MIDNIGHT

AT

EBERLY MANOR

K.P. Gillespie

Midnight at Eberly Manor

Copyright © 2025 by K.P. Gillespie

ISBN: 979-8-9986447-1-9 (paperback: AM)
ISBN: 979-8-9986447-3-3 (paperback: IS)
ISBN: 979-8-9986447-2-6 (hardback)
ISBN: 979-8-9986447-0-2 (eBook)

Cover Design: Tim Byrne

Published by: Chester Springs Press
PO Box 190
101 Fellowship Road.
Eagle, PA 19480
kpgillespiebooks@gmail.com

10 9 8 7 6 5 4 3

Dedication

To my loving and talented family, whose
encouragement made this all possible. Also, to the people
and places in Northeast Philadelphia who inspired this
book.

PART 1

Prologue

C assie feels the blood drain from her face, her body tingling with pins and needles as the grandfather clock's ominous chime announces ten minutes before the hour; *ten minutes remaining*.

The five strangers rush around in a panic, their movements illuminated by the sunlight streaming through the Grand Ballroom's windows. They seek to open their locks from the hundreds on the steel grids surrounding them.

All players are aware of the consequences they will face if they fail. Death. The trial demands that Cassie summon every ounce of strength to survive this unending nightmare.

Cassie's heart pounds in her chest as she nears the next lock, her fingers fumbling with each try. She twists another key, but an unsettling click echoes back, refusing to yield. *Dammit, come on*. Frustration evolves into anxiety with each failure, the metallic sound echoing.

The pendulum swings back and forth, ticking away their remaining time ... tick, tock, tick, tock.

One

C assie gently cradles the delicate pendant of the miniature Amish horse and buggy, a cherished gift from her mother. As she fastens it around her neck, tears well up in her eyes. Her fingers trace its contours, evoking memories of simpler times now overshadowed by the events of a deadly night. She takes a deep breath, letting her thoughts settle as she focuses on the steady beat of her heart.

By the window, her blonde hair glimmers in the soft October sunlight spilling through the glass, illuminating her cozy condo. The art nouveau paintings on the walls dance with hues of amber and jade, while the black leather sofa and vintage coffee table stand sentinel in the serene space. A gentle breeze wafts in, the fresh scent of river water and jasmine swirling around her like an old friend, coaxing her heart into a tranquil rhythm.

Cassie, in black yoga pants and a camisole, lays out her yoga mat on the balcony, grounding herself in each pose as the city hums below. Her thoughts flutter like leaves, but with every deep breath, she stabilizes herself, creating small pockets of peace amid the urban noise. After a quick, meditative pause, she heads back inside, sits at her vanity, and begins her makeup routine.

Stepping into her spacious walk-in closet, she selects a

tailored, camel-colored power suit from the neatly hung array, as if choosing armor for a battle she knows is coming. Her fingers move over eye-catching accessories, ultimately settling on deep-red Louboutin heels that shine with confidence. With a spritz of Black Orchid Eau de Parfum, the scent surrounds her, leaving a trail of determination behind.

Cassie glances at her phone, the glow reflecting in her eyes as her burgundy nails tap the screen. A buzz signals a notification from her real estate app, and a smile spreads across her face at the new opportunities. A message from her mom appears, drawing her in with a warmth that brightens her expression.

Hello, darling. Just checking in. Would you like to visit the Philadelphia Museum of Art this week? They have a Monet exhibit I have been waiting to see for ages.

Cassie types back:

Sounds like a great idea, Momma. I'll get back to you later to confirm, but Friday looks good for sightseeing.

Cassie adjusts her collar and grabs her black leather portfolio, feeling the weight of the essential legal papers inside. One document, marked in red, catches her eye—the unexpected email from yesterday could change the outcome of the case. Excitement and anxiety swirl inside her as she snaps the clasps shut, ready to face the challenge ahead. The immaculate polishing of the leather produces a subtle sheen, the brass clasps gleam, except for a single, jagged scratch along the side. It's superficial, but undeniable. Her fingers brush against the rough mark, a shadow flickering in her mind.

Brakes scream in anguish. An impact echoes inside her. A briefcase slams into the dashboard. A haunting memory replayed in a loop, etching itself into Cassie's thoughts with every passing day. She focuses on her breathing to quiet the mental chatter of these terrible memories.

It's only a scratch, she tells herself, pushing from her mind the tragic origins. She turns the briefcase, and the damage fades inward, hidden from view, hidden from the world.

Lost in thought, she struggles with the chaotic changes her life has undergone, questioning how she let everything get out of hand. Each day, her anxiety grows, and she feels past mistakes drawing near, as if those shadows are ready to catch her.

Cassie steadies her breath as she enters her condo's key code, the click echoing in the quiet. A familiar mix of anxiety and anticipation floods her as she secures the door and moves down the polished marble hallway, her heels clicking purposefully.

In the elevator, she catches a glimpse of herself—Cassandra Thompson, poised and polished at twenty-nine, a senior lawyer at DeMarco & Briggs. The lobby greets her with bright light reflecting off warm wood and elegant murals, awakening a flicker of hope that dances in her chest as she steps into the day.

As she enters the private parking garage, her heart races at the sight of her red Mercedes convertible. Sliding into the driver's seat, the cool leather beneath her feels like a second skin. She turns the ignition, and the engine roars to life. As Cassie speeds away, the wind whips her hair back, a thrilling signal of her departure.

She navigates her way through the light Monday morning traffic, her grip tightening on the steering wheel, knuckles whitening. The radio plays in the background, but her mind is elsewhere, filled with thoughts of the upcoming meeting. The sun, hanging low in the clear blue sky, casts long shadows across the road, but its warmth does little to chase away the chill running down her spine.

Two

As Cassie navigates the narrow cobblestone streets of Philadelphia, a sense of calm washes over her. This little corner of the city is a warm embrace, and she can't wait to make a quick stop at her favorite café for a well-needed dose of caffeine. *Only one more block*, she reminds herself, focusing on anticipating the first sip of her handcrafted latte. It's her small luxury, a moment of calm before the inevitable chaos of the workday takes hold.

Cassie spots a rare parking spot outside the café and thinks to herself, *What a great way to start the day!* The busy crowd is gone today, making it feel as if the city has paused just for her. As she walks up to the counter, the aromatic smell of roasted coffee surrounds her, drawing her into a cozy haze. The barista, a friendly young man with a warm smile and a name tag that says "Jake," welcomes her.

"Morning, Cassie! The usual?" he asks, reaching for a mug to prepare her drink. "I can add two shots of espresso if you need extra caffeine this morning."

Cassie smiles, "Thanks, Jake. This is why I tip you so well … and I'll treat myself to one of your delicious croissants at the expense of my diet."

As he smiles back, Cassie allows a moment of connection, a fleeting sense of camaraderie in this quiet moment before the usual Monday morning crowd descends upon the café— moments she misses.

Cassie settles into her usual booth, the familiar scent of roasted coffee beans surrounding her. She enjoys the rich aroma rising from her handcrafted latte, where a delicate leaf pattern of foam floats on top, a tiny masterpiece worth its steep price. Next to it, a flaky croissant glistens invitingly, each buttery layer catching the light. Her gaze drifts to the café's bustling scene. An older couple nestles in a corner, their fingers intertwined over a newspaper as they share quiet smiles between sips of steaming coffee.

Across the room, a group of college students collaborates animatedly, their laptops flashing with snippets of code and notes, laughter punctuating their intense discussion about an upcoming project. They radiate energy, filling the air with youthful exuberance. In contrast, a young mother sits nearby, her face lined with fatigue as she rocks her crying toddler, one hand clutching a crumbling muffin, the other gently bouncing the child on her knee. She whispers, her voice a tender lullaby over the café's chatter.

Cassie's fingers slip into her pocket, retrieving her phone. She intends to steal a moment of tranquility, scanning her work emails. But when a notification flickers on the screen, her heart sinks, tightening into a fist of anxiety. A troubling case requires her immediate attention, shattering the calm that had surrounded her moments ago. She can't believe it—*do people take their jobs seriously?* A curt reply forms swiftly on her screen, frustration boiling beneath each tapped key.

Stay frosty. I'll handle it when I get to the office.

Firm and assertive, the words remind her she can handle the chaos waiting for her.

Leaving the café, she tosses her briefcase into the back

seat of her car with a loud *thud*. The engine roars to life as she revs it, presses the gas pedal, and speeds into traffic, narrowly missing a silver Volkswagen.

The driver honks loudly, the screeching sound tearing at her nerves. Without thinking, she flips him off, feeling her fleeting sense of peace vanish in an instant.

Three

Dawn breaks as Detective Janelle Robinson steps into the boxing gym, the cool air inside wrapping around her, mirroring the embrace of a long-lost friend. The familiar scent of sweat and leather hangs in the air, mingling with a faint trace of tiger balm. The gym is empty except for the rhythmic thump of a lone boxer's workout on a heavy bag, its worn exterior a testament to countless battles over the years.

Janelle stands in the gym, her presence magnetic. At thirty, her tall and muscular frame moves with a purposeful grace, a testament to years of dedication. The short strands of her natural hair frame her face, highlighting the fierce determination etched in her features. Her smoky hazel eyes sparkle with intelligence, each glance keenly aware as she scans the room. On her left arm, the vivid outline of a phoenix tattoo catches the light. Its fiery colors tell a tale of resilience and rebirth, a reminder of her roots in West Philadelphia. On her right arm, a pink lotus flower blossoms, intricate and beautiful, embodying purity and spiritual awakening, a stark contrast to the tough fighter she is.

Janelle's hands, adorned with nails painted a bold crimson, rest on the speed bag, ready to release her energy. The vibrant color reflects her lively personality and also serves a practical purpose during her intense workouts. As she wraps her hands with care, the familiar tightness around her knuckles feels comforting.

With a quick movement, she throws her first jab, the sharp crack echoing through the gym and breaking the silence. Each punch flows into the next—jab, cross, hook—a rhythmic dance that matches the steady pounding of her heart. Beads of sweat roll down her forehead and drip from her chin, darkening the mat beneath her. The rhythm of her strikes echoes like a heartbeat, a powerful reminder of the strength she has built within herself.

Thoughts rush through her mind like fierce punches. Today will be tough; deadlines are approaching, and her life is in her hands. The burden of her role as lead detective in the 8th District weighs heavily on her, but in this sanctuary, she finds a moment of relief. Each punch is a prayer, each drop of sweat a sacrifice for the determination she needs.

She visualizes the faces of those she fights for, their stories blending with hers and driving her forward. As the minutes go by, the sound of her solitude fills the gym. It's only her and the bag; nothing else matters right now.

Janelle's muscles ache as she holds her fists aloft, savoring this moment of stillness. She closes her eyes, letting the adrenaline surge through her veins, feeling the energy transform her and ground her in the now. This is her sanctuary, where sweat and spirit merge, molding her into the fighter she has become.

She shakes out her arms, releasing the tension that has built up around her. The challenges ahead can wait; she reminds herself. A quick visit to her apartment to get ready for the day is all she needs. She stays calm amid the storm, feeling prepared for the obstacles that lie ahead.

Four

J anelle Robinson's cat, Jonesy, a sleek ginger shorthair, sits perched on a window ledge, watching the bustle of an early Monday morning in the Mayfair neighborhood of Northeast Philadelphia. His emerald eyes, twin slits of predatory focus, track the jerky dance of a yellow taxi, its horn a staccato blast intruding on the rising hum of the city.

As Janelle walks through the door, her gym bag in hand, a sharp, shrill voice cuts through the heavy silence of the room. It's time to rein in the chaos. "Jonesy! Get down from there, you fiend!" Jonesy, moving with the feline grace of Sigourney Weaver's on-screen companion, reluctantly leaves his vantage point. She tosses him onto the floor and begins the well-worn coffee maker, her morning ally.

Janelle steps out of the shower, steam swirling around her. The scent of lavender soap clings to her skin as she puts on a crisp white shirt, feeling its coolness against her warm skin. The silver gleam of her badge catches the light, a steady reminder of her duties. As she adjusts the collar of her dark blue uniform in the mirror, she sees not only herself but a warrior ready to face the day ahead.

As she steps into the kitchen, her eyes catch the stubborn remnants of time—a smudged, silver microwave and a fridge that hums softly but looks like it has seen better days. Sunlight streams through the window, casting a warm glow over yesterday's takeout sprawled across the scarred wooden bistro table, the tabletop worn down from countless meals shared. She glances at the aging blue couch and loveseat, their fabric frayed and whispering stories of lazy afternoons and laughter. The walls, once vibrant, now wear a muted coat of paint, shadows playing over spots where photographs have hung for a long time, leaving only ghostly impressions. The air hangs heavy with stillness, tinged with the faint, musty scent of dust that swirls in the sunlight.

In this modest apartment, just ten blocks from the lively 8th District, she feels a wave of peace wash over her. Here, she can breathe easily, away from the chaos of Northeast Philadelphia, ready to face the day ahead. Janelle pours herself a cup of coffee with two creams and one sugar, savoring this moment of comfort before the whirlwind begins.

As she moves to her desk, adrenaline kicks in, and she gathers essential documents. Her mind races with thoughts of tomorrow morning's meeting to review the case with the Philadelphia Chief of Police. Scribbling key points on a notepad, she reviews her materials one last time. Adjusting her blazer, she's ready for the day. As Jonesy brushes against her leg, she kneels to embrace him, letting his purr soothe her.

As she steps out the door, she takes a deep breath, savoring the peacefulness of the morning walk. It grounds her, reminding her of how far she has come and the strength she carries as she faces the challenges ahead.

As Janelle walks toward her destination, her focus remains on one main idea. Today is a pivotal day in a high-stakes investigation. Her team will collect the forensic evidence, witness statements, and cell phone tracking data requested yesterday. They will present this information to a judge to obtain a search warrant, which could influence the outcome of the case and impact the reputation of the 8th District.

* * *

Janelle bursts through the doors of headquarters, the precinct's familiar hum wrapping around her like a warm blanket. She offers quick smiles to colleagues as she weaves through the busy space.

Her desk comes into view, a chaotic stack of case files and half-empty coffee cups. With a soft click, she powers on her computer. The screen flickers to life, casting a pale glow on her face. Her eyes fixate on a series of vital files, each a puzzle piece waiting for her to fit it into place, igniting a sense of purpose within her.

With a solitary deep breath, she straightens her shirt. Adrenaline surges through her. This is her moment to crack the case wide open. Janelle grips her notes tightly. She is ready to lead the discussion and push for a warrant, which could change everything. *Once I write this name, there's no turning back.*

She pulls out the warrant affidavit and fills in the target's name: *Cassandra Thompson.*

Five

C assie's car screeches into the Liberty Towers parking garage as she races to the 34th floor. The elevator doors chime open, and she steps into DeMarco & Briggs Law Offices, inhaling the scent of polished wood and fresh coffee. The office is a blend of luxury and ambition, with plush furnishings and sweeping city views.

"Morning," she mutters to the receptionist, glancing at the anxious junior associates hunched over in their cubicles. After dropping her briefcase at her desk, she looks toward the break room as the tempting aroma of fresh coffee fills the air. The office hustle fades behind her as she steps inside, where a lively buzz of laughter and chatter creates an inviting atmosphere. Colleagues gather, exchanging quick smiles and light banter about the weather.

She heads to the coffee station, feeling the warmth of the chipped mug in her hand as she pours the rich, dark brew. This brief ritual offers her a pause—a respite—before resuming daily demands.

Cassie pulls out her phone and grimaces at the number of missed texts in the group chat about tonight's happy hour.

She texts back:

I can't make it tonight. I'll see everyone next time.

* * *

The partners' meeting starts at 9:00 am. Senior Partner Mr. David Harrison, whose face shows the passing years, addresses the small group. Alongside Cassie, two senior attorneys vie for Mr. Harrison's approval. Three junior attorneys prepare their presentations, and two junior law clerks take minutes during the meeting.

Mr. Harrison begins, his voice devoid of inflection. "First on the docket this morning, the Dougherty case."

Cassie leans forward, keeping her expression unreadable. Inside, the knot of anxiety tightens.

"Ms. Thompson, can you give us the details for those unfamiliar with the case?"

Cassie's heart races as she faces her colleagues in the conference room; anticipation fills the air. Their hopeful yet nervous expressions mirror her own uncertainty. The smooth table feels cold beneath her palms as she recalls the many late nights she spent preparing for this moment.

Every decision depends on today's outcome—not only for herself but also for DeMarco & Briggs. The firm's future is in the balance, and pressure weighs heavily on her. Failure means more than a setback; it could unravel everything she has worked tirelessly to build. She takes a deep breath, knowing she has to win—she has to.

With notes in hand, Cassie approaches the center podium. "This case is a wrongful death suit filed by the Wagner Law Group on behalf of plaintiffs Keith and Mary Dougherty. Their son, Kenneth Dougherty, a young man in the prime of his life, died during routine abdominal surgery at Chestnut Hill Hospital. The hospital board of directors has hired DeMarco & Briggs for its defense."

With a steady breath, she continues, her voice confident. "This case revolves around allegations of medical negligence and malpractice. The plaintiffs, the grieving parents, assert that their son's death directly resulted from the hospital's failure to support an adequate standard of care. Our role is to show that the hospital and its staff acted professionally, and that the unfortunate outcome was beyond their control."

As Cassie delves into the case, her mind races with practical strategies. Her focus on coworkers and superiors fuels her determination. She connects key evidence and witness testimonies, viewing them as vital parts of a larger truth. Mr. Harrison listens carefully as he takes notes on his legal pad. Her concentration stays sharp as she explains the case, silencing any doubts.

The conference table gleams under the bright lights, reflecting the sharp features of another senior attorney, Mark Weller. He leans back, the leather of his chair creaking softly. His dark, perfectly tailored suit absorbs the light, emphasizing the predatory glint in his eyes. Mark steeples his long, graceful fingers, nails manicured to perfection.

Cassie feels uneasy around Mark Weller. His charm and sharp suits hide an ambition that overshadows her, making her cautious of his true motives. As the son of a successful lawyer, he moves effortlessly through social circles, while she clings to her small-town roots and a fading accent, which he looks upon with disdain.

Landing the Young murder case two years ago, when Mark fell ill, was a fortunate break for Cassie that boosted her career and reputation. This success showcased her legal skill, and Mark has never forgotten it. The memory of her victory continues to fuel their simmering rivalry. To him, she is nothing more than "trailer trash," a term he has used within her earshot.

"With all due respect to my colleague, I believe we have reached an impasse, Mr. Harrison."

Cassie leans forward, ready to make her next move. She plays her ace-in-the-hole. "Yesterday, Mr. Harrison, I received an email from a new lead who could give us the inside information we need. Someone who was inside the operating room that morning. Someone unidentified until now." She pauses, her gaze flicking to Mr. Harrison before returning to Mark. "I intend to pursue this witness aggressively."

Mr. Harrison, his weariness forgotten, leans forward. The potential impact of this new witness on the case is undeniable.

Mark arches a skeptical eyebrow. "Does this witness have *inspired revelations?*"

Recognizing she is on the precipice of a high-stakes gamble, Cassie realizes this witness is a wildcard, one she has no choice but to play.

Cassie has baited her trap. "Even better, Mr. Weller, we have a witness who can *actually* support our hypothesis about the sequence of events that morning. Your input in this case has been unproductive at best. If we want to win, we need to focus on solid evidence, not wishful thinking."

Mr. Harrison stands and asks abruptly, "Can we continue the update, Ms. Thompson?"

Opening a file, Cassie reveals a single page with a name and contact information—the potential game-changer in the case. Mr.

Harrison picks up the page, and as he reads the contact's address, a spark of recognition lights up his eyes.

"*Eberly Manor* ... interesting," he mutters under his breath. He looks at Cassie. "Is this individual credible?"

"Yes, Mr. Harrison. His initial information matches well with the forensic evidence we have uncovered," Cassie explains. "It fills many gaps, including the inconsistencies the plaintiff's lawyers are trying to exploit. His testimony could sway the case in our favor."

Mark calms his anger. "We'll need to question this witness thoroughly. One more wrong move and the entire case is in jeopardy."

"I'm aware of the risks," Cassie replies. "That's why I've kept this information private. I'll contact the witness to schedule an immediate interview."

Mr. Harrison stands. "Ms. Thompson, I don't want this man anywhere near this case until you confirm his credibility. Keep me up to date on your progress."

Cassie's calm demeanor conceals the tension rising in her stomach. Securing this testimony is crucial to the case. Mr. Harrison's hesitation signals the high stakes involved. She knows no one in the corner office got there by playing fair; they've done whatever it takes to win, and Cassie hates losing. She felt a surge of pride when she realized she was a step ahead of Mark, with a witness who could sway the case in her favor. His skepticism only strengthened her resolve, knowing that this time she had the advantage in their ongoing rivalry.

The meeting proceeds at a brisk and efficient pace. Each participant provides updates and confronts Mr. Harrison's blunt critiques. The room buzzes with quiet competition, and the unspoken threat of facing the partner's anger hangs in the air. A subtle shift to more mundane topics gives Cassie time to plot her next move.

The meeting concludes with an explicit command: to make significant progress on the Dougherty case within the week. Cassie, as composed as ever, leaves the boardroom with the sun casting deep shadows over the tall skyscrapers. Her persistent plotting has resulted in a temporary victory.

Her life is a constant balancing act; each step and word measured, her flaws kept hidden. As pressure mounts, the burden of success feels like the last thread holding her together. Cassie fears if she stumbles, her world will come crashing down.

* * *

Cassie pushes open the door to her office, and the familiar scent of polished wood and ink fills the air. The clock ticks ominously—only two days before the crucial preliminary hearing. She scans the stack of files on her desk, and each one brims with details that could sway the case. Her stomach growls, reminding her of the cafeteria's irresistible call.

After a quick lunch of a hastily prepared sandwich and a lukewarm cup of coffee, she returns to her desk, determined. She leans over the files, tapping her fingers as she plans her next steps. Every second counts in the fight ahead.

She calls two junior associates to aid with the case. Fresh out of law school and eager to prove themselves, they file into Cassie's office, their faces a mix of anticipation and trepidation.

Cassie outlines their tasks for the upcoming preliminary hearing. "This hearing is our chance to stop the plaintiff's case from going to trial," she states, her voice carrying an air of authority. "Both of you need to be prepared, focused, and ready to adapt to the testimony, if necessary."

Emily Burke, a 24-year-old junior paralegal, fidgets as she listens, her long brown hair swaying. Her green eyes are wide with apprehension, and she adjusts her thick-rimmed glasses. It will be her initial courtroom experience.

"I've put together an outline of the evidence related to the plaintiff's witnesses," she stammers, biting her lip. "Everything is ready for Wednesday's presentation, with notes on each piece and potential exclusionary strategies in case they're needed. I'll be ready, Ms. Thompson," she says, her enthusiasm mingled with a hint of anxiety.

She turns her attention to Luis Hernandez, a junior attorney whose dark hair, engaging brown eyes, and broad smile contribute to a positive vibe on the team. His several months of courtroom experience enrich the team chemistry.

"Ms. Thompson," Luis begins, "I've created a detailed timeline of events, cross-referencing it with Emily's list of evidence. I developed possible questions to challenge the plaintiff's testimony and cast doubt on their recollection of events."

As the team wraps up its preparations, Cassie remains optimistic. As she reviews her notes, Emily feels a surge of confidence, gathering her thoughts and preparing for her next steps. With Luis's strategic insights guiding them, she believes they are ready for the preliminary hearing.

Cassie clutches her bag as the elevator doors slide open, releasing her into the dusky lobby. Stepping onto the street, a rush of exhilaration mingled with the evening chill, sending a thrill through her. She glances around, the vibrant city swirling with life.

Turning into a narrow alley, the sounds of laughter fade into whispers as she navigates past ivy-clad brick walls and colorful street art. It's a place of secrets, where the ordinary gives way to the unknown. Her heart quickens; she moves faster, eager to reach her hidden sanctuary.

Six

Moonlight spills through the arched windows of The Book Nook, casting silver streaks across the sidewalk. Cassie pushes the heavy oak door open, its hinges groaning softly in welcome. Instantly, the city's cacophony fades, replaced by the gentle rustle of pages turning and the murmured exchange of friendly voices. She takes a deep breath, and the rich scent of leather-bound books envelops her like an old, comforting blanket.

Tall shelves stretch overhead, their vibrant spines a kaleidoscope of colors and sizes, each book promising an escape into another world. Sunlight streams through tall windows, illuminating dust motes that float lazily in the air. As her feet softly pad on the worn wooden floor, each step feels like a heartbeat in this enchanting maze of stories. A wave of warmth washes over her—an unexplainable feeling that in this sacred space, she finds her way home.

Cassie notices an older man with a weathered face browsing the history section. His gnarled fingers trace the spine of a book about the attack on Pearl Harbor, and she senses his gentle touch represents his search for a long-lost friend. He closes his eyes briefly, and his expression softens, as if offering a silent prayer for the memories in those pages.

Standing near the fiction section, Cassie finds herself surrounded by vibrant spines and imaginative titles, beckoning her to explore thrilling journeys. The charm of science fiction and fantasy captivates her, evoking memories of her favorite childhood reads. She gazes around the store, feeling a sense of belonging among the diverse patrons drawn to this sanctuary.

She observes a young artist with striking purple hair and numerous piercings wandering through the art section. Cassie sees a spark of inspiration in the artist's eyes as she picks up a colorful purple sketchbook, and her eyes alight with imagination.

Nearby, a couple in their thirties walks hand in hand, their faces glowing with dreams of travel. Cassie senses their longing as they browse a guide to Scotland, filled with images of stunning landscapes and mysterious lochs. The couple leans in close, sharing hopes of 'someday'.

Cassie watches, amused, as two high school students, dressed in their blue and gold uniforms, walk over and ask where *Animal Farm* by George Orwell is located. As they complain about the required reading for the semester, a friendly bookseller gestures toward the classic section, guiding them along.

She watches the people around her, a gentle smile playing on her lips as she sinks deeper into the cozy nook of the bookstore. She blends into the background, a quiet observer among the bustling crowd. The lively chatter fades into a soothing hum, and the shelves lined with books create a comforting barrier.

She breathes in the distinct scent of old paper and ink, a blend that wraps around her like a warm embrace. As she pulls a book from the shelf, her fingers dance over its worn spine, feeling the texture and history within its pages. A wave of peace washes over her, and for a moment, she sheds the weight of her life outside—no longer the ambitious lawyer. Here, she loses herself in stories, cradling the freedom that anonymity provides.

Her eyes find a leather-bound copy of *The Odyssey*, and a pull at her heart draws her in. As she opens the book, the scent of aged paper and ink fills her senses.

As she reads, she feels a connection to Odysseus, the wanderer navigating storms and burdens. Each word resonates with her own struggles. In the empty library, she longs for peace and the ability to leave her past behind.

With every turn of the page, she reflects on her journey and considers her trials. Even as fear lingers, she finds a spark of strength within, ready to face the waves of her life with resolve.

Cassie closes the worn-out book, holding it as if it were a lifeline. This is precisely what she needed today. A gentle smile appears on her face, warmth filling her. After only thirty minutes in this dusty bookstore, her worries had eased, leaving her with a renewed sense of purpose. She stands taller, ready to face the world, each book reminding her of her inner strength.

"Attention, everyone! We're closing in five!" the bookseller announces.

Cassie retraces her steps to the car, clutching Homer's masterpiece tightly, its paper edges cool against her skin. Streetlights cast long shadows as she walks, and the night air whispers around her. The story of Homer's bravery wraps around her, serving as a comforting shield in the darkness that lies ahead.

Seven

The click of the lock echoes through the otherwise silent condo, and a burden lifts as Cassie steps inside. The sharp clatter of her high heels against the polished wood floor punctuates the stillness, each sound a reminder of the chaos of her day slowly fading. She collapses onto the plush couch, kicking off her heels, her body sinking into the soft cushions, muscles unwinding with a sigh.

With a flick of her wrist, she lights a scented candle. A warm flicker illuminates the dim room, casting shadows that dance and sway, creating a comforting glow around her, like a familiar embrace that keeps the outside world at bay. The scent of hyacinths fills the air. Cassie glances at the clock on the wall: 9:30 pm.

Pulling out her laptop, she gets to work on the immediate task. She needs to schedule a meeting with the mysterious witness in the Dougherty case.

The laptop screen glows as she types:

[Email - Cassie to eapoe1959:] Subject: Dougherty Case:

As lead attorney on the Dougherty case, I have reviewed the emails with your information regarding this case. According to our firm's partners, I require more corroborating details and information on the operating room timeline to proceed. Please provide the information below so we can verify with our timeline. Time is crucial.

Cassie prepares to hit send. She pauses, a sense of unease washing over her. Something feels off about this, but she can't afford to be cautious now. Cassie's mishandling of the case leaves her with no option but to pursue this last-minute witness.

A flicker of something unreadable—suspicion?—crosses Cassie's face as she hits send. Hope brightens her features. Her furrowed brow, illuminated by the laptop screen, reveals her emotional turmoil. The success is crucial to her entire professional future. It signifies not only a vital appointment but also a turning point that could transform her career and restore her sense of purpose.

Cassie's eyes snap back to the laptop, an incoming message notification blinking within minutes:

[Email - eapoe1959 to Cassie:] Subject: Dougherty Case:

I will share the required information during our meeting. I require that we meet at my estate on Saturday at noon. Both of us desire justice in this case. Please confirm.

Cassie responds.
[Email - Cassie to eapoe1959:] Subject: Dougherty Case:

I am available to meet on Saturday at noon. I look forward to speaking with you.

Another email dings moments later: [Email - eapoe1959 to Cassie:] Subject: Dougherty Case.

Be punctual; I do not tolerate lateness.

Cassie searches for the name and address given in the original email. The details catch her eye. Eberly Manor, built in

1926 in suburban Philadelphia, was the home of William Eberly, a former executive of the Pennsylvania Railroad Corporation. It is now owned by William Eberly's grandson, R.W. Haskins.

She closes her laptop with a sigh of relief. The meeting is confirmed. She hums a tune in her best Veruca Salt impersonation, *"Now I have a golden ticket,"* and laughs at her reference to her favorite childhood movie.

As she sinks back into the plush fabric of her couch, a chill runs down her spine as unsettling questions swirl in her mind. *How did he know she was the lead attorney on this case? How did he get her personal email address?* The air around her feels thick with uncertainty, as if shadows are closing in on her every thought. She needs this witness to succeed. The alarm bells must be silenced, no matter the cost.

Cassie's gaze drifts to a worn photograph on the end table, its corners beginning to fray. She leans in, memories flooding her mind. High school graduation day, once filled with promise, is now overshadowed by harsh reality. The faces in the photo—her mom and Aunt Barb—flicker like fading ghosts; their smiles tug at her heart. They remind her of the simple joys she left behind.

Eight

Cassie: 13 Years Earlier

In the summer of 2011, the Thompson farmhouse stood on a dirt road, its weathered wood visible through chipped, peeling paint. This aged home, a witness to old-world craftsmanship, had seen better days. The sun-bleached walls and sagging roof hinted at a long history. Inside, the creaking floorboards protested the passage of time.

In one such room, fourteen-year-old Cassie Thompson sat hunched over a worn copy of *To Kill a Mockingbird*. The silence of the Thompson farmhouse was a familiar companion as the ancient clock marked the approach of evening. The story of a small town's fight against racism resonated with Cassie, evoking unexpected emotions. She connected with Scout Finch's journey from innocence to experience, as well as her father, Atticus's commitment to truth and justice. As she read, her mind drifted back to her early childhood.

Cassie remembers the horse-and-buggy rides with her mom and dad through Strasburg, PA, and the visits to the railroad museum, ice-cream cones in hand. Summers imprinted on her mind. Running through fields, savoring fresh-picked strawberries, and listening to her mother's gentle voice reading enchanting bedtime stories.

Aunt Barb often took Cassie to the local library in the charming downtown area. Each visit filled her with awe. The tall ceilings and wooden shelves created cozy nooks, perfect for escaping. Aunt Barb, tall and graceful with a warm smile, led her to the young readers' section, where every book promised a new adventure.

Cassie admired her mother, Sarah, who faced many of life's toughest challenges. After Cassie's father left them, Sarah worked double shifts at the local diner. Despite carrying emotional and physical scars, Sarah's love and strength guided them. She was determined to create a better future for them.

Cassie remembers the many nights Sarah had stayed up late, whispering encouragement as she struggled with her homework. Sarah's steady belief in Cassie's potential was a constant guide, like a warm hand on her shoulder, helping her move forward even when the road ahead was dark.

* * *

Cassie walked to Strasburg High School on a cool fall morning in 2011. The shift from summer's warmth to fall's chill echoed her inner unease. With each step, her worn shoes and hand-me-down clothes seemed out of place amid the department-store chic of the other girls. The growing dread in her stomach felt sharper with thoughts of English class, especially as she remembered her book report from the week before. She could still see her classmates' expectant faces as her stutter stole the words from her lips, leaving her paralyzed with embarrassment.

Entering the classroom resembled stepping onto a battlefield. Her heart raced, each beat a frantic drum in her chest. But this time was different. Clutched in her hand was her masterpiece: an essay on the transformative power of literature, centered around *To Kill a Mockingbird*. This was her chance for redemption, and as she prepared to face her fears, a flicker of hope surged within her, pushing back against the shadows of doubt.

After Cindy Tepper finished her presentation, Cassie knew her turn was next. She tried to breathe and calm herself. The teacher called her up to the front to present her book project.

As Cassie stepped to the front of the classroom for her presentation, the students snickered. She tried to dismiss them and focus on the project. But as she read, her words twisted on her tongue. "M-m-my p-p-p-project ... i-i-is... a-a-about..." she stammers, unable to continue. Her classmates' cruel laughter hit her like a wave, shattering the self-confidence she'd built.

Yet, amidst the laughter, a familiar presence silenced the students with a single piercing gaze and a sharp reprimand. It was their English teacher, Mrs. Adams, a stern woman with an air of authority. As Cassie sat, she exchanged a glance with Mrs. Adams, who smiled at her. Cassie offered a wry smile in return.

The next day during lunch, Cassie sat alone, lost in her favorite book, when Abigail Clark and her clique of mean girls approached. Abigail, a struggling student, hated teacher's pets— those eager classmates who always won the teacher's favor while teachers overlooked her. The girls surrounded her, their voices loud and mocking, teasing her about her stutter and shabby clothes. Cassie tried to ignore them, but Abigail snatched her book and tore out pages, scattering them like fallen leaves.

"Good luck reading your stupid book now, you stuttering backwoods bitch." Abigail mocked. She added, "C-c-can't w-wait for your next b-b-book report, Cassie."

Cassie's heart sank; the humiliation of Abigail's cruel taunts and the destruction of her beloved book fueled a burning anger deep within her. The pages of *To Kill a Mockingbird* littered the floor like trash. Cassie ran from the cafeteria, tears streaming down her face.

As she stepped into her home, she rushed up the creaking stairs and slammed her door shut. Tears soaked her favorite pillow while the orange sun sank below the farm's horizon. Helplessness clawed at her, but a fierce determination ignited within her to confront the bullying that stifled her voice. In the dim light of her bedroom, she made a silent vow: no more tears in front of others and *never giving up on herself.*

The next day, during Cassie's free period, the principal's assistant approached her and asked her to speak with Mrs. Adams in her classroom.

"Cassie," Mrs. Adams said, her tone a mix of warmth and concern, "I see you sometimes struggle with speaking. But I believe there's a remarkable talent within you, waiting to shine. I'm here to help you discover it." Cassie nodded, her eyes wide with curiosity and hope.

"We can start with a few simple exercises," Mrs. Adams said. "Let's begin by reading aloud together. After that, I'll introduce you to breathing techniques and help you with articulation. We'll move on to more advanced exercises to further strengthen your diaphragm and improve your vocal control. Does this sound good to you, Cassie?"

"Thank you so much, Mrs. A ... Adams!" Cassie beamed, her eyes sparkling. With a bright grin, Cassie hugged Mrs. Adams, ready to take on the challenge.

Cassie's progress was gradual but consistent, supported by

Mrs. Adams's patient guidance and encouragement. Each day, her confidence in public speaking grew, and joining the school's debate team her junior year revealed a passion she had never realized she had.

The excitement of debate tournaments sparked something inside her. Standing before a mock trial with her peers, she relished her sharp arguments and powerful delivery as her stutter disappeared into the background. She had found her voice—a source of unwavering strength that shielded her from hurtful words.

Recognition from peers and teachers warmed her heart, lifting insecurities that had once held her back. No longer a timid girl with a stutter, Cassie embraced her new identity. When facing Abigail and her posse, she stood tall, ready to use her words as a weapon. Each taunt became a chance to prove her strength, and she vowed never to let anyone dull her spirit again.

* * *

In the spring of 2014, Cassie stood with pride in the wings of her high school auditorium, her cap and gown symbolizing the struggles she had overcome. She scanned the blue-and-gold auditorium, a flutter of excitement building inside her until she spotted her mom and Mrs. Adams.

Memories flooded her mind: late nights of studying, moments of self-doubt, and the perseverance that Mrs. Adams' guidance had helped her achieve, culminating in her role as salutatorian. Excitement filled the students as their classmates took their last steps into adulthood. Laughter and chatter surrounded her, creating a warm backdrop for the celebration. Her fellow students embraced her with warm hugs, offering support and affection through heartfelt gestures that symbolized their shared journey.

The rustle of caps and gowns echoed her journey, each sound resonating with her hopes and dreams. This moment belonged to her, and she was ready to embrace it.

Cassie stepped forward to deliver her senior class salutatorian speech. She stood tall and proud, her voice confident and steady. She shared her journey of overcoming obstacles and moving forward despite the challenges she faced. Her words resonated with her classmates, and they cheered as she finished her speech with a message of hope and resilience.

"The path ahead may be uncertain," Cassie said, "but our unwavering determination will shape our future. Let us embrace our struggles and use them as a fire to forge a brighter path." Cassie raised her diploma high. "Congratulations to the Class of 2014. It's our turn to go out and change the world!"

As Cassie stepped off the lectern, the thunderous applause from her classmates filled the air, and she caught a glimpse of her mother crying and Mrs. Adams' proud smile. There was a sense of satisfaction in that moment, yet it appeared to be only the beginning.

Cassie took a treasured selfie with her mom, Aunt Barb, and Mrs. Adams, all of them smiling. In three months, she would begin a new chapter of her life at Penn State University, eager to study law. With a mix of excitement and determination, Cassie was ready for the journey ahead.

Nine

J anelle sits in the conference room of the 8th District, detailing the documents and signatures required for the search warrant for Cassie Thompson. It's a busy morning as she works through her tasks. This afternoon, she will give an update to her CO and the Philadelphia police commissioner on their progress.

Across from her, Detective Derrick Coles, an athletically built Black man in his early forties, wears a dark blue suit, a white shirt, and a red tie, tapping a pen against the edge of the table.

Sitting next to Coles is Detective Carolyn Fenn, a petite woman in her early thirties with long brown hair and a light blue suit that complements her eyes. Janelle glances at her colleagues, meeting Detective Coles's anxious gaze and the quiet focus of Detective Fenn.

"We are still waiting for the cell phone tracking data for Cassie Thompson to be released," Janelle states, her voice steady despite the thoughts swirling in her head. "This morning's judicial review indicated we needed to place Cassie Thompson at the accident scene before considering a warrant," she said.

Derrick fidgets with the pen again, his anxiety clear as he nods in acknowledgment. "Makes sense. The cell phone data will support the evidence collected at the scene, along with the surveillance video."

Detective Fenn pulls up the relevant files on her laptop, her fingers flying over the keyboard. "I'll check the database for any updates we've made concerning the cell data request."

As Janelle watches Detective Fenn work, a flicker of urgency ignites inside her. Everything rides on this evidence. She maps out their approach, each step vital to closing in on Cassie and building their case. "Make sure to check the timestamps," Janelle urges, her tone sharpening. "We need to add as much corroboration as possible."

The precinct's sounds fade, leaving a quiet moment. Janelle checks her timeline slide of the accident investigation to present to the police brass this afternoon.

March 2023	Initial investigation
May 2024	Case classified as cold
August 2024	Re-open case, priority one
October 4th,2024	Suspect identified
October 5th,2024	Cell phone-tracking data subpoenaed
October 7th,2024	Search warrant documents prepared. Judicial review shows that proof of the suspect's location is needed for a search warrant.

* * *

Janelle sits in her office, enjoying her Philly cheesesteak hoagie from the local Wawa convenience store across the street from the station. She reviews her presentation for this afternoon's meeting, calming her nerves. The phone rings, cutting through the ambient noise of clicking keyboards and muted conversations. She picks it up and continues her workload.

"Hello, this is Detective Robinson."

"Detective, this is Patricia at the Overbrook Nursing Home. I'm afraid I have some sad news to share."

Her stomach drops. "Is it my mother?"

"Yes … She died this morning. I'm so sorry."

The news settled deep within Janelle. "Thank you for letting me know," Janelle replies, keeping her voice composed.

Janelle's breath catches in her throat as she struggles to suppress the tears threatening to spill. The overwhelming tide of her mother's loss envelops her, leaving her feeling both shattered and relieved.

Janelle's mother's heroin addiction cast a long shadow over their family, and now it feels like the storm has passed. Taking a deep breath, she pushes aside the terrible memories and steels herself for what's to come.

Janelle reviews the logistics: a funeral, informing family members of her mother's death, and managing the aftermath. A heaviness rests in her chest, stirring a mix of sadness and relief. This is what she's always done: handle things, manage the chaos. She tells herself, *I'll get through this, the way I always have.*

∗ ∗ ∗

The wail of sirens cut through the humid air of West Philadelphia in the spring of 2008, with the sound of gunshots echoing off brick row houses. This was Janelle Robinson's reality, carved from the turmoil of her childhood.

Inside their cramped home, the air reeked of desperation. At seventeen, Janelle moved through the darkness, burdened by her family's struggles: unpaid bills and her father's absence, a ghost in a faded photo.

Janelle stood in the doorway, overwhelmed by a deep sense of sadness as she looked at her mother, once so energetic, now sitting listlessly in a dusty armchair, her gaze vacant. The colors of her favorite shawl hung lifelessly on her, a stark contrast to the fading walls holding echoes of a joyful life lost.

One day in Mrs. Davison's social justice class, Janelle sat spellbound as a black police officer shared his passionate conviction about the vital importance of community and the transformative power of service. He emphasized the need to rise above poverty and improve one's own life and others'. His presence exuded strength, igniting a fire within her as she scribbled words like 'justice,' 'hope,' and 'change' in her notebook. To ensure the consistent application of social justice, guaranteeing humanity for every individual.

Later that night, the sirens outside transformed from a lament to a challenge. Gazing at the towering skyscrapers of downtown Philadelphia, a mix of determination and resolve washed over her. Taking a deep breath, she made a vow: "*I will become a police officer, and I will make a difference.*"

Janelle began her studies at Temple University in the fall of 2008, majoring in criminal justice. Excited about her future, she interned at the Philadelphia District Attorney's Office during her sophomore year, gaining valuable experience and making connections. Despite facing challenges at home and in her neighborhood, Janelle persisted and graduated in the spring of 2012 with a Bachelor of Science in Criminal Justice, magna cum laude. With her degree, she was determined to become a Philadelphia Police Detective and enrolled at the police academy.

* * *

Janelle arrived at the police training academy on a cool fall morning in 2012, eager yet nervous to join Platoon 42, a diverse group of recruits from Philadelphia. She thrived during the physical training, pushing herself through obstacle courses and hours of firearms practice to build her skills.

During a hostage situation simulation in a dimly lit warehouse, adrenaline surged through her as she prepared to test her tactical abilities. While others responded instinctively, Janelle carefully considered her options, prioritizing the safety of the hostages over rushing to capture the suspect. Her unconventional choice caught the instructors' attention during the review.

Reflecting on their comments about her strategic thinking, she felt proud, realizing that her quick decisions could yield practical results. In that moment, she embraced her identity as a police officer.

She graduated at the top of her class, receiving recognition for her performance in tactical and analytical assessments. Her graduation photograph with her classmates showed her confident smile.

* * *

Janelle sits at her desk, her eyes fixed on her police academy photo. The confident smile reflects her pride, a testament to the late nights and hard work she put into her training. Nearby, another picture catches her attention—her mother, full of life before the shadows took her. Tears stream down Janelle's cheeks as a wave of emotions washes over her: frustration, fear, and joy. She remembers the sacrifices of loved ones and the doubts that have shaped her journey, with each feeling intense and overwhelming.

It was time to bury the past and be the change she vowed to create in that West Philly classroom so many years ago.

Ten

J udge Robert Haskins walks through the dim halls of Eberly Manor, a mansion cloaked in grandeur yet shrouded in shadow. The heavy drapery pulled across the windows mutes the outside world, thickening the atmosphere inside with tension. The sharp click of his shoes echoes ominously, contrasting with the hushed murmurs of servants scurrying around, preparing for the upcoming games. He inspects the arrangements, noting how the flickering candlelight casts elongated, sinister shadows on the walls. All surfaces dusted and polished.

The game pieces are carefully arranged in different rooms. Each piece's position gives a clue about the game. The air smells of expensive cigars. This fragrance blends with the excitement of impending chaos. This gathering isn't about a friendly game night; it's a ruthless competition where only the most cunning will leave unscathed. Haskins cracks a thin smile, relishing the thought of the events to come.

He settles into his plush leather chair in the study and opens his laptop to check his emails. The judge glances at the last email messages displayed on the screen.

[Email - Cassie to eapoe1959:] Subject: Dougherty Case:

I am available to meet on Saturday at noon. I look forward to speaking with you.

[Email - eapoe1959 to Cassie:] Subject: Dougherty Case.

Be punctual; I do not tolerate lateness.

He reviews the email messages from a helpful associate at DeMarco & Briggs Law Firm. The previous Saturday, a message from one of Cassie's co-workers at the law firm caught his attention. The subject line "*Re: Dougherty Case Developments and Investigation*" piqued his interest, and the inside information provided the last piece of the puzzle needed to lure Cassie into his elaborate trap. Judge Haskins stands, straightens his tie, and strides out of the room, the weight of his intentions lingering in the air, an unspoken threat.

When Judge Haskins enters the library, a feeling of satisfaction grows inside him. He runs his fingers along the spines of many leather-bound books, each title carefully chosen. He picks up his favorite Edgar Allan Poe novel and places it by the fireplace. As he gently sets it down, the fading sunlight catches the embossed title on the cover, casting a warm glow that seems to whisper the promise of shadowy tales waiting to be uncovered. The room and the book will soon reveal their significance.

Six players received invitations, and six accepted. A curated list of participants for this occasion is prepared. Everything is ready.

Eleven

Wednesday, October 9th

C assie Thompson sits upright in Courtroom B of City Hall, her charcoal-gray power suit sharply contrasting with the warm, aged wood around her. The grandeur of the vaulted ceilings and intricate moldings envelops her like a heavy cloak, thick with echoes of the city's historic trials.

She glances at the worn wooden benches, imagining the anxious litigants and curious spectators who once occupied those seats, their fates hanging in the balance. Ahead, the imposing judge's bench looms, the American flag gently rippling in the background, a silent watchman over the proceedings.

Cassie's heart pounds, a surge of anticipation flowing through her veins. This space isn't only a courtroom; it's a crucible of justice, alive with potential. Today, she feels it deep in her bones—this is another moment to leave her mark on its legacy.

Emily Burke, Cassie's colleague, shifts in her seat, her fingers fidgeting with the edge of her notebook as she searches for a way to ease the tension in the air. Across the polished table, Luis Hernandez's fingers drum an irregular rhythm, the soft tap-tap-tap a subtle sign of the mounting anxiety. Silence presses around them like a dense fog.

The defendant, Jonathan Reese, sits beside Cassie, his slouching posture and shifty eyes a stark contrast to hers. He glances around as he straightens his tie. His dark blue suit hangs too large for his frame, as if borrowed for the occasion. He folds his hands in his lap, avoids eye contact, and keeps his gaze fixed on the judge's bench. His dark hair falls across his forehead. He tries to stay unnoticed, although everyone's eyes have already zeroed in on him.

A hum of anticipation fills the crowded courtroom. Today, the courtroom holds a preliminary hearing for a high-profile sexual assault case, with alleged victim Angela Marks at the center.

Cassie is familiar with her opponent. Prosecutor Lydia Blake is not the type to be caught off guard or to give up easily. This is just another contest for Cassie, one she fully expects to win.

The bailiff announces, "All rise. The First Judicial District of the Commonwealth of Pennsylvania is now in session. Judge Anne McCarthy presiding. Please be seated."

Everyone's attention shifts to the judge entering the courtroom. She is an older woman with silver hair pulled back into a tight bun; her black robe draped over her slight frame. With a steady gaze, she surveys the courtroom, the plaintiffs, and the defendant until her discerning eyes land on Cassie.

Judge McCarthy begins: "We're here today for a preliminary hearing in the case of People vs. Jonathan Reese. Mr. Reese has been charged with first-degree sexual assault. At this hearing, we will determine whether there is enough evidence to move to trial. The court has permitted witnesses to testify on both sides of the case. Are both sides ready?"

Cassie and Lydia rise in tandem. "Yes, Your Honor."

Lydia Blake steps forward. She is a formidable presence; her tall, slender frame draped in a tailored navy-blue suit. Lydia's relentless pursuit of justice is renowned, and today, she embodies it.

"Your Honor, we are here today to present a case of sexual assault against Jonathan Reese. The incident in question occurred at a party hosted by mutual friends of Mr. Reese and the victim, Angela Marks. It is alleged that, during the evening Mr. Reese asked Ms. Marks if she wanted a ride home, but instead took her to his house and assaulted her there."

"We will present evidence, including witness testimonies and forensic evidence, to corroborate Ms. Marks' account of the events. It will show a clear pattern of predatory behavior on the part of Mr. Reese, who used the party as an opportunity to commit this crime."

As Lydia outlines the case, the atmosphere grows heavy. Her voice is steady and focused; her words echo throughout the courtroom.

Lydia pauses and faces the judge. "Premeditation is admissible in a preliminary hearing for sexual assault cases and helps establish intent. We believe that the evidence will prove beyond a reasonable doubt that Mr. Reese planned and carried out a sexual assault on the night in question. We ask the court to proceed to trial."

As Prosecutor Lydia Blake concludes her opening statement, the courtroom remains in tense silence. The impact of her words presses down on the spectators, and eyes shift to Cassie, awaiting her response.

Cassie, exuding an air of confidence, rises to deliver her opening statement. Her steady and commanding voice fills the courtroom. She lays the groundwork to dismantle the prosecution's case.

"Your Honor, today we find ourselves faced with a grave accusation. An accusation that could ruin a man's life. We are here to examine the facts and determine whether sufficient evidence supports the charges against my client, Jonathan Reese."

With a subtle gesture, Cassie motions towards Jonathan, sitting beside her, his nervousness unmistakable. "Mr. Reese finds himself in this courtroom today due to unfortunate misunderstandings and circumstantial evidence."

"Although we acknowledge that he and Ms. Marks interacted at the party, we will show that the prosecution's account of events is inconclusive and not enough to move forward with a trial. The defense also wants to highlight that, so far, the prosecution has not presented any DNA evidence in this case."

Cassie steps down and joins her team at the defense table. The judge turns to Lydia. "Ms. Blake, you may call your first witness."

Silence settles as the first witness, Julie Miller, steps onto the stand. She is a young woman in her early twenties, with a pale complexion and hazel eyes, shifting her gaze between Jonathan and the judge. Lydia Blake begins the questioning, her voice calm and assertive. She prompts Julie to describe the night of the alleged assault, and her words paint a vivid picture of a troubling scene.

Julie describes the party as a blur of loud music and free-flowing alcohol, before her voice drops to a whisper, "I saw Jonathan Reese that night. He was ... he was drunk. I remember him spilling his drink on me." She takes a shaky breath, her eyes flicking to Jonathan, who sits stone-faced beside Cassie. "I saw him later in the hallway. He was ... he seemed upset and angry. Then I saw Angela. She looked scared and was backing away from him. That's what I remember."

Lydia nods, her expression grim, and turns to the judge.

"Your Honor, the prosecution believes this testimony provides context for the defendant's state of mind that evening."

Judge McCarthy studies Cassie as she rises for cross-examination and begins her questioning.

"Ms. Miller, you mentioned that Mr. Reese seemed angry at the party. Can you describe his exact behavior?"

"Well, he was … talking loudly. He seemed agitated, like he was mad about something."

Cassie's gaze sharpens. "And did you see him act aggressively toward anyone?" Julie hesitates. "No, I didn't see anything physical, but his behavior … was intimidating."

As Cassie approaches the defense table, Emily passes her a note. She glances at it before continuing her questioning. "Ms. Miller, you mentioned a crowded and chaotic party. Alcohol was readily available, correct?"

Julie nods, her face pale. "Everyone was drinking, but I only had two beers."

Cassie says, "So, it's fair to say that many individuals were intoxicated that evening, and emotions may have been heightened due to the influence of alcohol?"

Lydia rises, "Asked and answered, Your Honor."

Judge McCarthy says, "I'll allow it. Please answer the question, Ms. Miller."

Julie says, "I suppose that could be true."

Cassie pauses. "Now, Ms. Miller, you stated that you saw my client, Mr. Reese, in the hallway. Can you tell us how long this encounter lasted? Was it a brief or prolonged interaction?"

Julie hesitates, her eyes darting around the room. "It was …

brief. A moment or two." She adds, her voice unsure, "He seemed … distressed."

Cassie's tone sharpens. "Distressed, yes. But was he acting out Ms. Miller? Did you witness any aggressive behavior or harm inflicted by him on Miss Marks during that moment?"

As Julie fidgets in her lap, she replies, "No, I didn't see him touch her, but…"

Cassie cuts in, her voice steady. "But you assumed he was upset and angry based on his body language and the fact that he seemed to be looking for something or someone. Correct?"

Julie nods.

"Do you know who Mr. Reese was looking for?"

"No, I'm … not sure."

Cassie turns to the judge. "No further questions, Your Honor."

Judge McCarthy addresses the witness. "Ms. Miller, you may please step down."

Cassie addresses the judge. "Your Honor, we submit that Ms. Miller's testimony, while sympathetic, is based on assumptions and brief encounters. We ask that the court consider the impact of alcohol and the chaotic nature of a typical college party when evaluating her statements."

Judge McCarthy motions to Julie. "The witness may step down. Ms. Blake, you may call your next witness."

"Your Honor, I call Melissa Collingham to the stand."

As Lydia Blake questions Melissa about the party, Cassie turns to Emily and notices her searching through her briefcase. Her eyes show growing panic as she looks for a photo that could cast doubt on Melissa's testimony. Yesterday's prep meeting focused on this witness and the picture she took, which shows Jonathan and Angela smiling together at the party.

Cassie says to Luis, "Help Emily find that photo." He leans over to Emily, offering his help as she searches through her briefcase for the missing photo.

As the testimony ends, the judge announces, "Your witness, Counselor."

A heavy silence lingers in the air, thick with unspoken tension. Cassie leans in with her colleagues, their whispers blending with the rustle of frantic papers. Her gaze, intense, flickers between the witness and the judge. Without the photograph, her questions seem useless, slipping away before she can grasp them, leaving her frustration simmering just below the surface.

"No further questions at this time, Your Honor," and Cassie returns to her table, taking her seat, glaring at Emily.

Lydia calls her last witness: "Your Honor, I call Angela Marks to the stand." Small and pale beneath the harsh fluorescent lights, Angela takes the stand, her hand trembling as she places it on the Bible.

"Do you solemnly swear that the testimony you are about to give shall be the truth, the whole truth, and nothing but the truth, so help you, God?"

"Yes, Your Honor."

Lydia Blake's sharp questions cut through the tense silence; her words depict Jonathan Reese as the villain. As she guides Angela through the traumatic experience, Lydia carefully details Jonathan's threatening actions. Angela's voice quivers as she remembers her fear. Lydia highlights Angela's emotional pain, crafting a story of a volatile man whose drunkenness fuels aggressive behavior.

Angela, shaking, steps down from the stand. The judge calls for a lunch recess, allowing the courtroom to regain its composure before cross-examination begins.

As the courtroom empties, Cassie hurries out, her associates following her.

She says, "Emily and Luis, head to the office now and find that photo! Check the file server. We keep backups of all the evidence there." Cassie pauses. "Also, see if anyone has accessed your desk recently."

As Cassie hurries toward the cafeteria, a simmering anger rises within her, tangled with a suspicion that someone at the law office has tampered with the evidence. Emily's careful cataloging of the files during yesterday's prep meeting comes to mind. Uncertainty gnaws at her as she walks, intensifying her anger and suspicion.

* * *

The courtroom buzzes with anticipation. As Cassie prepares to begin her cross-examination, Luis and Emily slip back into the courtroom, their strides urgent. Emily's eyes are wide with worry as she gestures toward Cassie.

Cassie says, "May I have a brief sidebar with my associates, Your Honor?"

"Proceed, Counselor."

Cassie turns to Emily. "What did you find?"

"I checked my desk drawers, where our evidence was stored. It was opened last night. I'm sure of it. Several of my things had been moved around. I'm sorry, Ms. Thompson. I didn't notice it this morning. And the case files are missing from the computer."

Anger surges inside Cassie, but she quietly calms herself.

"Thank you, Emily," she replies, her thoughts racing through the implications. "This isn't on you. We need to stay focused during Angela's cross-examination."

Emily manages a smile and prepares the evidence for Angela's testimony.

Cassie seethes, aware of who had the motive and opportunity to sabotage her case. She takes a deep breath, her determination strengthening as she prepares to continue the cross-examination. Angela is unsure—press the issue. Make the courtroom hear it, she thinks, glancing up at Angela, who sits on the witness stand, her hands trembling.

"Ms. Marks," Cassie begins, her voice calm and collected, "you mentioned earlier that you willingly accepted a ride from Mr. Reese. Can you tell the court why you chose to get into his car, given that you had your own mode of transportation?"

Angela shifts in her seat, her gaze flickering around the room. "I ... I suppose I wasn't thinking clearly," she replies, her voice wavering. "I trusted him, and I wasn't able to drive myself. He had a new car."

Cassie's expression remains neutral. "You weren't able to drive yourself?" she repeats. "Can you elaborate on that statement, Ms. Marks?"

Angela hesitates. "I ... I had been drinking, only a few beers, and I didn't think it was safe for me to drive. I believed Mr. Reese was sober enough to drive us both home."

"I see," Cassie says, her tone measured. "So, you had no hesitation in going with Mr. Reese?"

Angela's eyes widened, and she stammered, "I-I don't think so … I mean, I trusted my judgment at the time."

Cassie pauses, allowing her words to hang in the air before continuing. "Alright, Ms. Marks, do you recall the color of Mr. Reese's shirt that evening?"

"I … I believe it was a dark color… I think it was blue, but I can't say for sure."

"You can't say for sure," Cassie repeats, her gaze unwavering. "Do you remember the color of his car?"

"It was a light color, white or gray, I think, but again, I'm not sure."

Lydia rises. "*Objection*, Your Honor, irrelevant."

"Overruled. You may continue, Counselor."

Cassie has a wry smile on her face. "Tell me, Ms. Marks, can you be sure of anything that night?"

Lydia rises again. "*Objection*, Your Honor, badgering the witness."

The gavel falls, a sharp punctuation to the judge's rebuke. "Sustained," she intones, her voice a low, unwavering censure. "Ms. Thompson, please keep your questions focused on this case."

Cassie replies, "Yes, Your Honor."

Returning to the counsel table, Emily speaks to Cassie for a moment. With a purposeful stride, she resumes her position by the witness stand.

"Ms. Marks, can you please tell the court what you remember about your interaction with Mr. Reese in his apartment?"

Angela's gaze drops to her lap. "I ... I remember him touching me... He smelled like beer. I remember feeling scared and trying to push him away."

"Scared," Cassie scoffs. "Can you describe to the court what scared you, Ms. Marks? Was it the situation, or some action by Mr. Reese?"

Angela's voice trembles. "I ... I suppose it was a combination of everything. I felt trapped and overwhelmed."

Cassie's expression stays impassive. "Trapped and overwhelmed. Can you clarify that, Ms. Marks? What specific actions or words from Mr. Reese triggered these feelings? Did he involve you in any sexual activity?"

Angela's eyes fill with tears, and she struggles to find her voice. "I remember lying on his couch. He was talking to me, touching me. I can't remember what he was saying ... It was ... a blur."

Cassie allows Angela's last words to resonate throughout the courtroom. She knows he has what she needs. "No further questions, Your Honor."

"The witness may step down."

After a brief deliberation with her associates, Cassie steps forward. "Your Honor, the defense would like to point out that the witness's memory of the evening is fragmented and unclear. We believe external factors may influence her recollection, including alcohol consumption, and request that the court consider this when evaluating her testimony."

The courtroom falls into a hushed silence as Cassie concludes her cross-examination. The judge calls for a recess so she can arrive at a decision.

Cassie invites Emily and Luis to join her in the cafeteria for a quick bite. She places a gentle hand on Emily's shoulders as she holds back tears.

Emily says, "I'm sorry, Ms. Thompson, I don't know what could have happened. I was so careful."

Cassie responds, "This isn't your fault, Emily. I know who tried to sabotage our case. And me."

* * *

Judge McCarthy re-enters the courtroom. Everyone waits for her ruling, filling the room. After a moment, she stands, her voice calm and commanding.

"After reviewing the testimony and evidence, I find it does not establish the probable cause necessary to proceed to trial," she states, her eyes sweeping over the courtroom. "While I appreciate the efforts of both the prosecution and the defense, I cannot overlook significant gaps in the facts of this case."

Pausing, she allows her words to settle in as the spectators shift, caught between disappointment and anger.

"The burden of proof rests with the prosecution, and we cannot move forward without adequate evidence. This decision is about preserving the integrity of our legal system, not about deciding guilt or innocence. Therefore, the charges against Mr. Reese are dismissed. I trust all parties will respect this ruling."

With that, she raises her gavel, signaling the court's adjournment and sealing the moment in the minds of everyone present. The murmurs of disbelief ripple through the spectators, but Cassie remains composed. She exchanges a glance with Jonathan, relief washing over his face.

"Mr. Reese," the judge says, "you are free to go. However, this case will remain open for future consideration should additional evidence arise. Court is adjourned." As she bangs her gavel, the sound reverberates, marking the end of the preliminary hearing.

Cassie turns to Jonathan, her voice low and reassuring. "It's not over yet, but this is a big win for us. Keep a low profile and take no questions from the press."

Jonathan swallows hard, still trying to process what had happened. "I ... I can't believe it," he stammers, a mix of shock and gratitude in his eyes.

As they gather their belongings and prepare to leave the courtroom, they can feel the weight of judgment lift, at least for now.

As the session ends, Cassie ignores questions from news reporters and crime bloggers gathering in the hallway. With a stoic expression, she leaves the courthouse, her associates following behind.

"We'll keep the missing evidence under wraps for now," she says, considering the implications. Emily and Luis nod in agreement.

They need to be cautious; every move matters in this delicate game, and she's determined to hide what she knows. Her mind racing with betrayal, Cassie heads back to the office to plan her next step—a chat with Mark Weller.

Cassie's mind races with possibilities; she can already picture the fall from grace awaiting him when she reveals the evidence of his deception. It is no longer only about the case; it has become personal, and she is determined to hold him accountable for his actions.

Twelve

Thursday, October 10th

Detective Janelle Robinson sits across from Detective Carolyn Fenn at the Mayfair Diner, a bustling breakfast spot frequented by locals. The rich aroma of coffee mingles with the savory scent of sizzling bacon, pulling at her senses. She glances around, noticing the clatter of plates and murmured conversations weaving through the air.

The silence between them feels heavy, charged with unspoken thoughts. Janelle fidgets with her gold chain, the cool metal brushing against her fingertips, as she shifts slightly in her seat, her eyes darting to the window and then back to Carolyn.

Detective Fenn looks tired, as if the stress of long hours and many investigations has worn her down. Janelle watches as she slowly sips her coffee, the dark liquid swirling in her chipped mug.

Janelle needs to choose her words carefully to start the conversation.

"Working in the 8th District can be tough," she says, leaning in as if to create a sense of intimacy in the crowded café. Her voice softens, underscoring how much she values this moment of connection.

Fenn nods, her face showing deep weariness that goes beyond simple tiredness. The lines around her eyes reveal a story of many sleepless nights, weighed down by an enormous sense of responsibility.

Fenn's voice is thick with emotion. "Janelle, the pressure can feel overwhelming," she said. "Some cases weigh on me. Each unsolved case weakens the trust we've built. Some days, it's hard to cope."

Janelle cradles her coffee cup, the porcelain warm against her palms. She savors the rich aroma as steam curls into the air— a fleeting moment of calm amidst the bustling diner. Around her, the clinking of forks and soft chatter blend into a gentle hum, leaving only Fenn's words hanging in the air. Janelle shares Fenn's concerns, bringing them closer together and forming a shared understanding of what's at stake.

Janelle shifts in her seat, focusing on Detective Fenn. "Look, I get it. It's tough to see past the next case. Everyone needs to have dreams beyond this job. We need something to hope for, right?" The moment feels meaningful to Janelle and could mark a turning point in their professional relationship.

Fenn offers a gentle smile, her eyes reflecting her deep desire to make a positive difference. "If I can support our community, that's what means the most to me. You know, my mom and dad always worried about me being a cop," she says. "They think it's too dangerous and often remind me of all the risks involved. I get where they're coming from, but this is what I've always dreamed of doing. I wish they could see that."

Detective Fenn takes a sip of her coffee. "Janelle, can I share something personal with you?"

Janelle nods and leans in to listen.

"I've been thinking a lot about my future—especially my personal life. I want to find the right life partner, someone who can handle the challenges of being married to a detective. My job is so unpredictable, and I need a partner who understands that and supports my ambitions. I also think about starting a family someday. My mom can't stop talking about having grandbabies."

Detective Fenn smiles. "It's hard to date when your cases can end with a body bag. I'm sure you must feel the same way. Is that a crazy thing to dream about?"

Janelle's voice softens as she thinks about her mother; the loss is still fresh in her heart.

"It's a struggle to balance a personal life with work," she confesses, her gaze drifting to the window.

"Every day I step into the precinct, it feels like I'm carrying two heavy burdens—one from the cases I handle and another from the grief of my mom drifting away from me. I wonder if I'm doing enough to honor her memory while managing the demands of the job. I try not to show my emotions in the precinct as a female detective."

Janelle's emotions hang between them, proving how deeply intertwined her life as a daughter and a detective has become. She pauses and manages a wicked smile.

"Fenn, imagine the shitstorm in this neighborhood if men ran this department."

Fenn laughs, "Copy that, Detective."

Janelle and Carolyn raise their coffee mugs and clink them together in a mock toast.

The two have lighthearted conversations, strengthening their bond as they work toward their shared goal of improving their neighborhood. Detective Fenn asks Janelle about a guy she met last week at a Philadelphia Eagles game. Janelle dismisses the question with a laugh.

Fenn admits, "I've been thinking about getting a tattoo," as she glances around. "Yours are so beautiful and a little badass."

Janelle smiles. "Thanks? What do you have in mind?"

"I want something that represents our work, like a badge or a symbol of protection," Fenn says, her eyes bright. "I'd like it on my wrist or forearm to keep it close. To be a constant reminder of who I am."

"That sounds great! The tattoo shop I mentioned has some talented artists who can help create a custom design," Janelle encourages.

Fenn smiles, appreciating the support. "It feels like a big step, but I think it could mirror my commitment to my work and my journey."

Janelle raises her coffee mug. "To new beginnings and meaningful ink!"

Fenn laughs, clinking her mug against Janelle's. "Cheers to that!" A pause in the conversation allows Janelle to take a bite of her cold but crunchy bacon as she dips it in ketchup. Her phone's vibration breaks the quiet atmosphere, signaling a significant message.

Janelle beams with a confident yet intimidating expression. After weeks of effort and a failed attempt at a warrant, there are signs that the detectives working on the case might be changing.

"Finish your coffee, Fenn. The cell phone data for Cassie Thompson is in. Let's get to work."

They both finish their coffee and head out the door.

Thirteen

Friday, October 11th

As the city awakens on a cool Friday morning, Cassie stands at the foot of the Philadelphia Museum of Art, captivated by its grandeur. She is grateful for a rare day off amid her busy professional life. A light mist adds a mystical touch, while the smell of soft pretzels fills the air, tempting her to indulge. Laughter and chatter mingle with the rumbling of the Market Street subway below as hundreds of people head across the city to work.

Cassie stands on the bustling sidewalk, her gaze fixed on the sun as it fights to break through the heavy veil of gray-blue clouds. The golden light dances across the museum's ornate façade, illuminating the intricate carvings and casting soft shadows. A group of tourists gathers on the iconic 'Rocky Steps', their laughter mingling with the rhythmic thud of joggers' footsteps racing by, puffs of mist escaping their mouths in the brisk morning air.

She shifts her weight from one foot to the other, a flutter of anticipation sparking in her chest as she checks her phone for the arrival of her mother's Uber. This outing is a cherished rarity, a break from the daily grind of their lives. As she waits, memories of her small-town upbringing wash over her—a sense of longing intertwining with a twinge of guilt.

The city, with all its chaos and vibrancy, had drawn her in, and she couldn't help but marvel at how far she'd come. Yet, the thrill of adventure had come at a cost. Shadows of tough choices linger in her mind, ethical lines etched into the fabric of her journey. She takes a deep breath, inhaling the crisp air, still clinging to the wide-eyed dreamer within her, even as she navigates the complexities of her new reality.

She looks up and spots her mother, who appears flustered as she steps out of her Uber. Her gray hair glints in the morning mist. Sarah Thompson, appearing older than her years, offers a weathered yet welcoming smile.

"Cassie, darling, I hope you weren't waitin' long." Although her face is lined with age, Sarah's voice still holds a youthful, backcountry lilt.

"Hi, Momma," Cassie greets. She leans in for a quick, controlled hug.

"Oh my," Sarah exclaims, "the ride from home was quite an adventure; people blowin' horns, going way too fast. Cars going this way and that way. For sure, I was thinking I wasn't gonna make it."

"It's okay, Momma," Cassie smiles. "You're here now, and we have the whole day to explore." Cassie and her mom walk up the famous steps, ready to begin their visit.

As they step into the grand atrium of the Philadelphia Museum of Art, a wave of admiration washes over her. She looks up at the soaring ceilings, where sunlight streams through large glass panels, casting a warm glow on the marble floor. Cassie can't help but feel awe as she takes in the stunning architecture around her. The intricate design of the atrium draws her in, with its elegant lines and arches guiding her gaze upward as if inviting her to explore every detail. The aroma of brewed coffee from the nearby café drifts through the air, creating a cozy atmosphere despite the museum's impressive size.

A group of laughing children dashes past, their joy contrasting with the contemplative clusters of older visitors admiring the sculptures. Cassie catches a glimpse of her mother's face, radiating awe and wonder, and it fills her with a sense of shared excitement.

As Cassie and her mom exchange an eager glance, the stresses of work melt away as they enter the line to show their tickets.

* * *

A hushed wave of murmurs parts as they reach the Monet exhibit. Before them, a sea of faces tilted upward, a silent congregation before the shimmering water lilies. Fractured by the high gallery windows, sunlight dances across the canvases and highlights the subtle gradations of Monet's brushstrokes, a dizzying swirl of blues and greens. The pink in the mysterious flowers suggests the color of dawn.

"Look," a woman gasps next to Cassie, "the way he captures the light ... it's alive."

Her companion nods, captivated by the water's hypnotic movement. Each lily pad is a tiny island in a changing world of colors. Cassie watches a group of students from a nearby prestigious art school studying the paintings, taking notes as if it were a final exam.

She turns to her mother. "Momma, how do you like the paintings?" Cassie asks, her voice playful, a whisper above the murmuring visitors.

Sarah chuckles. "They're wonderful, darling. Just lookin' at the light in these paintings, Cassie. How it plays on the water lilies. Reminds me of our creek back home. Only, it don't have any fancy French painters to make it beautiful."

Cassie scoffs, but a flicker of something akin to amusement softens her expression. "Is the muddy creek in Strasburg more beautiful than Monet's masterpieces?"

"Different beautiful, Cassie," Sarah corrects. "Just like ... different ways to live a life. Some shiny, some simple, but all holding their own kind of beauty." She pauses, her gaze lingering on a colorful canvas. "This ... it reminds me of the sunrise over the cornfields back home. Peaceful. Hopeful."

Cassie stares at the painting, a wave of unexpected emotion washing over her. The colors and delicate brushstrokes evoke a sense of calmness, a tranquility she hasn't experienced in a long time. For a moment, she is unaware of the storm raging within her, the secret guilt clinging to her like a second skin.

$$* * *$$

As they leave the gallery, Cassie suggests they get lunch at the cafeteria on the second floor. They settle at a table by the window, offering a view of Benjamin Franklin Parkway, where tall fountains spray a soft mist, shielding them from the midday sun. As Sarah looks over the menu, the sounds of conversation and the gentle clinking of cutlery fill the space.

"It's been a while since we've had the chance to do something like this, just the two of us," Cassie remarks, her gaze steady as she takes a sip from her glass of water. Sarah, her features softened by the warm light streaming through the window, nods in agreement.

"Surely a treat, Cass, especially with your busy schedule and all." She winks, her voice conveying warmth and affection.

The conversation shifts to life's unexpected twists. Cassie discusses the challenges of her job, including long hours and pressure to succeed. Sarah hopes Cassie finds a loving partner who cherishes her laughter and supports her dreams, envisioning a relationship rooted in respect, affection, and shared joy. She wishes for Cassie a passionate and enduring love built on trust and understanding.

Sarah reaches for Cassie's hands. "You always had the will and want in you, Cass," her mom says, a hint of pride creeping into her voice. "But remember to take care of yourself. Life isn't only about achieving and acquiring."

Cassie's features soften, and she reaches across the table to lay her hand on her mother's. "I know, Momma," she says, her voice muted. "I'm trying to find a balance. Sometimes, it seems like the world is moving so fast, and I don't want to be left behind."

Cassie feels the strain of painful memories trying to ruin this day and these precious moments. She tries to keep them away. She can't.

Cassie blurts out, "Momma, what would you say if ... if you knew I did something terrible?" The words surprise even herself.

Sarah turns her weathered face, creases of concern etched on it. "Depends on the terrible thing, Cassie darling. But I believe forgiveness is always possible. Forgiveness. ... for yourself... and maybe for others, too."

Sarah hugs Cassie. "I spent years hangin' onto the hurt your dad left behind. Bitter and angry with the whole damn world. I forgave him for walkin' out on us. It was a price I had to pay for you, Cass. I understand love outweighs the hurt, and I won't let bitterness hold me back. Whatever you're feelin' don't let it hold you back."

Tears well up in Cassie's eyes as her mother's words echo inside her. Taking a deep breath, she can only manage a smile and reach for her mom's hand across the table. Cassie shifts her attention to Monet's artwork; the muted colors now take on new meaning. Maybe she believes there's a way to find peace, make peace with the darkness, and still see the surrounding beauty. A life still possible.

Cassie and her mother continue exploring the museum. As they move through the final exhibit, Cassie and Sarah embark on a journey through time and across continents. They encounter displays that highlight the intricate beauty of Islamic art, the grandeur of ancient Egyptian artifacts, and the captivating stories woven into the textiles of indigenous cultures.

Cassie points to a stunning ancient Egyptian sculpture. "Momma, can you imagine the stories behind these pieces? They must have been so important to the people who created them."

Sarah nods, her eyes wide with fascination. "I know, darlin'. Every old thing tells a story from the past. It's amazing to see how much we've changed, but we're still part of where we came from."

Cassie smiles. Her mom has more wisdom than any other lawyer she has battled. Wisdom to do the right thing. To give, not take.

* * *

Cassie and Sarah fall silent as they exit the museum, each with a wonderful memory.

"Well, darling, that was something. I ain't seen anything like it," Sarah says, her eyes sparkling with wonder. "It's like stepping into another world, with all those different places and times right here in this building."

"It is something, Momma. I'm so glad we came. It's been a while since I've been so happy," Cassie replies, a soft smile playing on her lips. "I am so glad you enjoyed it too."

"Oh, I did, Cass. I did. It's a real treat to see all these beautiful things. And it's special to spend this time with you, just the two of us," Sarah says, her voice thick with emotion. "But now, I think it's time for this old lady to head back home."

"You don't have to rush off, Momma. We can take our time," Cassie says, her gaze fixed on the bustling city beyond the museum steps.

"No, no. I know you have your city life to get back to. Besides, I need to hold on to this moment; you understand? I want to keep this day perfect, just the way it is." Sarah chuckles, her eyes twinkling with affection and mischief.

The sun breaks through the clouds, shining a warm light on their faces as they hug. Amid the bustle of the art museum, a moment of calm surrounds a mother and daughter as they share a heartfelt goodbye.

"I love you, Momma," Cassie says, her voice soft and sincere.

"I love you too, darling." She hugs Cassie. "My momma used to tell me forgiveness is the only path to peace. Don't let darkness dim the light of your future, no matter how difficult the path."

Sarah's words hang in the air, a last piece of wisdom to guide Cassie forward. With a final wave, they part ways.

* * *

Cassie stands by the window, her eyes fixed on the city skyline as the sunset colors fade into gray, reflecting her inner chaos. Burdened by her past, she imagines a fork in the road, with each path whispering uncertainty and temptation. Her mother's voice softly echoes in her mind, offering comfort that both soothes and haunts her. The memories linger like ghosts, constantly reminding her that some burdens can't be escaped.

Trying to hide the truth about that tragic night from her conscience and the police has only bought her some time. The truth can't stay hidden for long.

Her day of reckoning is approaching. Fast.

Fourteen

C assie adjusts the rearview mirror of her convertible as she pulls out of her reserved parking spot, beginning the drive toward her noon appointment. She wears a dark blue business suit, appropriate for the crucial meeting. The city traffic pulses with a slow, frustrating rhythm. She navigates the gridlock with practiced ease.

She guns the engine, a low growl reverberating in the cockpit. Her car—a sleek red blur—slices through the concrete canyon, the rhythmic thump-thump-thump of tires echoing like a heartbeat against the fading hum of the city. Ahead, the expressway unfurls like a gray ribbon, stretching to the horizon. Cassie's grip tightens on the wheel, her eyes bright as she navigates the curves. Each mile brings her closer to a meeting that could inscribe her name on the firm's frosted glass door, the prospect shimmering like a mirage just out of reach.

The Philadelphia exurbs stretch out like a chaotic quilt of big-box stores and identical housing developments, a uniform landscape beneath an indifferent sky. Cassie speeds past manicured lawns, their bright greens clashing beautifully with the warm terracotta of the brick houses. She rolls her eyes at the sameness, the dullness of it all, leaving the city's distractions behind as she slips into the peaceful embrace of the countryside. As AC/DC's 'Hells Bells' blares from the stereo, she cranks up the volume, hoping to drown out the tightness squeezing her chest—a persistent unease that clings to her like an unwanted passenger.

The last leg of the journey takes her through the picturesque countryside of Chester Springs. Rolling hills, farmhouses, and ancient oaks frame the road, heralding a serene, idyllic way of life.

The air is thick with the sweetness of freshly cut hay, blending with the sharpness of wood smoke, wrapping Cassie in a nostalgic embrace. She watches red-tailed hawks glide effortlessly overhead, their wings outstretched as they soar against the blue sky, symbolizing the wild freedom that both charms and eludes her. Below, along the winding road, charming stone walls create a tapestry of history, whispering stories of days gone by.

A horse-and-buggy clatters past, the rhythmic clop of hooves punctuating the warm silence. Inside sits an Amish family, clad in their traditional garb, faces serene and focused as they navigate the gravel path. The sight draws Cassie in, a wave of nostalgia washing over her as her childhood memories flicker like fireflies in the twilight. The scene before her, steeped in rustic simplicity, feels like a window into a life untouched by the relentless pace of the modern world.

As Cassie rounds the bend on the Chester Springs road, the breathtaking view of Eberly Manor appears before her. The Gothic mansion's dark outline stands out against the blue fall sky, flanked by the granite formations of Welsh Mountain and Barren Hill. Cassie's eyes widen with wonder as she drinks in the sight of the grand house.

Eberly Manor stands as a guardian of 1920s neo-Gothic architecture, surrounded by well-maintained grounds and ancient trees whose branches conceal their secret stories. Each tree, with its twisted trunk and spreading limbs, holds the mysteries of the ages, honoring the generations that have come and gone. The manor's grand stone façade rises against the sky, embraced by century-old trees, blending nature and architecture into a living tapestry of history.

As Cassie approaches the gray behemoth, the detailed craftsmanship of the manor becomes clear. Weathered by time, the stonework tells a story, with each brick carefully placed. Tall arched windows with stained glass catch the fading sunlight, while steep roofs adorned with finials and gargoyles stretch upward. Ivy-covered stone walls hide old secrets, and ornate wrought-iron railings surround the terrace. Towering spires display exquisite craftsmanship. An eerie silence fills the air, carrying a damp earth smell that invites curiosity about the manor's mysterious history.

Two large stone ravens stand guard at the approaching gate, always alert. Cassie notices more details that make the estate unique: intricate ironwork on the balconies, leaded glass windows that reflect the fall leaves, and ornate wooden doors that beckon her inside. The gates swing open to welcome Cassie as she arrives.

This mansion looks straight out of a Hitchcock movie, Cassie reflects as she parks on the gravel driveway. The crunch of tires on stones breaks the stillness. The manor's massive wooden door, etched by skilled hands, stands before her. Carved from aged oak, it features a delicate pattern of interlocking vines and leaves. The iron knocker takes the shape of a raven's head, poised to strike. Its dark eyes pierce right through her.

She moves toward the door, her heels clicking on the cobblestones—the only sound breaking the quiet. A shiver runs down her spine as her fingers grip the cold brass handle. With a hesitant knock, a wave of dread grows inside her, as if something sinister waits beyond the threshold, expecting her arrival.

After a few moments, the door creaks open, and Cassie steps inside. The space is vast, with high arched ceilings and elaborate moldings. A large man, his presence filling the foyer, greets her. His expression is stoic, but his eyes hint at curiosity.

"Ms. Thompson, we've been expecting you. Please follow me."

We? Cassie thinks. *Who the hell is 'we'?*

The air feels heavy with an old stillness, broken only by the soft sound of their footsteps. Sunlight streams through the large windows, illuminating the fireplace's flickering flames and casting a warm, amber glow across the room. Cassie's eyes wander over the manor's interior, inspecting the detailed carved wooden panels, delicate frescoes, and shiny antique furniture. Each detail hints at wealth and a refined history, inviting her to delve further into its secrets.

The man leads her to a set of double doors, which he pushes open with a creak, inviting her to enter.

The scent of beeswax and seasoned wood envelops Cassie as she steps inside. A large mahogany table gleams in the candlelight, surrounded by six chairs, one of them empty. Five strangers sit around the table, their faces a mix of curiosity and fear. The flickering flames create dancing shadows, and suddenly, footsteps echo in the hallway. Everyone's gaze snaps to the entrance, anticipation thick in the air.

A commanding presence fills the doorway, sparking a flicker of familiarity in Cassie. He is a tall, imposing man in his sixties. He has silver hair and wears a tailored charcoal gray suit. His aura dominates the room.

"Welcome to Eberly Manor. I am your host, Judge Robert Haskins," he announces. His resonant baritone voice cuts through the silence with precision. "As all of you may now realize, your presence here is not for the reasons you expected. Soon you will learn the true purpose of your visit."

"For now, please give all your electronic devices to my associates; you will all need to focus on the tasks ahead. If you intend to leave my estate prematurely, my associates will make sure that you stay until *I* decide you can leave."

Cassie's heart races as she observes the threatening surroundings. *This is bad. I need to get out of here.* She steps toward the door, but the guards block her way, their hands reaching for pistols from their shoulder holsters.

The judge's cold voice cuts through the moment: "I recommend you reconsider any thoughts of leaving my manor, Ms. Thompson." His gaze locks onto hers, and the weight of the scene presses upon her. Whatever secrets Eberly Manor harbors may cost her everything.

Stupid move, Cassie. Way to take the fucking bait. The Google search. Eberly Manor is owned by William Eberly's grandson, R.W. Haskins. Judge Robert William Haskins. The Young murder case.

The judge has perpetrated a profound deception. This is not a meeting with a helpful informant, but a visit to the sanctuary of someone she knows and fears—a powerful man with a score to settle.

Fifteen

Cassie: Two years earlier

The stress of the upcoming Young murder trial weighed on Cassie's shoulders as she hunched over her desk, poring over every detail of the prosecution's evidence. The case was a murder accusation against Michael Young, the son of a high-profile client. She experienced a desperate need to secure a favorable outcome. The calendar read October 22nd, 2022—two weeks until the trial.

Cassie was a last-minute substitute for a colleague, Mark Weller, who had fallen ill. She understood the impact of her performance on her career and was determined to do whatever it took to succeed. Cassie checked the clock. It was 5:00 pm. It had been a long day, with no end in sight. A file listing evidence and witnesses held her attention. Her thoughts wandered back to simpler times when stress was not a daily, unwelcome companion.

Cassie's rise within her firm was steady, punctuated by her move to a modest apartment on Broad Street in Center City. Transitioning from her life in Strasburg, she navigated the new city and her role with ease.

She spent her evenings in her obsessively organized apartment, dedicating most of her free time to reviewing documents and preparing for cases.

Cassie received a promotion to attorney in the spring of

2022, and with the new title came a small office. One evening, Mr. Thomas DeMarco walked in with her to her new office.

"Ms. Thompson," he said, extending his hand. "Congratulations on your promotion. I trust you find your office suitable?"

"Yes, thank you, sir," Cassie replied, her tone eager yet even.

"You know, Cassandra," he adds, his voice dripping with an unsettling familiarity. "With your ambition, the right partner could put you on the fast track in this firm." He lets out a low chuckle, his gaze lingering a moment too long on her silk blouse, making her skin crawl. He reached out and touched her shoulder. "Just remember, appearances do matter in this business. A little charm goes a long way."

Cassie managed a smile, her hand clenching her briefcase, knuckles turning white.

After his initial greeting, Mr. DeMarco left, the door clicking shut behind him. Cassie, now alone, unpacked. The memory of Mr. DeMarco's lingering gaze—dark—and his suggestive comments sent a chill, a cold prickle, down her spine. The lingering taste of his words was unwanted and unsettling.

* * *

Cassie looked up from the Young file as the cleaning crew tidied the empty offices. Time was pressing as she scoured the case for any evidence to leverage. The 'Commonwealth v. Young' file was thin on crime scene photos and evidence.

She noted inconsistencies in the witness testimonies from the 8th District police reports but found little to aid the defense. Drumming her fingers on the desk, she examined Michael

Young's financial records, looking for an alibi, someone with a motive, or weaknesses in the prosecution's case. The documents showed a privileged young man with an otherwise ordinary life.

While examining the forensic evidence, she noticed inconclusive lab results—no fingerprints or DNA linked Young to the crime. This lack of definitive evidence raised reasonable doubt but didn't offer her an obvious strategy.

Cassie reviewed the potential witnesses by checking their personnel files for any criminal history or biases. She identified a key witness with ties to a Young family competitor, who could bolster the case.

After hours of watching security camera footage from the crime scene, she zoomed in on the grainy images, her heart racing with hope, but the flickering screen revealed no clear evidence to support their case. The prosecution's key witness stayed in her mind; their testimony was heavy with uncertainty, casting a menacing shadow over her efforts. Cassie leaned back in her chair, rubbing her temples as frustration gnawed at her gut. The ticking clock above mocked her, each second slipping away as the pressure built.

Senior Partner Mr. Patrick Briggs stepped into her office, his presence filling the space. He had listened in on the case updates at the morning meeting and spent the day looking for an opportunity to get measurable results in the defense's favor.

He leaned over Cassie, touching her shoulder, and said, "Cassandra, I can help you with that witness's testimony. Come, let's discuss it in my office."

Cassie felt a mix of relief and curiosity as she followed Mr. Briggs. His senior partner's office was a sanctuary; its walls draped in rich mahogany, and its shelves lined with leather-bound books.

Mr. Briggs closed the door behind them and gestured for Cassie to sit down. "I understand you've been working hard on the Young case," he began, his voice gravelly. "It's a challenge, but I believe you have the potential to turn the case around and succeed."

Cassie experienced a surge of satisfaction and hope.

Mr. Briggs said, "I may have insight into one of the key witnesses. Someone who could offer an extra push to sway the jury in our favor."

As Cassie listened, Mr. Briggs revealed details of a prior connection between the prosecution's key witness and a rival of the Young family. The witness seemed to have a hidden agenda and was seeking personal gain.

"This could be our leverage," Mr. Briggs said, his eyes gleaming. "With the right approach, we might be able to shape his testimony to fit our needs. Creative framing, if you will."

Adapt his testimony—creative framing. Is he talking about witness tampering? As Cassie's mind raced with tough decisions, she was aware of the potential danger. She understood that influencing a witness's testimony carried significant risks. Given her emerging career might be at risk, what options did she have?

Mr. Briggs leaned forward, the faint smell of expensive cologne filling the air with a sharp, citrusy scent. "This is part of doing business as a lawyer, Cassie," Mr. Briggs said with a serious tone. "Your position at the firm is at risk, and you need to understand what's required to succeed."

As Cassie went over Mr. Briggs's instructions, a knot formed in her stomach, mixing anxiety with moral conflict. The words felt heavy in her mind, betraying the ideals that had initially attracted her to law. She remembered her favorite class at Penn

State, Legal Ethics with Professor Collins, where she had poured her heart into an assignment that earned her an A+. The pride she felt then now seems a distant memory.

Cassie's gaze drifted to the window, where the heavy clouds in the sky mirrored the weight inside her. The pressure to succeed loomed over her like the sword of Damocles, a constant reminder of the high stakes involved. She pondered the potential outcomes, the thought of betraying her values gnawing at her mind, leaving her caught in a storm of conflicting emotions.

Mr. Briggs placed both hands on Cassie's shoulders. "Let's take a break. The Marriott on Broad Street. Drinks are on me."

The words carried significant weight: they were an invitation, a promise, and a threat.

Sixteen

Cassie: *Two years earlier*

November 2022 in Courtroom A1 at City Hall held day four of the Young murder trial. A diverse assembly of Philadelphians, their faces a mix between grim curiosity and anxiety, filled the packed benches of polished dark wood. A handful of reporters sat in the back seats, each vying to record the pivotal evidence.

The courtroom doors swung open, revealing Judge Robert Haskins. He moved with purpose, his dark robes perfectly tailored. His silver hair was neatly combed, and his expression remained stoic. His polished shoes muted footsteps as he entered. Cassie, with her sculpted blonde bob framing a composed face, watched him from the defense table.

"All rise," the bailiff announced, his voice cutting through the silence. Everyone in the courtroom, including the defendant, Michael Young, dressed in his well-tailored dark-gray suit, stood at attention.

Cassie steadied herself. Beside her was her trusted paralegal, Sienna, who organized their legal pads and documents and was ready to assist at a moment's notice. Standing next to her was Cassie's junior associate, Ryan.

Melissa Rourke, the prosecutor, stood out in the courtroom with her fiery red hair and discerning green eyes, ready to catch any deception.

Judge Haskins stood quietly, his sixty-plus years of observing the familiar surroundings. The faint pallor of his skin reflected the aged wood and dust clinging to the ceiling and walls.

"You may be seated," Judge Haskins's deep, resonating voice commanded, drawing the attention of everyone in the courtroom. He settled into his chair, the gavel resting beside him, a physical symbol of his authority and the seriousness of the proceedings.

The first three days of the Michael Young murder trial unfolded, featuring strategic legal maneuvers. The prosecutor presented forensic evidence and witness testimonies implicating the defendant, while Cassie unsuccessfully objected to their inclusion.

When Detective Janelle Robinson took the stand, Cassie's defiance only grew stronger. Janelle's commanding presence fueled Cassie's determination to challenge the story about Michael Young. She thoroughly scrutinized Janelle's testimony, searching for flaws in the prosecution's case.

With each mention of Michael, Cassie's resolve strengthened. She was determined to confront Janelle and dismantle the prosecution's carefully crafted narrative. As Janelle's compelling testimony concluded, silence enveloped the courtroom, closing the third day of the trial.

∗ ∗ ∗

The fourth day began, and Cassie and her team were prepared. Janelle Robinson was called to the stand by the bailiff. She stood confidently and walked over to the witness box. Sitting down, she straightened her posture and looked around the courtroom as she got ready to continue her testimony.

"Ms. Robinson, you have already been sworn. Ms. Thompson, you may begin your cross-examination," Judge Haskins' voice boomed.

As Cassie readied her cross-examination, she was reminded of something one of her undergraduate professors at Penn State had told her years before: *Never ask a question in court if you don't know the answer.* She'd follow his advice today.

Cassie approached the witness stand. She paused, her gaze locked on Detective Janelle Robinson, an experienced police officer but new to detective work—a potential weakness to explore. Janelle met Cassie's gaze.

"Detective Robinson," Cassie began, her voice a low purr, "you previously testified that Mr. Young was seen near the crime scene. However, your report lacks precise and consistent details. Could you please refresh the court's memory about the exact circumstances?"

Janelle said, "The witness account places him within a three-block radius of the murder at approximately 10:15 pm. The murder occurred between 10:00 pm and 10:30 pm."

"A rather broad window, wouldn't you agree, Detective?" Cassie pressed, her smile brittle. "Plenty of time for someone else to commit the crime."

"There's corroborating evidence, Counselor," Janelle countered, her voice calm but firm. "Cell phone tower data placed his phone near the scene at the relevant time."

"Convenient," Cassie said. "There was no mention of this in your initial report. Perhaps this 'convenient' evidence appeared after the defense requested a full disclosure."

Melissa rose. "*Objection*, Your Honor. I want to remind the court that the defense has been given every opportunity to obtain this data. The prosecution or the investigation team is not at fault for your failure to acquire it."

"Sustained, noted for the record."

Cassie leaned forward, unfazed. "Detective Robinson, are you familiar with the concept of *data dumping* as a strategy to overwhelm and distract opposing counsel?" Her voice was laced with an outright challenge. "A common tactic used to obscure important information among irrelevant documents, hoping it remains unnoticed."

Melissa jumped up. "*Objection*, asked and answered."

"Overruled. The witness may answer the question."

Janelle's gaze stayed fixed on Cassie. "I am familiar with the strategy, Counselor," she replied. "However, I assure you we did not use any such tactics in this case. The cell tower data was part of a broader analysis," Janelle said. "It wasn't deemed crucial to the initial report, but became relevant as the investigation moved forward."

"Evidence being 'lost' is convenient, I'd say," Cassie countered, her voice dripping with sarcasm."

Melissa stood with rising anger. "*Objection*, Your Honor, the defense is badgering the witness."

"Sustained. Ms. Thompson, enough of the theatrics, please."

"My apologies, Your Honor," Cassie grinned to herself as she turned away from the bench.

Cassie walked to the defense table and studied a photograph held by her associate, Sienna. She sauntered back toward the witness stand.

"Detective Robinson," Cassie began, "this photograph, *Exhibit B3*, which is a still from a security camera, purports to show the defendant near the crime scene at 10:47 pm. Is that correct?"

"Yes," Janelle replied.

"But the photo is grainy and dim. It could be anyone," Cassie said. "We processed that exact photo against our facial recognition software database, and it could not come up with a match with anyone. With that in mind, how can you definitively identify Mr. Young?"

Janelle counters, "It's called forensic analysis, Counselor. His specific gait. I've observed him on security video. The way he walks is consistent with the figure in the photo."

Cassie says, "A subjective assessment, Detective. No concrete evidence. No timestamp verification besides your assumption. This 'evidence' is quite feeble, don't you think, Detective?" Cassie's voice dripped with disdain.

Melissa rose. "*Objection*, Your Honor. The defense is *again* badgering the witness."

"Sustained." Now visibly agitated, Judge Haskins said, "Ms. Thompson, one more of those and I will hold you in contempt of court. Do I make myself clear?"

Cassie replied with fake humility, "Yes, Your Honor."

"Well then, please continue, Ms. Robinson."

Janelle's face showed growing anger toward Cassie, whose relentless probing and disdainful demeanor were dismantling her testimony.

Janelle took a breath. "It's one piece of the puzzle, Ms.

Thompson. Combined with other evidence, including eyewitness testimony and forensic findings, it paints a clear picture."

Cassie chuckled out loud. "What about the metadata? Have you checked the photograph for timestamp accuracy?"

"The metadata was corrupted during the data transfer, Counselor. We could recover the image but not its associated metadata," Janelle explained.

"Corrupted? So, you're trusting a blurry photograph with questionable origins to place Mr. Young at the scene? This isn't a police sketch, Detective. It's supposed to be evidence."

Janelle replied. "It's supporting evidence, a piece of the investigation. Combined with other..." Cassie cut her off.

"Enough with the *other evidence*! This photograph, as it stands, is inadmissible. It's unreliable, lacks verifiable timestamps, and is based on your subjective interpretation of a vague image and a ... walk." She paused, letting her words sink in. "Your Honor, with your permission, I move to exclude *Exhibit B3*."

Judge Haskins considered her request. He tapped a pen against his desk as the courtroom waited. "Motion denied, Counselor," he said, his voice flat. "Detective Robinson, you may please continue."

Janelle countered, her voice calm but firm. "Counselor, while the image isn't crystal clear, the individual's build and clothing are consistent with the suspect's description. We will present corroborating witness testimony that places Mr. Young in the vicinity."

Cassie took a deep, cleansing breath and stepped toward the bench. "No further questions, Your Honor."

Judge Haskins motioned to Janelle with his hand. "You may step down, Ms. Robinson."

Cassie followed Janelle back to her seat in the gallery, noticing her tense shoulders and the look of distress on her face. Cassie felt a sense of satisfaction; she had completed her mission. Everything was going as planned.

Melissa Rourke stood poised as she called her final witness to testify.

"Your Honor, with your permission, I would like to call Mr. John Simmons to the stand."

Mr. Simmons rose. Over fifty years, etched into the fine lines around his eyes and the slump of his shoulders, had worn him like a well-loved glove. His tan suit, once sharp, now carried a faint sheen of dust and the subtle imprint of many sittings. Each step was slow, with the worn leather of his shoes creaking against the subdued murmur of the gallery.

He paused, his hand resting on the witness stand. His gaze swept over the assembled faces before settling on the judge. A single bead of sweat traced a path along his temple.

The bailiff addressed the witness: "Mr. John Simmons, please raise your right hand. Do you swear to tell the truth, the whole truth, and nothing but the truth, so help you God?"

"I do."

Cassie shifted in her seat.

Melissa began. "Mr. Simmons, can you please tell the court why you were at the crime scene the night of the murder?"

"I was a security officer at the warehouse that evening."

"And what are your duties there, Mr. Simmons?"

"I patrol the street that borders the building and check the doors for suspicious activity."

"I see Mr. Simmons. So, please tell the court what happened on the night of May 2nd, 2022, between 10:40 and 11:00 pm?"

"I thought I heard shouting from the other side of the building. When I arrived, there was chaos, but I remember seeing a man carrying something that looked like a knife. It seemed like he was attacking someone on the ground, but I couldn't see everything clearly."

Cassie watched as the courtroom's fluorescent lights cast a sterile glow. The stale air, thick with unspoken tension, prickled her skin. This was the moment she had been waiting for.

Melissa said, her face showing growing alarm, "Mr. Simmons, in your sworn statement to the police, you stated you saw the defendant, Michael Young, at the scene of the crime, and that he was the man who stabbed the victim identified as Carl Kallinase. Could you please elaborate on that?"

Mr. Simmons shifted in his chair, his nervousness heightening the intensity of the cross-examination. He looked around the courtroom with apprehension. "Well, I ... I saw someone who looked like him. I mean ... it was dark... I guess it could have been someone else." His voice dropped to a whisper.

A ripple of surprise surged through the courtroom. Cassie watched with a barely perceptible smile playing on her lips.

Judge Haskins banged his gavel hard on his desk. "*Order in the court, please. Order.*"

Melissa's voice hardened. "Mr. Simmons, your sworn statement states you clearly identified Michael Young. Saying it looked like him is not the same as giving a positive identification.

Are you claiming you perjured yourself in your earlier statement?"

Cassie rose. "*Objection*, Your Honor, the defense is leading the witness."

"Sustained. Ms. Rourke, please let the witness testify."

He said, avoiding eye contact, "I ... I was under pressure. I wasn't sure, but ... the police... like they were... insistent. You know how they can be..." Melissa tightened her face, the sudden shift in demeanor casting a shadow over the witness.

Cassie noticed the unexpected testimony was weighing heavily on Melissa, threatening her case. As the murmurs faded, she saw Melissa stand, anger clear in her eyes, fixed on the judge. Cassie felt a knot in her stomach, sensing the moment's significance and believing the testimony had shifted the case in her favor.

"Your Honor," she asserted, "I request a sidebar."

Judge Haskins replied in a measured tone, "Ms. Rourke and Ms. Thompson, please approach the bench." The air crackled with anticipation as Melissa approached the bench, her anger barely contained. Cassie followed, struggling to conceal her amusement at this calculated turn of events.

The judge welcomed them to the bench, and a hushed conference ensued, with only the participants aware of the words being exchanged.

Melissa pleaded, "Your Honor, the prosecution requests a continuance in light of this new development. They believed it was necessary to investigate the matter further and ensure the integrity of their witness's testimony."

Cassie countered, "The witness is under oath. I see no reason to delay his testimony." The courtroom buzzed with implications, and the tension grew as the judge considered the request.

Judge Haskins furrowed his brow, weighing the request.

After a few moments, he responded. "Very well, Ms. Rourke, I will grant you a continuance until Monday morning. As per Ms. Thompson's request, Mr. Simmons' testimony and your request will be considered admissible."

He turned to Melissa, angry. "In the future, Ms. Rourke, please be sure to have your witness statements verified before you enter the courtroom and waste the court's time." He shot a glare at Cassie, suspicion etched across his face.

Judge Haskins tapped his fingers on the bench, the sound echoing in the silent courtroom. "The prosecutor's request for a continuance is granted," he intoned, his voice carrying an air of finality. "Court will resume on Monday at 9:00 am sharp."

With that, he brought the gavel down, signaling the end of another dramatic day in the Young murder trial.

As she walked by, Cassie observed Janelle grabbing her briefcase and leaving the courtroom in disgust.

Cassie and her team stepped out of the courtroom, and a flood of mixed emotions swept over her like a tidal wave. Satisfaction coursed through the group, but Cassie grappled with a deep sense of unease. She had made a deal with the devil—a victory that tasted both sweet and bitter.

Cassie traded her guiding principles for the tempting promise of a corner office. As the weight of that decision settled in her chest, she felt a strong sense of betrayal. The images of her former life lingered in her mind, urging her to reconsider the path she had chosen as she moved through the polished halls of her new world.

Seventeen

Janelle: Two years earlier

J anelle slammed the door of her apartment shut, her frustration
boiling over as she threw her bag onto the couch. The memory
of her day in court replayed in her mind, each moment more
infuriating than the last. Janelle fought the urge to throw her coat
across the room, her face twisted in anger. *They tampered with my
witness! she seethed*, her thoughts swirling with frustration and
disbelief. How had they undermined Mr. Simmons, filling his
mind with doubt and fear? This wasn't a careless mistake; it felt
like a deliberate betrayal.

As she pictured Cassandra Thompson's smug expression, a
fresh wave of anger coursed through her. The wicked satisfaction
that must have spread across Cassandra's face at the chaos she
had orchestrated only fueled Janelle's resolve. What depths had
Cassie sunk to, manipulating his testimony so brazenly? Janelle
clenched her fists, vowing that this underhanded move wouldn't
go unchallenged. The game had shifted, and she was determined
to expose the scheme and strike back.

Gazing out the window, she watched the day fade into
twilight, reflecting her own turbulent emotions. She opened the
fridge and grabbed a cold Yuengling lager; the icy bottle promised
a brief escape. When she hit play on her phone app, soft jazz filled
the room with a calming presence. The mellow tunes washed over
her, offering a brief respite from her dark thoughts.

As Janelle sank into her chair, tension coiled in her muscles, and the weight of the courtroom's scrutiny pressed down on her. Jonesy, sensing his mom's turmoil, jumped onto her lap and curled up against her. She stroked his fur; the familiar texture and warmth offered a trace of comfort amid her chaos. The soothing sound of his purring, mixed with the soft jazz, gradually calmed her racing heart, allowing a flicker of solace to emerge.

"I had a terrible day, Jonesy," she said, burying her face in his fur. Jonesy purred and settled on her lap. Janelle's mind remained troubled with thoughts of the trial. Jonesy's gentle companionship was only a temporary comfort for her wounded pride.

Janelle learned two crucial lessons today. First, never underestimate how far a defendant's lawyer will go to sway a case in their favor. This betrayal left a lasting mark on her conscience. Second, never underestimate Cassandra Thompson again. Her cunning was a formidable force. Janelle realized every move mattered, and the courtroom was a battleground where trust was a valuable commodity. The stakes were high, and in this game, she had to be sharper, faster, and always one step ahead. The battle was only beginning.

She knew they would challenge each other again, and this time she would be ready.

Eighteen

Judge Haskins: Two years earlier

As the sun dipped below the horizon, casting long shadows across the countryside, Judge Robert Haskins sat in his study at Eberly Manor, a brooding figure in the heart of his 100-year-old Chester Springs estate. The many legal victories and two decades on the bench felt like mere trophies accumulated over the years. Despite the accolades, a gnawing emptiness clawed at him, an unrelenting visceral beast.

He swirled the exquisite fifty-year-old scotch in his snifter; the ice softly clinking against the glass, disrupting the steady tick-tock of the clock echoing in the hallway. His thoughts drifted to the recent Young homicide case, its weight pressing heavily on his mind. The word "acquittal" flickered through his mind, souring his gut. A cruel smile curled his lips as he traced his finger over the weathered surface of his desk, lingering on the faint imprint left by a drink spilled long ago. In that instant, the room—once his sanctuary—transformed into a suffocating tomb, each shadow a reminder of the crushing defeats he couldn't shake off.

He had reviewed the trial proceedings. Every detail, including a surprising last-minute testimony from a crucial witness, was inconsistent with his earlier sworn statement.

He wrestled with the two options presented in this confusing case. Either a well-meaning yet flawed memory from the witness, distorted by the pressures of police questioning, or a calculated manipulation orchestrated by the defense. But which one was it?

A growing unease crept into Judge Haskins as he studied the evidence before him. His suspicion increased when he saw a direct link between the witness and DeMarco & Briggs, a firm he loathed with simmering hostility. This law firm had been involved in unethical actions in several recent trials he presided over, fueling a deep rage that felt personal.

It wasn't only the possibility of a compromised witness troubling him; it was the battle with the ghost of his younger, more ethical self. His reflection in the polished wood of his desk served as a haunting reminder of that past self.

Jurisprudence, once his guiding principle, had hardened over the years into a crippling cynicism that seeped into every part of his life. He recognized it in the defendant's lawyer, a woman embodying the amorality Robert had once embraced. The emotions she stirred in him were complex, encompassing both envy and disgust, prompting him to scrutinize the moral standards he had always upheld.

As Judge Haskins grappled with the ethical dilemma before him, memories of his late wife, Eleanor, resurfaced. He recalled her gentle eyes, always filled with steady moral clarity, guiding them through even the toughest ethical challenges. In his mind, he pictured her standing in their garden, surrounded by the fragrant flowers she cared for with such love and attention. Her soft smile and graceful movements eased the turmoil inside him.

As Judge Haskins' thoughts returned to the compromised witness and his moral decline, memories of Eleanor continued to haunt him. Her gentle spirit motivated him to remember himself as a man who valued integrity and justice above all else. He had promised her he would uphold those principles, but now he felt he was on the brink of a betrayal deeper than any legal mistake. He struggled with the fear of dishonoring the values that once defined his life and career.

Unethical legal maneuvers driven by ambition, whispered in the silent corridors of Eberly Manor, would serve as his instrument of revenge.

As the judge finished reviewing the Young murder case, he understood this undeniable truth: Cassandra Thompson and his destinies were now connected, destined for another encounter if she continued down her dark path.

At this moment, Judge Haskins concentrated on creating a complex scenario to deliver justice through his grand plan. But his role as a sworn judge required absolute certainty, beyond any reasonable doubt. He owed just as much to Eleanor as to his legacy on the bench.

Those who met these criteria would become hesitant participants in a high-stakes, secret spectacle. Once again, they would play games at Eberly Manor, and this time, the stakes would be much higher.

Nineteen

Now

The judge begins, "Ladies and gentlemen, if I may have your attention." He smiles; his eyes fixed on Cassie. "It is now time to reveal why you have been chosen as my guests this afternoon. All of you have been in my company at one time or another, either in my courtroom or under other circumstances."

As the judge's words echo in her mind, a knot of dread tightens in her stomach. The men with guns stand watchful and unyielding; their icy stares pierce her skin. Panic floods her—there's no way to escape, no way out.

She remembers her encounters with Judge Robert Haskins, most notably in the Young murder case. The judge's reason for bringing Cassie here is confusing to her. She looks around the room and doesn't recognize anyone else. *Where are the other lawyers or witnesses if this is about what I did during the Young trial? Who are these people?* Cassie wonders.

Judge Haskins continues, snapping Cassie back to reality. "I intend to right the wrongs I once allowed. Each of you has something in common: involvement in evading justice. I will not stand by and let justice be perverted or denied."

A chill runs through Cassie's body. An ominous thought crosses her mind: *What if this isn't about the Young case, but ... something else?*

Judge Haskins approaches the players and holds up six walnut wood boxes. "Players, there is a box for each of you with your name on the front. Inside, there is a welcoming gift for you."

"In a moment, I will ask each of you to step forward to receive your box. But before that, there is a name tag on your chair. Please pin it on so each player can identify you."

A wistful look crosses his face. "I have played games in this manor house my entire life, and so it will be today with you. However, these games will be different. Each game will involve skill, patience, and even a touch of luck."

The judge gestures to the boxes on the table.

"Let's begin."

* * *

Elizabeth, a tall woman in her mid-thirties, sits upright like a delicate bird on her perch. Her cardigan, with its faded floral pattern, drapes over her curvy frame, and her skirt, a matching muted shade, hangs to her knees. A noticeable tremor passes through her clasped hands. Her face, pale and lined with worry, shows no expression.

The judge says, "Elizabeth, please step up and take your box."

Cassie watches as Elizabeth approaches Judge Haskins, a tense silence hanging in the air. Elizabeth takes the box and returns to her seat. She opens it, revealing a library card. She stifles a sob. Cassie tries to understand. *What does this gift mean? Why is Elizabeth so upset?*

Elizabeth's terrified expression reflects her anxiety, and

Cassie experiences a surge of empathy. Every instinct tells her this is more than a simple artifact; it's a reminder of the judge's potential wrath and a deadly challenge.

Elizabeth sits in silence, her words inaudible above the ticking clock in the corner. She turns to the judge. "I want to go home. I can't do this," she says, putting her head in her hands.

Cassie wonders, *Why is this woman here? Is the judge insane?* She glances at the other players; their dazed looks mirror her own.

The judge says, "Emilio, please step up and take your box."

Cassie's gaze lands on the man with the name tag 'Emilio.' He's tall and athletic in a fitted tracksuit. His dark eyes scan the room with intensity. A stray lock of black hair falls over his forehead, and he brushes it aside, clearing his throat before stepping forward with a box in hand. He opens it, revealing a stethoscope inside, and sets it on his chair. His expression is blank as he takes a seat, calm amidst the surrounding buzz.

While the other players fidget, Emilio stays unfazed, radiating a calmness that intrigues Cassie. She feels he could be someone to watch out for.

Cassie watches as a woman named Judith approaches the judge. Her hands mirror the intensity in her sharp gray eyes. Wrinkles mark her features from over sixty years, as her gaze shifts within the dim space. A halo of unruly gray curls contrasts with the neat lines of her bright blue cotton dress. The afternoon sun breaks through the gloom, illuminating the confidence on her face.

As Judith, expressionless, opens her box to reveal two red roses, Cassie notices she didn't react. She wonders what if this older woman isn't what she seems? Cassie vows to stay alert and observe each player. The stakes are too high for her to let her guard down around anyone.

The fireplace's flickering light touches the worn velvet of the chair where Regina sits, illuminating her grim expression.

Regina, in her mid-thirties, has curly red hair framing her face, hinting at a personality as lively as her curls. Her outfit exudes authority, reminiscent of a schoolteacher. She wears a fitted blouse, a dark cardigan, and a gray pencil skirt. Her black shoes match her purposeful steps, enhancing her commanding presence. She opens her gift, a gold cross, which she quickly clasps around her neck.

As Regina fixes her gaze on her, Cassie meets her eyes with unwavering intensity, but inside, fear and doubt churn like a storm. At this moment, she's not only facing a rival; she's risking everything she's fought for. Cassie steps forward, determined but aware that any misstep could change her fate. Her instincts tell her to stay alert, and she cannot let Regina outsmart her.

Cassie scans the room, focusing on one man who stands apart—Thomas. In his late forties, he exudes a disturbing mix of determination and anger, his dark gaze remaining steady. There's a deep intensity about him that quickens her heartbeat.

His worn brown shoes tap against the hardwood floor, and she notices how his button-down shirt strains against a once-strong frame, now yielding to the passage of time. Gray threads pepper his short brown hair, serving as another reminder of the years he's lived.

He doesn't talk to anyone, isolating himself from the other players. Instead, his gaze scans the room, dark and intense, lingering too long on each face until it lands on hers. A shiver runs down her spine. What's that expression? Fear? Anger? What stories hide behind his stormy exterior?

He steps up and takes his box. He sits gripping the lid, unwilling to reveal what it contains.

Cassie's heart pounds as Judge Haskins speaks her name. She steps forward, every person's gaze heavy on her. The judge hands her the walnut box, a symbol of his decision.

Back in her seat, she hesitates before opening it, glancing around to ensure no one is watching. Inside, there's a brass key, heavy yet insignificant. What does it mean? Does it unlock a door in the manor?

Cassie expected her gift to be a token from the Young murder case, the only direct link she had to Judge Haskins and his desire for retribution. For now, only the judge knows the purpose of the key. Whatever game Judge Haskins is playing, she's now an unwilling participant.

$$* * *$$

Judge Haskins chuckles as he approaches the players. "As you enjoy my welcome gifts, it should be clear why you have been chosen to take part in this special gathering. Now, I will reveal the stakes."

"This evening, five games will be played, each lasting one hour. There will be no conversations or scheming among players during the games. I want to prevent any alliances from forming, as they could give certain players an unfair advantage. The loser of each round will be eliminated. More about that in a minute."

"The player who wins the last game will get to make an important decision about their fate and avoid the harshest judgment. Trust me, the privilege is worth winning. Sadly, the losers of each game will immediately face the consequences of their actions. For some, the unfortunate outcome will be death."

As Judge Haskins chuckles, a wave of tension sweeps through the room. Elizabeth's face turns even paler, tears streaming down her cheeks as her hands tremble in her lap, and her breathing quickens in panic. Emilio's composed manner briefly wavers, a flicker of doubt flashing in his dark eyes before he quickly masks it with a stoic expression. Judith's sharp gaze narrows, determination crossing her features. Regina tightens her hold on the gold cross around her neck, her jaw set with resolve.

Thomas's brow furrows, his eyes darkening as they shift from the judge to Cassie, hinting at either rage or fear. Each person's reaction sharpens in the moment, a mix of dread, defiance, and curiosity, woven with anxiety that hangs over them like a specter.

The judge's words echo in Cassie's mind—losing means death, and that thought twists through her spine, igniting panic. She scans the room; the armed men are now lurking predators, their eyes gleaming with malicious anticipation. Every person here feels like a potential enemy, their fear blending with the thick tension in the air, choking her. There's no way out, a voice repeats inside her head—the walls of Eberly Manor close in, trapping her in a nightmare.

Twenty

The polished wood of the grand staircase gleams under the weak light filtering through the high, arched windows above. With each cautious step, Cassie ascends, drawing closer to an ominous fate that hangs in the air like a heavy fog. A judge's associate gestures her into a spacious bedroom; the heavy oak door creaks shut behind her, muffling the unsettling stillness that envelops Eberly Manor.

She remains still, her pulse racing as she hears footsteps fade down the hall. This isn't a mistake; Judge Haskins has laid a trap. Anxiety settles in her stomach. No one knows where she is—not her mom, friends, or coworkers. This meeting is secret; trust is a luxury she can't afford, especially after the disturbing incident with the missing photo. She turned off her phone's tracking after DeMarco & Briggs' policy on client meetings, but now that choice feels heavy in the surrounding silence.

Her gaze flits around the room, absorbing the cozy decor that starkly contrasts with the icy dread gripping her heart. A four-poster bed looms, its silk curtains taunting her, while the fireplace casts a sinister glow, shadows dancing in the corners like whispers of her fears.

A chilling sensation shocks her; it feels as if the walls of Eberly Manor are scrutinizing her every move. Her mind races, sorting through fragments of recent conversations about the Dougherty case. Mark Weller's name surfaces, an insistent thread woven with suspicion. She recalls his love of gossip, and a troubling thought takes hold: could he have betrayed her by feeding information to Judge Haskins? Did he destroy evidence to throw her off in the preliminary hearing? If he shared sensitive details, that might explain her precarious situation now.

The urge to run and escape hits her so hard she loses her balance. *I have to escape—now before it's too late*, Cassie thinks, but footsteps in the hallway crush the thought. She gazes out of the thick glass windows and sees a three-story drop.

A small antique trunk sits on the bedside table, its keyhole tempting her to look inside. Remembering the brass key she received from Judge Haskins, she scans the room for any signs of danger. Ensuring she is alone, she picks up the box, inserts the key, and opens it. Lifting the lid, she sees the item Judge Haskins chose for her: a single red brick with a dark red stain on its surface. Blood.

Cassie staggers to the floor. She closes the lid as if to hide the brick and its secrets. Hyperventilating, she sinks beside the trunk on unsteady legs, legs that can no longer hold her. She squeezes her eyes shut and presses her hand to her chest to quiet the rising terror that grips her. *He knows.*

The judge holds all the cards. She's trapped in his Gothic prison, watching her carefully built life fall apart. The game, she realizes, has only just begun. And she isn't playing to win. She's playing to survive.

Outside, the wind howls, but in her mind, it's drowned out by the screech of tires and a terrible scream …

Twenty-One

Cassie: 18 months earlier

C assie stormed out of the Somerton Bar & Grill, her face a mask of silent rage. *Well, that was a total waste of my time*, she fumed. The evening had been a disaster—another poorly planned blind date arranged by a well-meaning but oblivious friend. Her steps were unsteady as she stumbled toward her car. The dangerous combination of high heels and too many mojitos nearly caused her to fall.

Cassie fumbled with her keys, an alcohol-fueled buzz dulling her usual sharp coordination. Once inside, she slammed the door, jabbed her finger at the push-to-start, and started the engine. The powerful purr of the car calmed her frayed nerves, and with a screech of tires, she sped out of the parking lot, the Somerton Bar & Grill fading behind her.

She checked the time—10:00 pm—and set her phone's GPS to "home" before rolling down the convertible top, letting the cool night air rush in to tangle her long hair. The dashboard's glow cast an eerie light on her features.

Cassie felt the strain of the day pressing on her as she navigated the chaotic streets, the blaring horns a constant reminder of her frantic state. She drifted over the center line, unaware of the warning honks from other drivers. Her GPS blared, "*Continue straight to Frankford Avenue and Route 95*," but towering orange cones blocked the road ahead. *Fucking road construction.*

She turned left at the next unfamiliar intersection, Sheffield Avenue, hoping it would lead her back to a recognizable landmark. Instead, it only increased her confusion. The street lined with identical twin houses and the occasional convenience store offered Cassie no clues about her location relative to where she needed to go. Her mind felt foggy from alcohol and frustration. A barking dog, a flickering streetlight—the streets were dark and quiet. The once-soothing hum of the engine now seemed mocking as she realized she was lost. Her GPS kept shouting, *"re-routing ... re-routing in 500 feet..."* Her coordination faltered, and she glanced down at her phone, desperately trying to pull up the directions.

"Where the fuck am I...?" The words ripped from Cassie's throat were raw and panicked.

A sudden, horrible scream. *Thud.*

The impact jolted her—a brutal, bone-jarring collision that stole her breath. Her chest clenched, her fist tightening around her heart. The leather of the steering wheel dug into her palms as she slammed on the brakes, screeching in protest before shuddering to a stop.

A sudden feeling of dread washed over her. She had hit something on the road.

She swung open her car door, revealing a shadowy street. Her eyes, wide with growing horror, fixed on a terrifying sight: a tiny figure lying still, sprawled across the crosswalk bricks. She stumbled forward and took in the scene. Her eyes locked onto the unmoving figure—a little girl with pink glittery butterflies in her hair, friendship bracelets on her wrists, and her denim shorts stained crimson.

Cassie rushed back to her car. She sobbed uncontrollably as her mind raced.

She screamed, "I didn't mean to hit her. Oh my God, I didn't even see her. My life is over ... What have I done?"

She can't breathe or think. Cassie collapses into the driver's seat, her hands trembling. Without hesitation, she guns the engine and drives away from the scene.

PART 2

Twenty-Two

Janelle: Six weeks ago

Lead Detective Janelle Robinson sat at the head of the 8th District conference room table, reviewing her meeting agenda. Her CO informed her this morning that she was to reopen a cold case that had embarrassed the district a year ago. Across from her were Detective Derrick Coles and Detective Carolyn Fenn.

"Good morning," Janelle started, her tone welcoming. "As you know, we have been short-staffed for the last few months. We need to allocate their resources accordingly. This means certain cases have to be prioritized, and others, unfortunately, closed prematurely."

A slight frown appeared, signaling her displeasure with the situation. Janelle added, "One case is being reopened, priority one." She knew they were both aware of the 6-ABC news report on the Lily Cochrane case.

Detective Coles and Fenn nodded in agreement.

"The case is a heavy burden for us. Lily's family and friends are still grieving, and every update—or lack of one—hits hard. The neighborhood is crying out for justice, and we have a duty to fight for that, not only for Lily but for all victims. The Cochrane case has also been a source of embarrassment for our district. We have orders from the police commissioner to revisit the case and bring it to a quick conclusion. We can settle with fresh eyes and our combined expertise."

Detective Fenn said, "It was hard watching Lily's father choke back tears on live TV, pleading for anyone who knew something to come forward."

The room remained still as Fenn's words settled. Janelle knew the Cochrane case had been challenging, with few clues and significant public interest. She placed the manila folder sharply on the table between them. She paused, glancing at Coles and Fenn. "Effective immediately. You are both assigned to the Lily Cochrane case."

Coles leaned in, his youthful eagerness masking the apprehension in his eyes. He traced the edge of the folder with a fingertip, his breath catching in his throat. "Detective Robinson, is this straight from Commissioner Regan?"

"Yes, Detective Coles. Philly HQ wants fresh eyes on the case. We should be aware of how high-profile this is."

Detective Fenn shifted in her chair. Her fingers drummed a nervous rhythm against her thigh. She muttered, "I was on the original team ... hard to believe they'd want me back after I came up short." She ran a shaky hand through her hair.

Janelle said, "HQ wants a head start on this, Fenn. Someone familiar with the case. Someone who can bring us up to speed but also re-examine the evidence with a different lens."

She handed Detectives Fenn and Coles copies of the original list of witness statements and opened the evidence box.

"Let's start with the witness statements. As with most of the original evidence, there was enough to understand where and what to look for, but not enough solid leads to move forward.

The only witness at the scene did not see the accident, but only heard the collision. By the time they ran out into the street, the car had already fled. Other witnesses on nearby blocks also could not identify the vehicle."

"What about the doorbell cam footage?" Detective Fenn asked. "There should be plenty on Sheffield Avenue in the area of the accident scene."

Janelle answered: "About twenty to thirty cameras were available, but the driver turned off their running lights soon after the accident, presumably as a forensic countermeasure. Without lights, the car appears as a dark shape. We will also see this repeatedly in other evidence and potential leads."

Detective Coles offered, "Drivers in such situations typically lack the foresight to consider that possibility."

"The perpetrator in this case was meticulous and calculated," Janelle explained. "They knew exactly how to cover their tracks and avoid detection. But we also know no plan is perfect, and that's where we come in."

"Did the vehicle leave any evidence behind?" questioned Coles.

"Investigators found no identifiable evidence on the victim herself. Forensic analysis revealed the blood at the scene belonged to Lily. But there were identifying tire marks left on the street," Janelle responded. "And we also have this."

Janelle took out two small bags from the evidence box: one containing a piece that looked like a red plastic bumper, and the other containing shards of glass. She placed them on the table.

"This is the only identifiable forensic evidence found at the scene of the accident. The red plastic piece made of urethane originated from the lower front panel of the vehicle, next to the fog light. Investigators believe the shards of glass came from the right headlight."

Detective Fenn asked, "Did they identify a vehicle make and model from these pieces and the tire marks?"

"Yes, mass spectrometry analysis shows the bumper and glass belong to a 2018-2023 Mercedes coupe or convertible. Tire tread analysis also revealed a mid-size Mercedes."

"Unfortunately, there are thousands of vehicles of this make and model within a 50-square-mile area around the scene. I have the list from June of this year; it's a lot to review," Janelle adds. "Detective Fenn, can you follow up on those leads and try to narrow down this list?"

"On it." Detective Fenn grabbed the list.

Janelle said, "Detective Coles, you and I will revisit the accident scene to see if we can find anything overlooked in the original investigation."

＊ ＊ ＊

As Detective Robinson and Coles stood at the crosswalk where ten-year-old Lily Cochrane had lost her life, they gazed at the memorial, a poignant reminder of the tragedy.

Photos of Lily were everywhere, highlighting her bright smile and personality. A large teddy bear, its fur worn and weathered, sat among the flowers, offering comfort amid the grief. Personal items, like her favorite book—a well-loved copy of The Secret Garden—and a handmade bracelet with her name, were among the many cards from well-wishers.

Janelle noticed the fresh flowers at the cross, a touching symbol showing the community hadn't forgotten Lily. She understood the heavy burden of seeking justice and peace for Lily's family. Seeing the memorial strengthened her resolve. Janelle knew it was their team's mission to pursue justice and clear the 8th District's name.

Derrick, his eyes scanning the surrounding area, said quietly, "We'll find who did this, Janelle. We owe it to Lily to find who hit her and left her to die."

Janelle inclined her head, her gaze firm. "Let's advance along those intersections," she proposed, pointing to the converging streets ahead.

Derrick volunteered, "I'll take the right side of the street, and you take the left."

They examined every walkway and curb on the intersecting streets as they continued north on Sheffield Avenue. After covering ten blocks, the detectives found no sign of the car.

Janelle said, "The original investigators stopped here at Frankford Avenue, believing this major artery would be the best escape route. This perpetrator shows more advanced thinking, so let's continue until we reach the T-intersection with Rowland Avenue."

The afternoon sun cast long shadows, adding to the somber atmosphere. With each step, the realization grew they were far from solving the mystery. Janelle and Coles maneuvered along the intersecting streets, their eyes scanning every inch of the pavement and curbs as they searched for overlooked clues from the tragic accident.

After several more blocks, Janelle's keen eyes caught

something, and she signaled to Coles, "Over here, look."

A section of the right curb on the cross street caught her attention. At the bottom were deep, three-inch-long streaks of red paint. "Gotcha".

Janelle walked toward Coles, deep in thought. "The car's speed on the curve most likely affected the evidence," she said. "Even after eighteen months, the high-speed impact and the low traffic would have kept the paint fresh on the curb." This would have preserved the evidence.

The scene unfolded around her, igniting a whirlwind of thoughts about the crucial night of the accident. As she gathered more information, a theory began to take shape, connecting the past to the present in a complex web of events that led to the tragic moment.

Janelle hypothesized, "The perpetrator was speeding away from the scene, having switched off their headlights. They took this right turn too fast." She gestured to the cross street. "The car's lower bumper clipped the curb at high speed, leaving that deep gash and a trace of paint behind." She paused; her gaze fixed on the mark.

Derrick nodded, his eyes widening as the scenario unfolded in his mind. "We can match the paint to the original sample. This could prove that the marks came from the same car. I'll get forensics down here ASAP."

Janelle's sharp eyes scanned the surrounding area, noting the details of the street and nearby buildings. "If it matches, we also know which direction the vehicle took after the accident. We can focus our camera search in that direction."

* * *

Janelle and Coles hurried back to headquarters as they considered the implications of this fresh evidence. While driving to the station, they discussed their next steps, their voices full of excitement and resolve. They understood their investigation was gaining speed and were eager to follow this fresh lead.

Upon their return, Detective Fenn greeted them with enthusiasm. "I've made progress with the vehicle leads," she said. "I called the local Mercedes dealership and updated the paint and tire combinations for various models. We've eliminated 2018 cars, narrowing the list from over 1200 to 800. It's not a big change, but it's a step in the right direction."

Janelle turned to Coles. "If we can verify whether the paint we found matches the evidence from the accident, then we can show its direction afterward. Fenn, compile a list of unchecked camera locations, focusing on major retail spots with long-term footage storage. Prioritize areas off the direct path from Sheffield Avenue, starting with this intersection and heading east or west on Rowland Avenue. The car's lights had to turn back on at some point. Start with a five-mile radius and expand outward from there."

Janelle scanned Fenn's updated list, a sea of names and address details. She knows the answer to the riddle before them was on these pages; she needed to find it.

Twenty-Three

Game 1: Locks

L ed by Judge Haskins' burly associates, Cassie and the other
five players descend the grand staircase, their footsteps
echoing in the vast space. The large oak door swings open,
revealing the Grand Ballroom's grandeur. Soft light filtering
through the dusty windows casts an otherworldly glow on the
group, highlighting the fear and anticipation on their faces.

Cassie steps into the room like a soldier on a death march.
The late sun streams through the arched stained-glass windows,
casting long shadows that dance across the polished hardwood
floor. She observes the detailed paintings of hunts and mythical
creatures, noticing the quiet intensity in their gazes. Although
crystal chandeliers sparkle above, their light isn't enough, leaving
the corners in shadow.

Her eyes shift to the walls draped in dark crimson fabric,
where the stern-faced ancestors of the Eberly family watch her
every move. Cassie shivers under their intense gaze. In the corner,
the steady tick-tock of the clock adds a sense of urgency,
heightening her anticipation. But she remains focused on the dark
wood table at the center of the room. She notices six numbered
open boxes, each holding a ring of keys, arranged neatly, and a
wave of unease washes over her as she steps closer.

Cassie looks at the other players, their faces lined with
apprehension, mirroring her own. The macabre nature of the

room heightens the tension of the upcoming game.

The soft squeak of Judge Haskins' footsteps drifts through the door. His presence commands the room, and the players watch his every move. With purposeful steps, he advances, his eyes scanning the players with an ominous glint.

"Welcome, players," his voice booms, breaking the tense silence. His eyes, sharp and assessing, sweep across the assembled group. "I hope everyone enjoyed their welcome gift as a reminder of why you are here. The gravity of the situation is now, I hope, understood."

"We will play five games this evening. Some will be parlor games you may have played before, while others will require higher-level thinking. All will test your character and your ability to react under pressure. The stakes cannot be higher. Each round's loser will be removed from the competition, and I'm afraid they will face dire consequences."

Cassie's pulse quickens, and she feels a chill as she scans the room, where the shadows seem to stretch and undulate as if alive. A taunting reminder of the choices that led her to this haunting moment.

Judge Haskins continues, his voice taking on a grave tone. "The first contest you are about to play is not only a game of chance, but will separate those with ingenuity to win this game from those who pretend to have it."

As he finishes speaking, the players shift nervously, glancing at each other from the corners of their eyes and sizing up the competition. Cassie clenches her fists until her hands go numb.

"It is now ten minutes to 3:00 pm, and it's about time for the games to begin. This first game is called 'Locks' and is as simple as the name implies."

Judge Haskins flicks his wrist sharply, silently signaling his three associates, unnoticed in the vast room. With precise, quick movements, the men untie the ropes to push aside the curtains, revealing a massive, gleaming steel grid ten feet tall. An array of hundreds of identical locks lines up in rows and columns across three separate vertical panels.

The ballroom air crackles with murmurs of confusion, reflecting a spread of unease. Eyes wide, catching the glint of the revealed challenge. A shiver snakes down Cassie's spine, a cold premonition of Judge Haskins' cruel design. Her senses sharpen, ready for the labyrinthine game that demands laser focus. Scanning the room, she sees disbelief and horror carved on the other competitors' faces. Cassie assesses: three grids of locks, each with ten rows and ten columns—300 locks to attempt. She tries to calculate the best way to approach them.

Cassie watches Thomas, his body rigid and unmoving, fists clenched so tightly that his knuckles have turned white. The tension around him feels tangible, as if the air has thickened with unspoken words, a storm of simmering thoughts ready to burst. He deliberately avoids meeting anyone's gaze, which only heightens the atmosphere, creating an electric charge that crackles between them. It's as if the silence itself is alive, building up and poised to explode at any moment.

Cassie observes Regina. The metallic tang of blood fills the air as a crimson stream trickles from Regina's lip. She can see the frantic glimmer in her wide eyes as they flick anxiously from lock to lock on the towering, impenetrable walls around them. It is like watching a desperate hummingbird flit between blossoms, searching for a way out, a moment of solace in a world that feels more confining with every breath.

Cassie watches Emilio, feeling the intense tension radiating from him like heat off a sunbaked stone. He stands there, firm and unmoving, as if carved from granite—a stark presence in the courtroom's oppressive silence. His intense gaze remains fixed on the judge, a silent challenge etched deep into the lines of his rugged face. Cassie notices a single bead of sweat trickling down his temple, catching the light and shining like a solitary gem amid his hardened exterior. The air is thick with unspoken words, and she can feel the crackling energy between them, heightening the moment's weight.

Judith recoils, her body instinctively tensing as a wave of unease washes over her. A shiver, delicate yet intense, runs along her spine, a physical sign of the turmoil within. The tremor spreads through her entire body, a subtle but persistent reminder of her growing anxiety. Her fingers tighten around the cool, smooth surface of her necklace, clutching it as if it were a protective charm.

As Elizabeth stumbled back into her chair, Cassie saw the discomfort as the hard edge dug into her. A strangled sob catches in Elizabeth's throat, and Cassie sees her shoulders heaving with the effort to hold back emotion. A single tear escapes, carving a glistening path down her cheek. "It … it wasn't … supposed to be like this," Elizabeth says, her voice cracking like brittle ice. Cassie's heart aches at the sight, the weight of Elizabeth's pain palpable in the air between them.

As Cassie watches the other players, she notices the fear etched on their faces, each showing a distinct form of dread. Cassie wonders if anyone has the intelligence and determination to survive this sinister game, or if the darkness will eventually take them. She recognizes the players' apparent weaknesses and knows she can exploit their fears and vulnerabilities to gain an advantage.

Judge Haskins continues with dramatic flair. "Now, each of you will come up and draw a number." He gestures to a drawstring bag lying on the table in front of the players, alongside six numbered boxes containing sets of keys. "The number you choose will be significant, as you will soon discover."

"Cassie," the judge grins, "please step up and select the first number."

Cassie steps forward, her gaze fixed on the judge, calmly confronting him. "What is the meaning of this unlawful detention, Judge Haskins?" Her voice stays steady, even as her hands shake. "What do you hope to accomplish with these games?"

Judge Haskins's smile doesn't reach his eyes, and his expression remains cold and calculating. "Ah, Ms. Thompson, always so quick to question authority. I should have expected no less from a lawyer like you." He deliberately steps closer, narrowing his eyes. "As for the meaning of all this, let's say I have a particular interest in each of you, and these games will reveal a lot about everyone's character. Your reputation in the courtroom precedes you, Ms. Thompson."

"And if I refuse to play?" Cassie presses, her tone defiant. Judge Haskins' eyes flash with a mixture of amusement and something darker.

"Oh, you'll find that refusal is not a choice. If you don't play, you will be eliminated immediately and face your destiny. And I assure you, it will not be pleasant. Besides," he adds, "don't you want to uncover the truth about yourself and the other players? I know how much you enjoy competing when the stakes are high."

Cassie turns with disgust and selects a number from the bag.

Two. She steps forward and takes the keys from box number two.

Glaring at the judge, Thomas selects his number and quickly grabs his keys from his box with a look of disgust. Regina approaches hesitantly, her hand trembling as she reaches into the bag for her number and takes her keys. Emilio follows close behind, his face set in a serious expression. Judith and Elizabeth finish the ritual, their eyes flicking around the room, searching for answers or possible forgiveness.

The judge says, "You will notice ten keys on your rings, which will open only ten locks on the steel frames. Be aware each grid has one ladder to allow players access to the topmost rows of locks if needed. The winner of this game is the person who opens their locks in the shortest time. For anyone who has not opened their locks within one hour, the order of final placement will depend on the number of locks you have opened. Please place the open locks into your slotted box on the table."

The imposing wall of locks and the enigmatic Judge Haskins transfix the players. The tension in the room is substantial, and a heavy silence hangs in the air. With a dramatic flourish, the judge breaks the quiet. "Get ready, players. When the clock strikes three, you will have one hour to open your locks."

* * *

3:00 pm.

An eternity passes, but the clock strikes three times, and the players run to the wall to begin their challenge.

Cassie takes a moment to assess the situation. She realizes

trying the locks at random will be inefficient and time-consuming. Instead, she starts with the locks closest to the floor and works her way up; a methodical approach might save time. She thinks, *This is a game of luck, designed to see you fail. Move with purpose and prove the judge wrong.*

With steady hands, she inserts the first key into the nearest lock and twists it. No click. *Keep moving.*

Judith is next to her, imitating Cassie's strategy. She chooses the row above Cassie and moves in the opposite direction.

"This one's stuck," Judith shouts as she jiggles a key in a stubborn lock. "Come on … there we go." In a stroke of luck, the lock clicks open, and she moves on to the next. Her movements are deliberate and steady.

Cassie watches as Judith approaches, her brow furrowed and a determined frown on her face. The sound of the other players fades away into a distant hum. Cassie's heartbeat matches Judith's rapid breathing as she skillfully manipulates the locks. Each move is precise, yet Cassie senses an underlying tension. When Judith switches to a different lock, Cassie's focus sharpens, and her pulse quickens as she expects what happens next.

"Open, come on, damn," Judith exclaims, more to herself than anyone else, as the lock refuses to budge. She sighs and continues.

Watching Judith try to open her locks, Cassie mutters under her breath, the words sharp and desperate: "*Focus, Cassie. Pay attention to your locks.*" A cacophony of raised and desperate voices fills the room.

"Get the fuck out of my way," Thomas yells at a guard who is momentarily blocking his path as he moves to the center section of locks. *Better Judith than Thomas next to me*, thinks Cassie.

Cassie is starting the fourth row when she hears another *'click'*. "Yes, another one!" Judith exclaims as her lock clicks open. Cassie hears another triumphant voice from the far wall as Thomas rushes over to his box, two locks in hand. She looks up at the clock, which reads 3:15 pm. She considers choosing a different wall to work on, but decides against it.

One minute later, Cassie's decision pays off; her lock yields with a tiny *click*, drowned out in the noisy ballroom. Two locks later, another success. *Quick and steady, eight locks to go*, she implores, her voice a low, urgent mantra, each word spurring her on. *Cassie Thompson, you are better than them. Prove it.*

* * *

3:20 pm.

As the game progresses, the tension in the ballroom intensifies. Cassie shifts her focus to the center section, where Emilio and Regina move through the locks with clockwork precision. She has a nagging sense of being left behind, having opened only two locks. Observing her competitors, she is determined to close the gap. With focused intensity, she tries key after key in the locks, her hands moving with purpose.

Emilio and Regina work efficiently; their eyes scanning the locks with sharp focus. Emilio's tall frame moves quietly as he works along the wall, his face set in a determined expression. Standing on the ladder, Regina reaches up to the higher locks with a steady hand, her arms straining as far as she can. Their progress is steady, and they soon find a rhythm, working in sync as they tackle the intricate challenge before them.

In the left section, Cassie notices Elizabeth struggling. Her hands tremble as she grips the keys, and her breath comes in short, anxious gasps. She moves along the wall; her pace is slower than the others'. Her eyes dart around the room, taking in the imposing surroundings, and her face shows her panic. Cassie feels a surge of confidence. Elizabeth is panicking; a weak player is just what she needs right now to survive.

As the players continue their efforts, the tension in the room intensifies. The soft creak of the old floorboards and the ticking of the clock fill the silence between the players' strained breaths and the occasional click of a successful unlock. The air is heavy with anticipation, and the players are aware of the passing time, each driven to protect their secrets.

A short scream is followed by a "*bang*." The sound of the ladder falling to the ground. Regina sprawls on the floor next to Cassie, pleading, "Please help me," as she struggles to escape the ladder on top of her.

Without a thought, Cassie rushes to her aid, attempting to move the heavy ladder. Her hands move before her brain catches up. Helping a competitor? Maybe not the smartest choice. But her body had made its decision.

She lifts the ladder enough to let Regina wriggle out. "Are you hurt?" Cassie asks, scanning to see where the judges' men are located. "I'm okay. Thank you," Regina sobs, and resumes her focus on the waiting locks.

* * *

3:30 pm.

The sound of scraping metal and the loud celebrations of opening locks continue to fill the ballroom. Cassie's hands are slick, her eyes fixed on the minute hand ... 3:30. Two locks opened; she is behind. Not enough. Time is slipping away. She must stay calm and focused. She takes a steadying breath and presses on.

A minute later, Cassie unlocks her third lock. A small victory is enough to keep her going. She moves to the next, her hands steady as she works with renewed energy. The ballroom fills with the sound of desperate breathing and the soft scrape of keys as the players focus on the task.

Another lock opens for Cassie —two locks in a row, a minor miracle. Four locks in total. A sudden surge of adrenaline rushes through her body.

Next to her, Elizabeth sobs, "I can't do this. I don't understand why we have to do this!" Regina limps by Cassie, moving toward the next wall of locks.

* * *

3:45 pm.

The clock's pendulum swings through the room like a scythe, moving back and forth, closer and faster, ready to provide a lethal blow to any one of them.

The players continue their frantic attempts to master the secrets of the gleaming grid. Cassie maintains a calculated pace, trying each key in a systematic pattern. Thomas and Emilio are now vying with Cassie for the locks in the center panel.

Thomas looks agitated. Profanity follows every lock that won't open. As Cassie moves along the row of locks, he glances at her with a grim expression. He opens the next lock beside Emilio and slams it to the ground in victory, bouncing on the floor and hitting Emilio's leg. Emilio turns angrily to face him, but Thomas rushes to his box to put the lock away.

One minute later, Judith yells, "I'm done!" as she rushes over to deposit her last lock. With this development loud enough for everyone to hear, the group's pace quickens.

The ballroom fills with desperation as the players continue their attempts to open the locks. The tension mounts with each passing minute, the players' gazes flicking between the locks and the relentless clock, their hearts pounding in time with the harsh tick of the second hand.

Cassie runs across the ballroom to the left panel, where Elizabeth is still working. Eager to make up for lost time, Cassie has yet to try her keys on this section of the gleaming steel grid. She works with precise calculation, trying each key in every lock. Within minutes, another lock opens.

As the players work, the ballroom echoes with their efforts. With each minute, the harsh tick of the clock serves as a metronome, reminding her that time is slipping away. Cassie glances at the clock: 3:55 pm. *Five more minutes, damn it, come on.* The second-hand jerks forward, each tick like a hammer blow against Cassie, her anxiety building.

The turn of a key. A metallic *click*; the sound of a padlock yielding. A rush of air, a breathless gasp.

"Yes! Thank God!" Elizabeth's triumphant cry cuts through the air as she runs to the table and hurls the lock into her box, the impact a soft thud against the hammering in Cassie's chest.

Judge Haskins moves to the center of the room. "Players, you have one more minute remaining.

Panic wells up inside Cassie as she glances at the clock, its hands moving ruthlessly forward. Elizabeth's sudden streak of luck feels like a death knell for her; each missed click becomes a countdown to failure. The room spins around her, voices fading into a chaotic blur. Cassie struggles to breathe, but her rising anxiety clings to her, drowning out her focus and urging her to move faster—like quicksand, the more she fights, the harder it gets.

As Cassie tries one final lock, she prays, *Please let this be the one.* She twists the key. *Click.*

* * *

4:00 pm.

The clock chimes four times to signal the end of the first game. The tension in the room is electric as the players stand before their boxes on the table, their gazes fixed on the locks within that hold the key to their fate.

"Congratulations, players, on a game well played," Judge Haskins begins, his voice carrying a hint of approval. "You have all shown successful skill and determination in facing this challenge. This game may be over for one unlucky player, but for everyone else, your journey has only begun."

He pauses, his gaze sweeping across the group, taking in their reactions. "Now, the moment you've all been waiting for:

the results. I will announce the order in which you were able to open your locks." He gestures to the table, where the players' boxes sit, each containing a different number of locks.

"Our winner of this round is ... Judith. She was the only player to open all of her ten locks. Well done. Please stand over next to the boxes."

As Judith walks over, she stifles a sad smile.

Thomas, you also opened ten locks, but after Judith opened her final lock. You finished in second place and will play in the next game.

The judge stands beside Thomas. "However, any further disruptions will result in your next game being your last."

Thomas nods, stone-faced.

"Third place belongs to ... Emilio, with nine locks opened. Well done."

Outwardly composed, Emilio walks over next to Judith, rubbing his leg and keeping his distance from Thomas.

Judge Haskins steps forward, his eyes glinting. The players, their faces filled with emotion—from relief to lingering dread— watch him expectantly.

"In fourth place, we have ... Regina with eight locks open. You will also play in the next game. Please step over next to the others."

Regina's eyes briefly meet Judith's as she stands beside her.

A murmur ripples through the group. The judge will now reveal the name of the player who placed last.

Cassie's thoughts whirl. *If Elizabeth opened seven locks, I'm running for the door. I would rather be shot than face whatever fate the judge has in store for me.*

Judge Haskins turns to face Elizabeth and Cassie. "And now to reveal the loser of the round. Unfortunately, I am afraid to announce ... it is you, Elizabeth, with only five locks opened."

Elizabeth's shoulders slump further, and she closes her eyes, silently accepting her fate. Judge Haskins's associates surround Elizabeth and lead her away. Her muted sobs fill the Grand Ballroom.

Regina, Emilio, and Judith silently accept Elizabeth's departure, tears forming in their eyes. Thomas appears disgusted with the outcome and turns his back on the group.

Cassie surveys the chaotic scene unfolding before her. She thinks *the judge has gone mad. Why would anyone create a game like this?* The pressure and chaos represent a judgment that has gone too far. The sight of a sobbing Elizabeth being led away by the judge's men leaves Cassie wondering what she can do to escape this nightmare.

As Judge Haskins's men take the players back to their rooms, Cassie's mood settles heavily upon her. She sits on the edge of the bed, her mind replaying the game, the riddles, and the now-eliminated Elizabeth. Cassie thinks, *Will Judge Haskins consider taking deadly action against players in this game. He's a respected judge, not a killer.*

Cassie is unaware of any misdeeds the other players might have committed. But this is not the same man she faced in court. He acts as if he has nothing to lose, in sharp contrast to his respected role as the top judge in the Philadelphia courts. She must keep playing his games, but will look for ways to exploit his unpredictable behavior.

Cassie attempts to dampen her mind, preparing for whatever Judge Haskins may have planned for her next.

A sudden, sharp bang reverberates outside her room, breaking the silence. Cassie's heart races. Her eyes widen in recognition, and she sits frozen, the terrifying sound pulsing in her ears.

Twenty-Four

The lamp's gentle glow highlights the judge's satisfied expression as Judge Haskins leans back in his chair, holding a glass of Rémy Martin 1738 Accord Royale brandy. His study is a sanctuary of refined taste and comfort. Expensive vintage furniture decorates the spacious room, shining in the lamplight. A large desk, polished to a mirror-like finish, dominates the space. Leather-bound books with gold-embossed spines line the walls on eight-foot-high solid oak shelves.

A plush leather armchair by the fireplace beckons one to relax with a book. The fireplace, crafted from Italian marble, lends elegance to the room, its mantel adorned with delicate porcelain figurines and family photos.

The space offers glimpses of his passion, scattered throughout the room's decor. A brass telescope stands in one corner, its lens catching the warm light of the setting sun. The desk features a carefully arranged display of antique pens and inkwells. Exquisite art pieces adorn the walls, including genuine works and well-meaning imitations.

As the judge sips his favorite brandy, his eyes drift to the multiple screens mounted on the wall, each showing a live feed from different rooms in his mansion. The players in his game are unaware that every move they make is being watched and analyzed. One screen shows an empty room.

Players are pacing the room, searching for a way out of their predicament. The judge's associates, who roam the halls, serve as a deterrent. Regina sits on her bed, glancing at her gold cross, its surface shining in the afternoon light streaming through her window. She runs her fingers over the delicate chain, lost in silent prayer.

Judith sits at her small desk, gripping her pen. The judge watches her, sensing the mix of excitement and dread surrounding her. She writes with purpose; each stroke of the pen carries the weight of her recent experiences. She pauses and begins to cry.

The judge next observes Thomas, whose unmistakable agitation reveals a mix of desperation and anxiety. As he searches the room for an escape, his quick breaths and tense posture reflect deep turmoil. Recognizing the risk of impulsive actions, the judge remains alert, knowing that any lapse could lead to unintended consequences.

Judge Haskins leans back in his chair, his eyes fixing upon a black-and-white photograph on the mantelpiece. It is a portrait of his grandparents, William and Beatrice Eberly, the proud builders of Eberly Manor.

Judge Haskins's mind wanders back to his childhood, reflecting on the magnificent manor. On the wall is another dusty photo. Along with his grandparents, his father, John Haskins, his mother, Anne Eberly Haskins, and his sister, Constance, pose in front of the estate's entrance, the raven statues ever watchful.

The judge's gaze softens as he remembers his grandfather, a formidable man with a vision.

* * *

In the early 1920s, William Ryan Eberly, an executive at the Pennsylvania Railroad Company—the world's largest transportation firm—built an impressive mansion on a private thirty-acre estate in Chester Springs, Pennsylvania. It showcased his wealth and status, and he spared no expense during its construction. William oversaw every detail, from the Gothic-style architecture to the finest furnishings. The estate reflected his power and prestige.

William's construction of Eberly Manor was a labor of love, using the finest materials and skilled artisans. The result was a breathtaking mansion that embodied his success and legacy for the Eberly family. He and his wife, Beatrice, raised their daughter, Anne, in the upscale Main Line community of Philadelphia, surrounded by privilege and prominent social circles.

Judge Haskins harbors a grim memory of his grandfather's legacy. William Eberly, a well-established figure within Philadelphia's legal elite, shared with his grandson the unethical methods he employed to obtain building permits and other essential documents to expand his holdings.

Judge Haskins recalled how his grandfather had met with town officials at Eberly Manor, where they exchanged favors for money. This discovery permanently tainted Robert's view of his respected ancestor, revealing a hidden desire for power and status. It left him uneasy about the moral compromises behind a facade of public respect.

* * *

The judge's attention now shifts to another family photo. His mother and father, along with himself and his sister Constance, stand at the entrance of Market West Station, a grand railroad terminal designed and built by his grandfather.

His father, John Haskins, was a successful and dedicated businessman who often worked long hours at his Philadelphia CPA firm. John's strong work ethic and ambition left a mark on Robert, who witnessed the power of perseverance at a young age.

He was distant from his son, a reality embodied in one of his favorite songs, "Cat's in the Cradle," by Harry Chapin. It is a sad tale of opportunities wasted, which Robert experienced too often.

Robert's mother, Anne, was the opposite, embodying gentleness and intelligence. She nurtured her son's curiosity by exploring the many sights and sounds of the Philadelphia landscape. Their favorite place to visit was the Franklin Institute, a science museum that Robert and his sister loved. Hours passed as they explored the ten-foot-high Heart, a large interactive exhibit where a rhythmic heartbeat echoed through the hall. They enjoyed running around the open atrium and climbing on the statue of Benjamin Franklin.

As Robert navigated his childhood, his sister, Constance, six years older than him, was his constant companion and partner in crime. Her adventurous spirit and leadership influenced Robert, nurturing his curiosity and courage. Together, they created imaginary games and stories, their youthful energy bringing the mysterious manor to life. The house became a character in their tales, with its grand halls and hidden passages inspiring their young imaginations.

The Philadelphia Library Main Branch was their favorite destination, where they explored the extensive collection, seeking literary treasures to read on a lazy afternoon.

Robert's sister's influence had been a guiding force, keeping him grounded and compassionate. His ambitious, privileged world seemed different from her daily life. Judge Haskins pursued a life of power and prestige, following in his grandfather's footsteps.

* * *

In his teens, Robert grew to dislike playing chess with his father and cards with his grandmother, as he found them dull. Instead, he longed for the complexity of war games, where he could show his sharp observation and strategic thinking. Risk and Stratego were two of his favorites; their conquest-driven gameplay fueled his natural desire to dominate and outwit his opponents.

Clue, the quintessential murder mystery board game, also held a special place in his heart. He and his sister both relished the intellectual duel, the intricate process of piecing together the truth, identifying the culprit, their instrument of death, and the precise scene of the crime.

Each piece of the puzzle, painstakingly gathered, fueled his strategic analysis, pushing him to piece together the mystery from his opponent's actions. The judge recalled the excitement of moving his token across the board, each player a suspect in the mysterious murder. He remembered his sister, always quick to accuse with a theatrical declaration, her eyes sparkling with mischief. Their mother, Anne, played with gentleness and light-hearted fun, her soft-spoken nature contrasting with the rest of the family's intense gameplay.

* * *

As the judge continues to sip his brandy and reminisces about game nights at Eberly Manor, he feels a sense of purpose as he orchestrates his complex set of games. The judge relishes the tension in the air as he watches the players in their quarters. Their anxious faces, filled with fear, give him satisfaction. Every furrowed brow and tentative step proves his power. He can control their fates with just a flick of his wrist.

The judge finds it exhilarating to watch the players' mental and emotional unraveling as they face the fear of elimination. He enjoys the game's complexity, sensing their anxiety with each new riddle and twist. Surrounded by elegant decor in his study, he feels a firm control over the emerging drama, taking pleasure in his roles as both puppeteer and spectator. The thrill of uncertainty sparks his curiosity about how far they will go to escape the inevitable.

But Judge Haskins still harbors doubts, even as he revels in the power of the games he controls. He often recalls his mother's warnings to avoid his grandfather's mistakes and to stay true to his inner voice, ensuring he doesn't go down a dark path from which he can't escape.

He now wonders whether she feels burdened by the family legacy's shadows weighing on him. The sight of five players desperately trying to find a way out of Eberly Manor. To escape his judgment.

Twenty-Five

Game 2: I Spy

C assie returns to the Grand Ballroom, only to find the wall of locks draped in red fabric once more. The other four players remain silent. As the room quieted, Judge Haskins entered.

"Welcome back, players," his voice booms, breaking the tense silence. "I hope you enjoyed your respite in your quarters and are ready for another challenge. I'm sure at one time or another, as a child, you played 'I Spy.' A simple game in reality, the concept of finding an item designated by a list or another player."

Cassie remembers her carefree childhood days playing I Spy, a game she excelled at, where the only challenge was spotting what hid in plain sight, unlike the darker, more dangerous games she faces now.

Judge Haskins states, "In this game, you will find what I seek and present me with information about what you find and where you find it. Each of you will receive a list of ten items to 'spy' on. Players will receive unique lists to prevent direct competition. Only unlocked rooms on this floor will have items you need to find, and each room will contain at least one item."

"However, I decided to make your task more challenging. The items you seek are obscured by riddles, which you must solve. Only then can you begin your search. Be warned, the riddles may not be as straightforward as they appear." He lets his words sink in as the players look around the room. The complexity of the upcoming task is bound to challenge them.

Cassie clears her mind and prepares herself for the challenge. She decides the best way to begin is to solve as many clues as possible before venturing out into the hall to try opening doors. A favorite debate preparation technique —*analyze, then prioritize* —she thinks.

Judge Haskins calls each player forward and gives them a notebook with their unique items to find. The air is thick with anticipation as they gaze at the mysterious riddles, their confused faces illuminated by the soft light filtering through the dusty windows.

As the last player receives their list, the judge's voice booms again, "You may begin your search when the clock strikes five. Remember, only the open rooms will contain the items you seek. Do not leave this floor. My associates will be watching. Return here with your findings by 6:00 pm sharp."

The clock strikes 5:00 pm, signaling the start of the game. The five players disperse, and the floorboards creak as they run in different directions. Cassie stays alone in the ballroom; once filled with nervous energy, it now feels like a tomb—empty, cold, and silent.

The fragile paper of Cassie's notebook cracks beneath her fingertips as she opens it. The first page, yellowed at the edges and resembling an ancient map, contains her quest: a simple, ink-stained list. A tremor passes through her hand as she traces the first item with her fingertip.

Okay, she deliberates, her voice soft, a puff of air against the challenge of the task ahead. *Clear your mind, Cassie. This is a game of skill, not of luck.* Her eyes narrow in concentration. As she scans her list, each item is a challenge etched in sharp black script.

I spy the following objects:

---

1) What begins with an 'e' and only has one letter?
2) I roam at night and sleep during the day; I have yellow eyes, dressed in sable when I play.
3) What has many keys but cannot open a single lock?
4) What has thirteen diamonds but isn't rich?
5) What starts with T, ends with T, and has T in it?
6) I am a book where yesterday follows today, and tomorrow is in the middle.
7) Thirty men and two ladies gathered for festivities, dressed in black and white, yet with movement, turns into a nasty fight.
8) A fragile container without hinges, a lock, or a key, yet a golden treasure lies inside me.
9) Where can you add two to eleven and get one?
10) I have keys but no locks. I have a space, but no room. You can enter, but you cannot leave.

Cassie finishes skimming the list of riddles. Some of these don't sound difficult, but others…

The sound of the other players' movements in adjoining rooms vibrates in Cassie's ears, a companion to the frantic *thump-thump-thump* of her heart. The paper list is brittle beneath her fingertips. *Okay, deep breath. Solve the easy ones first.*

Her unsteady fingertip traces the intricate path of the spiraling script. A ragged breath eludes her lips: *Cassie, you've got this.* These words, etched onto the parchment's delicate surface, serve as an anchor amid the room's oppressive silence. A lifeline if she can grasp it.

Cassie reads the first riddle, this time out loud: "What begins with an 'e' and only contains one letter?" Her first thought was 'eye', with a 'y' between the 'e's. But that wouldn't work since there is more than one letter.

A moment's contemplation yields a sudden epiphany: *an envelope!* Cassie grins and scribbles the answer beside the cryptic verse: *one riddle solved, nine to go!*

She continues to the second riddle: *I roam at night and sleep during the day; I have yellow eyes, dressed in sable when I play.*

Cassie recalls her childhood fear of the dark and the creatures lurking at night. Owls, foxes, and raccoons inhabited the nearby woods, stalking their prey.

Her instincts, honed in the courtroom, lead her to see connections others might miss. I have yellow eyes … sable. Sable, the mammal … or sable, the color black?

Cassie tries to put the clues together. *What has yellow eyes … is nocturnal…and black?* She ponders for a moment. *A cat … a black cat! I'm sure they have yellow eyes!* Jotting down her answer, the pen glides over the page, leaving a confident ink stroke. She wonders which room holds this valuable item.

Negotiating the riddles, Cassie continues her gentle murmur of self-encouragement in the quiet ballroom. For the third riddle, she considers the idea of keys that can't unlock anything. Her eyes narrow as she contemplates the abstract nature of the riddle, and then it clicks. *A piano!* A piano has many keys but can't open any locks. She writes her answer with a flourish.

Cassie successfully solves the following two riddles. A deck of cards has thirteen diamonds; a teapot fits the riddle for number five.

A frown appears on Cassie's face when she reaches the sixth item. *I'm a book where yesterday follows today, and tomorrow is in the middle?* she thinks. *That doesn't make any sense; it could be anything.* She shakes her head, a sense of frustration building within her. *How can I find something when I don't understand the riddle?* She settles herself, lets it go for now, and keeps moving down the list.

As she reads the seventh riddle, Cassie's concentration deepens. *Thirty men and two ladies gathered for festivities, dressed in black and white, but the movement turned into a nasty fight.* Cassie racks her brain for events with thirty men and two women.

She thinks of formal events—such as balls and religious ceremonies—and ... a wedding? Cassie dismisses the idea and starts again. *It can't be an event; it must be something else. Think about objects; we need to find them.* She is ready to move on when she focuses on the last part of the clue.

Black and white objects ... two women...fighting, attacking... objects attacking each other. The answer reveals itself. A chessboard! Thirty-two chess pieces, black and white, with two queens attacking one another. With a sigh of relief, she scribbles her answer.

The eighth riddle also proves challenging. Cassie ponders a fragile container without hinges, a lock, or a key, yet holding a golden treasure. She thinks of delicate glass boxes, ornate jars, and even paper envelopes, but none fit the description.

How can something be fragile and hold something so valuable? she wonders, her eyes scanning the room as if the answer might hide in the shadows. For now, she leaves this riddle unsolved, her instincts telling her to trust her first impulse and move forward.

The ninth riddle is a play on words, and Cassie relaxes as she realizes the answer. *A clock! When it strikes twelve, you add two to eleven to make one*. She notes the clock sitting in the room and writes the object and location in her notebook. *Item #1 found*.

The final item stares at Cassie with unflinching eyes. *I have keys but no locks. I have a space, but no room. You can enter, but you cannot leave*.

As she grapples with the tenth riddle, unease creeps into her voice. *I have keys but no locks. I have a space, but no room. You can enter, but you cannot leave*. She repeats the riddle under her breath, her eyes narrowing in concentration. *It's a riddle within a riddle*, she wonders. *A place with keys and a space, but no room to move?*

She shakes her head; the answer eludes her. Despite her best efforts, the solution stays out of reach, and Cassie notes she should revisit it later, hoping her subconscious might provide insight.

Cassie reviews her updated list of objects.

1) What begins with an 'e' and only has one letter? (envelope)
2) I roam at night and sleep during the day; I have yellow eyes, dressed in sable when I play. (black cat)
3) What has many keys but cannot open a single lock? (piano)
4) What has thirteen diamonds but isn't rich? (deck of cards)
5) What starts with T, ends with T, and has T in it? (teapot)
6) I am a book where yesterday follows today, and tomorrow is in the middle (????)

7) Thirty men and two ladies gathered for festivities, dressed in black and white, yet with movement, it turned into a nasty fight. (chessboard)

8) A fragile container without hinges, a lock, or a key, yet a golden treasure lies inside me. (????)

9) Where can you add two to eleven and get one? (clock) (Hall)

10) I have keys but no locks. I have a space, but no room. You can enter, but you cannot leave (????)

* * *

The Study, 5:10 pm.

Cassie rushes out of the ballroom and into the hallway. She enters the first door and finds herself in a dimly lit study. Her eyes adjust to the light, and she spots one of her opponents, Thomas, standing by a bookshelf, his eyes scanning the titles. His brow furrows, and he taps his fingers on the table, caught up in his own world, unaware of her muted approach. She moves to the other side of the room so he remains out of sight.

Cassie scans her list. *What could be in a study?* She circles 'envelope', but no other item on her list fits. As she steps further in, she notices an ornate desk that dominates the room. It is a grand antique piece; its surface polished to a high sheen. The desk shows a well-organized arrangement, featuring a neatly stacked pile of papers, a vintage inkwell, and a quill placed beside it. A brass lamp with a green glass shade illuminates the space, casting a soft glow on the surrounding objects. In the center of the desk are several envelopes addressed to the judge.

Cassie records this discovery: *Clue 1: an envelope found on the desk in the study.* She continues to examine the items in front of her, searching for another that fits.

As she examines the items, a few catch her eye. A crystal paperweight sparkles in the lamplight, its facets catching the light. Next to a small, leather-bound book with pages filled with intricate calligraphy, a red jester's mask sits below, decorated with lace and shimmering gemstones. It possibly reveals a vestige of a previous masquerade.

But what draws her attention is a silver-framed photograph. It shows a teenage boy and a young woman, their faces lit by the sun as they stand in front of Eberly Manor. They are hugging, and their happiness is clear even in the black-and-white picture. Cassie assumes the teenager is Judge Haskins. She wonders who the woman might be, but soon goes back to work.

She avoids Thomas's presence and gazes at the bookcases, filled with legal manuscripts and writings. Classic titles, including works by Sir Arthur Conan Doyle and Edgar Allan Poe, fill one section. The books appear to be early editions, with brittle and discolored spines. Cassie notices a book is missing from the middle of the collection.

As Cassie continues her search, her mind returns to the tenth riddle that has eluded her thus far. *I have keys but no locks. I have a space, but no room. You can enter, but you cannot leave.* She repeats the words under her breath, eyes scanning the study for clues. She spots a typewriter on a small table in the corner. It is an old-fashioned model, its keys glinting in the lamplight. *A typewriter. It has keys but no locks. It has a space bar and a carriage return, like a laptop's 'Enter' key.*

A wave of contentment washes over her upon discovering the third item. Cassie sees Thomas's menacing gaze as he approaches to examine the objects on the desk, and she retreats from the study and down the corridor.

* * *

The Games Room, 5:20 pm.

Cassie ventures down the hall, her fingers brushing the doorknobs, considering the thrill of possibility—but frustration mounts as several doors remain locked. One opens, revealing a spacious chamber adorned with intricate wood paneling and a soaring vaulted ceiling.

Soft light filters through leaded glass windows, warming the games and collectibles scattered about. Cassie steps inside, her excitement growing as she spots a billiard table with inviting green felt. She scans the unique items on the shelves, each promising adventure. One stands out: a well-worn board game, "Stratego," with general and faded red and blue pieces.

Walls of cabinets may also hold potential answers. "A room dedicated to board games", she says, shaking her head. "Only in a mansion."

She spots Judith in the left corner, checking out the game tables, list in hand. Cassie checks her list; two items are immediate possibilities, but she needs to be thorough.

Her attention shifts to the right corner, where a chessboard sits on a small table. The black-and-white pieces are carefully arranged, awaiting the players' return. *Thirty men and two ladies*, she thinks, recalling the riddle's description. *A nasty fight ensues. Yes, this is it.*

Cassie makes her way over, her footsteps soft on the plush carpet. She runs her fingers over the smooth, carved pieces, their intricate details a sign of an expensive, handmade set. *Four down, six to go;* a sense of satisfaction washing over her.

As Cassie continues her exploration, Judith leaves the room, excitedly writing in her notebook as she moves toward the study.

She examines the shelves for other items to solve the remaining riddles. Her eyes narrow as she sees various games and curiosities, each offering a potential clue or red herring, leading her astray.

Amid the room's clutter, an eclectic mix of items draws Cassie's gaze. A vintage Ouija board sits invitingly, its planchette poised at the center, as if eager to summon the spirits that linger in the manor's shadows. Beside it, a stack of battered puzzle boxes leans precariously, the top one yawning open to reveal a dusty, neglected interior.

Cassie shifts her focus, scanning the vast shelves that stretch out before her, her heart racing with anticipation. Her eyes land on a poker table, where a deck of cards lies scattered, their backs facing up like a discreet invitation. A familiar riddle echoes in her mind: *What has thirteen diamonds but isn't rich?* A smile creeps across her lips as she connects the dots, her pulse quickening with each realization. She checks clue four off her list, satisfaction warming her. Five items found, five to go—the thrill of the hunt surges within her.

As Cassie continues her survey of the game room, her eyes narrow when she spots Emilio and Regina entering. Their hushed voices carry a sense of conspiracy as they glance around the room.

Her curiosity is piqued, and she adjusts her position, trying to get a glimpse of what they're doing. Their muted exchanges suggest a shared strategy, with their heads tilted together as Regina studies Emilio's notebook. Cassie remembers that any collaboration is forbidden and considers the potential consequences. Maybe something to use as leverage?

Cassie moves through the rest of the game room, giving Emilio and Regina a wide berth as they continue marking their lists. She sees Regina stop to examine a weathered 'Go' box, rattling its contents while glancing back at her list.

Cassie checks her list for other possible items to discover: a black cat, a piano, a teapot, books ... *No, nothing like that here.*

The eighth riddle still puzzles her: *a fragile container without hinges, a lock, or a key, yet holding a golden treasure*. While walking, she reviews the description, her mind quickly exploring different options. A container without hinges ... that could be a bag or a pouch. But how can it be fragile and hold something so valuable? Cassie bites her lip, unsure. She will have to wait to see if other rooms could contain an item that fits the description.

Cassie leaves the game room and makes her way along the hall, her hands trying doors to find her next destination.

* * *

The Kitchen, 5:30 pm.

Cassie pushes the ancient door open, its creak echoing in the quiet hallway. Inside the kitchen, sunlight spills through the window above the deep porcelain sink, illuminating the spacious room. A large central island gleams, surrounded by copper pots and pans that dangle overhead, their surfaces catching the light.

The air is rich with the lingering scent of spices, hinting at the life once lived here. In one corner, an antique refrigerator stands, its metal reflecting the sun's warmth. Cassie glances at the brass faucet, and a whisper of laughter, along with the sound of water splashing, resonates in her mind.

Cassie's footsteps pad on the tiled floor as she moves further into the room. Her eyes scan for any items that might match those on her list. She eyes the teapot, its silver surface gleaming on the stove. *What starts with T, ends with T, and has T in it?* She scrawls *'Teapot', 'kitchen',* next to clue number five. *Six items found.*

As Cassie moves further inside, her eyes settle on the antique refrigerator in the corner. Its off-white metal surface, reflecting the warm light, creates a distorted image of the room. She approaches it, her curiosity piqued. The refrigerator stands tall, with a brass handle on the front door.

Cassie reaches out for the handle and pulls it, sensing the cool metal under her fingertips. The door opens with a soft creak, revealing the interior shelves, stocked with a variety of perishables. Her eyes scan the assortment of jars, bottles, and containers.

As Cassie is ready to close the refrigerator, her eyes land on a carton of eggs, and the eighth riddle comes to mind once more. *A fragile container without hinges, a lock, or a key, yet a golden treasure lies inside me,* she recites. She considers the eggs, their delicate shells containing golden yolks. "It has to be an egg," she yells out loud, a sense of satisfaction washing over her. She writes the answer and the location in her notebook.

As she leaves the kitchen, she is relieved that she has solved another riddle. She continues through the hallway, her footsteps reflecting on the polished floorboards.

* * *

The Conservatory, 5:40 pm.

Cassie steps into the vibrant sanctuary, her eyes adjusting to the dappled light from the glass ceiling. The warm, moist air wraps around her, carrying the sweet scent of jasmine and rich soil.

She takes in the bright greens and vivid tropical flowers as she follows the winding gravel path lined with towering palm trees. To her right, lush ferns and delicate mosses thrive beneath a miniature willow tree, accompanied by the soothing sound of trickling water and chirping birds.

For a moment, she savors the conservatory's beauty before focusing on her task, scanning the room for the items on her list.

At that moment, Judith steps into the conservatory, her breath coming out in a quick, shallow gasp. She looks at Cassie and wanders around the room.

Cassie's eyes return to her immediate task, and the grand piano in the corner of the conservatory draws her attention. It is a magnificent, polished Steinway piano; its white wooden frame stands proudly in the soft light.

She approaches it with reverence, her eyes tracing the smooth lines of its instrument. The keys are yellowing with age, but they still shine with a gentle luster. Running her fingers over them, Cassie feels connected to the music that once occupied this space.

She remembers the third riddle: *What has many keys but cannot open a single lock?* The answer had come to her in a flash, and now, seeing the piano, she knew she was right. *Piano ... keys! So obvious.*

As Cassie stands there, she finds a moment of calm in the peaceful retreat, surrounded by lush greenery and quiet. Her mind shifts to the challenges ahead. One more room to explore, two more items to find: a black cat and a book. *I am a book where yesterday follows today, and tomorrow is in the middle.*

As she leaves the conservatory, Cassie sees Judith wandering among the blooming flowers. She has sympathy for Judith, who often appears lost and in need of guidance. But in this deadly game, there is no time for that now.

* * *

The Library, 5:45 pm.

Cassie races toward the last door, her heart pounding as she spots Regina and Emilio close behind her. She pushes open the last door and bursts into the library, breathless with anticipation.

The grandeur of the space surrounds her, with towering shelves filled with books reaching up to the high ceiling. Each title seems to whisper her name, urging her to come closer. Thomas stands nearby, his eyes scanning the spines of the volumes, lost in a world of words. Sunlight streams through the tall windows, casting a golden light that dances across the polished wooden surfaces, illuminating the spines of the books and creating playful shadows.

In the center of the room, a large oak table stretches out beneath the warm glow of the lamps, its surface bearing the marks of countless hours spent studying. Sturdy chairs, cushioned in soft green fabric, invite her to sit and stay. The flickering light from the lamp casts a gentle glow, silently encouraging her to dive into the ancient books and discover the treasures hidden within their pages.

Cassie's eyes scan the knick-knacks on the library wall. Her gaze falls upon a small black cat figurine. Its eyes glint in the lamplight, as if they glow. She recalls the second riddle: *I roam at night and sleep during the day; I have yellow eyes, dressed in sable when I play.* The figurine fits the description. With a sense of satisfaction, she adds it to her list. Cassie addressed the room. "Just one more to go, Cassie … Find the fucking book!"

The diverse tomes draw Cassie's attention. The library holds many books, which could be sources of knowledge and secrets. She runs her fingers along the spines, her eyes scanning the titles. *A book where yesterday follows today*, she thinks, recalling the sixth riddle. Could it be related to a particular book? She considers the concept of time and its relationship to the arrangement of the library's collection.

As she nears the reference section, her eyes fall on a pristine dictionary resting on one of the shelves. The words of the final riddle echo in her mind: A book where yesterday follows today and tomorrow is in the middle? A rush of clarity washes over her as realization hits. *It must be a dictionary!* Cassie's heart swells as she completes her list. The answer is a beacon of light piercing the fog. She closes her eyes for a moment, savoring the clarity. The unassuming book cradled in her hands is filled with knowledge, waiting for her to uncover its insights. In this stillness, the noise of the manor fades, and she relishes the sense of relief in finishing the task.

Cassie takes a moment to notice Emilio exchanging heated words with Thomas as she moves toward the exit. *Stay focused and pay close attention to Thomas.*

With only two minutes left, Cassie rushes out of the library, her heart pounding with pride. She returns to the Grand Hall with Thomas close behind her.

Cassie's mind races with thoughts of what will happen next in this devious funhouse. The large, imposing doors stand before her, and with a deep breath, she pushes them open and steps inside as the clock chimes the hour six times.

* * *

The Grand Ballroom, 6:00 pm.

Reverberating footsteps announce the judge's return to the Grand Ballroom. An obvious tension hangs in the air as the competitors surrender their notebooks. The subsequent wait is stifling, a heavy blanket woven with anticipation.

A rasping cough, contrasting with the heavy silence, precedes the judge's pronouncement. "The dedication you are showing to this competition has been nothing short of extraordinary," he says, his voice resonating with authority. "I am now prepared to announce the results."

"Congratulations, Cassandra," he proclaims. "You have found all ten items and solved the riddles with skill and precision. You are the winner of 'I Spy'."

As the judge announces her as the winner, a wave of emotions washes over her. Her game strategy has proven fruitful, bringing her relief and confidence. That, and her attention to detail, have proven to be her greatest assets in this game of riddles.

"Thomas, you have found eight items, an impressive feat, and you are our runner-up for this round." Thomas stands tall, but a hint of frustration is clear on his face. His jaw tightens, and the setting sun casts long shadows that mirror the growing unease within him.

The judge's voice resonates through the ballroom, announcing the next results. "Judith and Regina, you found seven items, a commendable effort."

Cassandra's eyes flicker to the pair, and their faces tell of relief. They have allied, and now they stand together, their gazes shifting to the one remaining player.

The room goes still. "And that means, Emilio, you are last this round with only six items found."

Emilio stands alone, his face shrouded in silence. The judge's decision echoes in the still air, an unsettling tension settling over the players, hinting at the dark storm of consequences that awaits them if they fail.

Judge Haskins steps toward the players. "Emilio, your time with us is over ... unfortunate. However, for the remaining four combatants, the next game will rely solely on intellect to help navigate a challenging course and secure a win. Consider the possibilities as you rest up."

Maintaining his stoic demeanor, Judge Haskins gestures for the other players to leave the Grand Ballroom. As they ascend the stairs to their rooms, they hear loud voices and a deafening bang.

Twenty-Six

Janelle: Friday, October 4th, 2024

Detective Janelle Robinson leaned forward, her dark eyes fixed on Chief Gregory Vanover as he entered the room. Excitement coursed through her; she was eager to update him on the Lily Cochrane case. For five weeks, her team had poured their efforts into this investigation, and it was now yielding results.

As the lead detective, Janelle felt a personal connection to the case. The weight of responsibility drove her, fueling her determination to scrutinize every detail. Her open notebook, filled with notes and theories, showed her relentless drive to solve the case.

Detectives Derrick Coles and Carolyn Fenn, key members of the team, sat next to Detective Robinson, eager to share their findings. Their strong rapport and collaboration had been crucial to the investigation's progress. Fenn adjusted her blouse as Coles rotated his neck to relieve tension from hours spent reviewing evidence photos.

Chief Vanover commanded respect with his tall, broad frame and precise military haircut. His salt-and-pepper hair, coupled with the wrinkles around his eyes from years of service, added gravity to his formidable presence. With a blend of expectation and authority, Janelle felt the weight of the chief's unwavering gaze upon her.

"Detective Robinson, could you please give us your latest

update on the Cochrane case?"

Janelle sat up straight in her seat, her dark eyes gleaming with excitement. She held Chief Vanover in high regard and was eager to share the results of her team's hard work.

"Yes, sir," she began, her voice confident. "We've made significant progress in the five weeks since we reopened the case. Detectives Coles and Fenn have helped analyze key evidence and follow new leads."

She gestured to her colleagues, acknowledging their vital contributions.

"Through our collaboration, we've developed a clearer timeline of the perp's movements after the accident and analyzed fresh evidence we found near the scene."

Detective Derrick Coles stood. "The paint transfer we found on the curb during our re-canvassing provided crucial information. Earlier investigations revealed fragments of the urethane bumper and headlight glass, as well as tire marks, which helped identify potential makes and models of the car."

"The new paint transfer confirmed the initial findings and revealed a unique layering with a specific primer, base coat, color, and clear coat. We traced this rare combination back to a local auto body shop."

Janelle stepped up. "With this information, we can narrow the search to a few vehicles, like a car's fingerprint. We're collaborating with the shop to identify those painted from that batch."

Chief Vanover was stoic. He asked, "How does that help us, Detective Robinson? We would need a warrant to get paint samples from a particular car for the match."

Janelle replied, "We understand that, sir, which is why we are searching for video footage that can identify cars that match the profile. Detective Fenn, can you elaborate?"

Detective Carolyn Fenn stepped forward, nervous as she glanced at Janelle. Janelle winked at her and mouthed, *You got this.*

Fenn took a deep breath. "Over the past few weeks, I've reviewed security footage from over two hundred businesses in the vicinity of the paint transfer."

She showed a street map of the neighborhood where the accident took place. "My search focused on businesses within a two-mile radius of the intersection where the paint transfer was found. Businesses typically have off-site, long-term video storage, unlike residential cameras. This helped me narrow down the potential areas in the footage."

"Initially, we couldn't find any video of a late-model red Mercedes with noticeable front-end damage in the footage we reviewed. We suspected the perpetrator turned off their car lights shortly after the accident. This was based on a doorbell video on Sheffield Avenue showing a car without lights rushing down the street. With that in mind, Detective Robinson suggested we focus our search on businesses north and east of the accident."

Chief Vanover asked, "Why focus on that specific area, Detective Fenn?"

"The initial investigation spent two months scrubbing through PennDOT camera footage that evening with no leads."

Detective Fenn brought up a graphic showing PennDOT's active cameras within a five-mile radius of the scene.

"Notice the lack of cameras on secondary streets in this

area," Detective Fenn pointed to the streets. "If the perp had prior knowledge of that information, that is where they would head to avoid detection."

"Northeast of the accident's location," the chief nodded in agreement.

"Yes, sir. With that in mind, we focused on contacting businesses in that direction, and yesterday we found the video we've been looking for. Let me bring up the footage from that evening from the Keystone National Bank on State Street, north of Pennypack Avenue."

She scrolled to a video on the desktop and clicked play. The grainy video showed the bank's exterior at night. Then, at 10:37 pm, a red Mercedes sedan was observed, matching the same make and model as described in the evidence. Although the video was grainy due to lighting conditions, the car appeared to have front-end damage.

Chief Vanover asked, "Can we enhance the image and get a better look at the license plate? Is there anything that might ID the driver?"

Fenn shook her head. "It's grainy, sir. I've tried enhancing the image, but the resolution is too low; all we can see is front-end damage that matches the evidence, and a partial view of the first character of the license plate. Even with video enhancement software, this was all we could see from the footage. But with this location as our starting point, we can better identify other cameras that offer a clearer view."

Chief Vanover nodded. "Nice work, Fenn. Detective Robinson, I want you to prioritize this lead. Use every resource at your disposal. We need to find where the car went and who was driving it. This could be our breakthrough."

Janelle's response was just a brief nod. Yet, many thoughts raced through her mind. This was not only another case but a potential turning point in her career—one that could shape her future as a detective. The image of the car, fleeting in the darkness, burned into her memory. Their team was close. It was time to finish what they had begun.

* * *

The sun was setting as Janelle studied the case files, her eyes narrowed and focused. The intricate web of evidence and theories surrounding the Lily Cochrane case had consumed her for several weeks.

Detective Fenn ran into Janelle's office, her eyes sparkling. "Detective Robinson, I've got a lead on the video footage."

Janelle looked up, her curiosity piqued.

"I've accessed security footage from a Dunkin' north of the Keystone National Bank. It's a bit distant, but the camera angle and lighting might help us. And the footage is high definition."

Janelle smiled as she rose from her seat. "Nice work, Fenn. Let's take a look."

Fenn pulled up the footage on her computer, and a gas station came into view. The timestamp showed it was from the night of the accident. They watched as a steady flow of vehicles came and went.

Then, at 10:39 pm, a late-model red Mercedes sedan approached a red light next to the store. The car hesitated before running through the red light and down the street.

"There," Fenn said, pointing at the screen. "See the front? It matches the damage from the accident scene." Janelle leaned forward, her eyes fixed on the car. "Can we enhance the footage to get a clearer view of the license plate?" she asked.

"Let me try the brightness and contrast controls," Fenn replied. As she adjusted the settings back and forth, Janelle shouted, "Stop there. Now increase the sharpness."

As Detective Fenn adjusted the settings, the plate came into focus.

"There you are..." Janelle announced. "Check that plate number against the VLN."

Fenn searched the plate against the Vehicle License Number database, and registration details came into view.

As Detective Janelle Robinson examined the recently revealed license information, her eyes widened in shock. She noticed a name in the registration details—one she recognized, someone unexpected, someone owed a well-deserved debt. An unethical and venomous lawyer who had humiliated her in court eighteen months ago and allowed a killer to go free.

Janelle's stunned expression spoke volumes, and a hush fell over the room.

Fenn spoke up. "What's the matter? Do you know her?"

"Know her?" Janelle echoed, her words tinged with a dangerous calm. She pushed away from the computer, and the chair scraped against the cold tiles. "Let's just say we have met in court once or twice." Her gaze hardened, fixating on a point beyond the walls of the precinct. A slow smile spread across her face, a promise of retribution hanging in the air.

Robinson's team entered Chief Vanover's office with excitement in their eyes.

"Detective Robinson, what have you found?" Chief Vanover asked, his voice steady but laced with curiosity. "Have you identified the vehicle?" Janelle nodded.

"Yes, Chief," she replied, her voice solemn. "The vehicle is registered to someone I know. Someone who would know how to keep us from tracking her car and try to destroy any evidence of the accident."

Chief Vanover looked at the registration information. He tried to stifle his excitement. He recognized the name.

Prepare the paperwork to obtain a warrant for the GPS and cellphone tracking data of this vehicle from the night of the accident. This will provide the information needed to verify the suspect's movements that evening. Also, get a search warrant for the suspect.

As Coles and Fenn left the office, Chief Vanover picked up the phone to make a call, a smile crossing his face. Janelle was unsure who he was talking to, but as she listened, she realized it was a call to someone providing essential updates for the case. After making the call, he placed the registration information on his desk.

> Cassandra Thompson
> 127 South Front Street
> Condo 1505
> Philadelphia, PA 19154

Twenty-Seven

J Judge Haskins observes the remaining game participants from his secluded command center, isolating them in their private rooms. He recognizes their emotions, desperate attempts to grasp why they are here, and their impending fates. Each handpicked contestant is essential to their sinister design. His motivations are shrouded in darkness, as is his execution in bringing them here, and the damning evidence is far removed from the courtroom's purview.

Haskins accessed ex parte materials and ongoing case information through back channels, a practice usually reserved for extreme situations. This access depended on a network of colluding Philadelphia law enforcement officers and was a web woven throughout his extended time on the bench.

His focus returns to the contestants on the screens before him, each one a caged specimen waiting for his next instruction.

For his game's subjects today, absolute precision is essential. Proof beyond a reasonable doubt is required to deliver long-overdue justice to those who have evaded it.

* * *

Two months ago, Judge Haskins received a tip about a cold case involving a hit-and-run that killed a ten-year-old girl from a source within the Philadelphia Police 8th District. Last Friday, video surveillance confirmed his suspicions about Cassandra Thompson, a rival lawyer known for her sharp mind and questionable ethics. The police have now proven her involvement in the accident that killed Lily Cochrane beyond a doubt. He confirmed her involuntary participation in his masterpiece.

Haskins sent a brief email with a simple question about a high-profile case to lure Thompson. He had previously gained insider knowledge from Mark Weller, another attorney at Thompson's firm, by pretending to discuss a partnership. The information he collected was crucial leverage in his plan against Thompson. He sent the email from an anonymous account, attaching a redacted document to draw her into his trap.

He needed to be precise with his timing to ensure each player was available for an invitation to his manor, perfect specimens to play his games.

A smile creeps across Judge Haskins's face as he reviews the last game's results. The competition's intricacies have unfolded exactly as he had expected, revealing the strengths and weaknesses of the remaining players. Judge Haskins observes Cassie, Thomas, Judith, and Regina, noting their every move and decision to gain valuable insight into their psyches.

Cassie has proven to be a formidable player, as expected. As a lawyer experienced in courtroom battles, she has a natural advantage over the other players. It will be interesting to see how she handles the upcoming challenge.

His mind shifts to Regina and Judith, two quiet yet steady players in their approach. Regina is a skilled game player. Her calm demeanor hides a sharp, strategic mind. She excels at reading clues and identifying the most effective approach to tackling each task. This was clear in 'I Spy'; the next game he has planned could benefit from the same strategy to allow her to advance. Regina's alliance with the now eliminated Emilio from the previous game will need to be addressed in the future.

Judith embraces her age as an advantage, navigating the game with a careful strategy. Her calm demeanor enables her to observe group dynamics quietly. She gathers important information by listening more than speaking, all while staying under the radar. In this high-stakes game, her composure sets her apart amid the growing tension.

Judge Haskins leans back, watching Thomas and his growing aggressiveness. While Thomas's intensity had its benefits, it was raising concerns. Haskins understood that letting emotions take control could cause unforeseen issues for the group and his goals.

With each tick of the clock, Judge Haskins enjoys the intricate web he's created. This is more than a game; it's a psychological battle where each decision impacts their fates.

He smiles to himself, anticipation running through him. The upcoming games will display his desire to deliver a twisted form of final justice while keeping the players unaware of the bigger implications of their involvement in his sinister plan.

Twenty-Eight

Game 3: Jeopardy

T he familiar Grand Ballroom looms large, its tall windows now showing a darkening sky that mimics the players' faces as they step inside. Judge Haskins stands at the front, wearing a smug expression on his face as always.

Before them, a Jeopardy-style game board flickers to life, each square illuminated with a glowing menace. The categories vary, hinting at possible questions: Periodic Table, Books, State Capitals, American Presidents, and Words. The players take their positions, glancing at one another with weariness and dread.

"Players," Judge Haskins begins, his voice smooth yet laced with an undercurrent of authority. "Welcome to the next stage of our game. Tonight, we will decide your fates, and your choices on this board will decide whether you will emerge unscathed or succumb to the darkness that binds us all."

Cassie exchanges wary glances with the other players, each aware that the game is not only a test of knowledge but also a battle of wills. As the judge gestures toward the board, the lights dim further, amplifying the sense of foreboding.

Judge Haskins states, "This is the game board you will play. While it resembles a popular game show, there are key differences. Each player will take turns answering clues; there's no buzzing in to answer a question. The order of play is Judith, then Cassie, Thomas, and Regina. You can select clues worth ten to fifty points. Correct answers add points to your total, while incorrect ones deduct points."

The game comprises three rounds. The first two are similar, differing only in categories and having equal values. In the final round, everyone answers a single question of their choice and can bid only what they've earned.

The judge walks next to Regina, wearing a serious expression. "Regina," he scolds, "I made it clear at the start of our games that you may not collaborate with any other player. You violated that rule in the last game by getting help from Emilio with a clue. So, your point total starts at minus 100 as a penalty."

Regina avoids the judge's gaze and wears a look of resignation as her hands tremble.

With the other players seated, Cassie wanders the Grand Ballroom, lost in thought about how to approach the game. The flickering lights of the game board cast a pattern on her face as she assesses the competition.

The categories on the board resonate with Cassie. Her knowledge should be an advantage, but she knows she needs to play smart, not aggressively. Each clue is a double-edged sword; a correct answer can push her forward, while a mistake could cost her valuable points. She must choose her moments carefully, selecting categories that suit her strengths.

You don't have to win this round, Cassie. Pick the categories you know and the higher point values. Words and books should be targets. Stay near the top and wait for mistakes.

With a determined glint in her eye, Cassie waits for the first round to begin.

* * *

7:00 pm.

"Judith, please begin," the judge announces.

Judith selects State Capitals for ten. 'Colorado?'—' Denver,' she answers.

"Correct," says the judge. "Cassandra, your choice, please."

Cassie takes a deep breath. "Books for fifty points." Who wrote *The Picture of Dorian Gray*? Cassie panics. She read the book but can't remember the author. She thinks. *Five seconds, Cassandra* ... She has no answer.

"Time's up. The correct answer is Oscar Wilde." The judge mocks, "Minus fifty points."

Cassie reminds herself that one missed question doesn't define the game. She focuses on the board, determined to regain her composure and strategize her next move.

"Thomas, please select."

"U.S. Presidents for thirty points." The question reveals, "Who was the youngest elected president?" Thomas answers, "J.F.K." The judge nods. "Correct, Thomas. Regina, please select."

Regina looks bewildered, as if she has never seen a 'Jeopardy' board. She pauses, studying the board as if it were a final exam paper.

The judge says curtly, "Please select a question now, or we will move on."

She blurts out, "Words for ten points." A letter added to a kidnap victim's salvation produces this small window found above a door. Regina stares at the board…

Judge Haskins has a bemused look on his face. "Time's up, Regina. The correct answer is transom."

Judith selects State Capitals for forty. 'Illinois?'—' Springfield,' she again answers.

"Correct again," says the judge. "Cassandra, your choice, please."

Cassie thinks *Regina is out of her league here. Relax, be positive, and stay calm.* "Books for forty points." Cassie smiles as the question reveals: Who wrote *Charlie and the Chocolate Factory?* "Roald Dahl," she answers with a sigh of relief. "Correct for forty points," the judge says.

He takes glee in his role, embracing it with enthusiasm and charisma akin to that of a game show host. His demeanor is lively and engaging as he navigates the proceedings with theatrical flair.

The first round continues, and Cassie correctly identifies *Henry David Thoreau* as the author of 'Walden', *Glinda* as the Good Witch of the East, and *Winston Smith* as the main character in '*1984*'. She also correctly identifies *Na* as sodium and answers questions about *Abraham Lincoln* and *John Adams*. She misses only one question.

* * *

7:20 pm.

After round one, Cassie is in third place, 150 points ahead of Regina. Judith and Thomas are each over fifty pts ahead of her.

The Round 2 categories are revealed: 1960s Events,

Astronomy, Automobiles, Cooking, Movies, and Before and After.

Cassie ponders the categories. *Astronomy and Movies look solid; stay away from Automobiles and Cooking.* Focus on your breathing, Cassie.

The second round begins.

Judith selects Cooking for fifty points. Pancetta is derived from the meat of which animal? Judith correctly answers, "A pig."

Cassie is up next. "*Movies* for fifty points." Which movie is the quote 'What's in the box?' from? Cassie smiles. 'Seven.' "Correct," Judge Haskins pronounces.

Thomas selects Automobiles next for forty points. In what year did the Ford Mustang go into production? His answer is swift: "1964." Judge Haskins announces, "Correct."

Regina's turn is next, and she selects *Astronomy* for fifty points. "Named for a professor of mathematics and astronomy at Ohio Wesleyan University, what structure in Delaware, Ohio, was completed in 1931 and included the third-largest mirror in the world?" Regina announces, "The Perkins Observatory."

"Well done, Regina," Judge Haskins says. "Judith, please select next."

Judith picks Cooking for forty points. Which spice is derived from the crocus flower and is one of the most expensive spices in the world? Judith looks puzzled as she searches for the answer.

The judge interjects, "I need your answer now, Judith." She guesses "paprika." "I'm sorry, Judith, the answer is saffron."

The second round continues. Cassie, Thomas, and surprisingly, Regina sweep their initial categories. Judith misses one more Cooking question. Each player readies for their last turn of the round. *Before and After* is untouched.

"Before and After for ten points," Judith selects. The players' expressions are puzzled about what this category could mean. The first astronaut in space, followed by the person who plays live-action Cruella De Vil. Judith does not know what the answer could be. The judge smiles, "Who is John Glenn Close?"

Cassie manages a grin. The two clues share a common word, and the answer is a new phrase. She is ready for the next question. "Before and After for thirty points." The seventh president was followed by a painter who splashed paint around and created high art. Cassie works through the answer. *Seventh President is … Andrew… Jackson… a painter named Jackson…* "I need your answer, Cassie," says the judge. "Andrew Jackson … Pollock, Judge."

"Correct."

Cassie breathes a sigh of relief. She has one more round left. Cassie estimates she's near the top of the scores.

The round ends with Thomas and Judith guessing correctly, and Regina missing Bill Nye the Science Guy Fieri.

* * *

7:50 pm.

The atmosphere in the Grand Ballroom shifts as Judge Haskins prepares to announce the scores. A heavy silence blankets the room, filled only with the rhythmic tick of the clock.

"Contestants, listen closely," Judge Haskins begins, his voice low and measured, sending a chill through Cassie and the others.

"I have calculated the totals up to this point in the game." Here are the results. He pauses dramatically, the silence becoming thick, like a chilling gray fog that envelops the room.

"In first place ... Thomas, with 520 points. Well done, you have a significant advantage going into the final round."

"In second place, we have Judith with 480 points. Cassie, you have secured third place with 470 points. Both of you still have a chance to place first or drop to last, depending on your performance in the final round."

The totals do not surprise Cassie; the results are crucial to her strategy.

"And finally..." He lets the silence stretch before delivering the final blow. "Regina, at a mere 390 points."

His words hang in the air, a specter of doom. Eyes dart around the room, calculating who is the biggest threat. With that, the contestants shift in their seats, aware that the next round will decide their fate in this deadly contest.

Judge Haskins walks over to the board, showing three different categories. "Players, in our final round, you must answer one question in your chosen category. You may wager as many points as you wish or choose to wager nothing. Based on the current point totals, any player has the potential to finish in any position, depending on the results. So, choose wisely!"

Cassie studies the categories: U.S. History, Shakespeare, and Mammals. She wants to wager cautiously; she is neutral on the three categories. Regina is right behind her, but Thomas and Judith could drop below her with aggressive wagers. But with aggressive bids and successful answers by any player, nothing is certain. There is only one goal —stay out of last place.

"Players, please write your wager and chosen category now."

Cassie chooses Shakespeare, believing her teacher, Mrs. Adams, is guiding her.

"Alright, players, here are the questions you must answer."

The questions are revealed.

What was the name of the British passenger ship that sank after being torpedoed by a German U-boat, which killed 128 Americans and became one of the reasons the U.S. entered World War I?

What is William Shakespeare's longest play, with over 4,000 lines?

Which cat has tufts on its ears and has the widest territorial range of any feline?

Cassie considers her decision. The first question about the British passenger ship instantly clicks, as does the third question about the tufted feline.

Cassie reasons, *Okay, Cassie, the longest play is Hamlet or Othello. Which one...*

She considers two possible plays. Neither choice is certain. She struggles to recall the precise information she needs. *I can't afford to get this wrong;* the stakes weigh on her consciousness.

She has fifteen seconds left to make a choice. She writes her answer and closes her eyes.

Judge Haskins steps forward. "Players, time to reveal your answers. First, U.S. History."

Thomas turns his card over with a smug look on his face. *Lusitania,* 300 points.

"The correct answer is the RMS Lusitania. Thomas now has 820 points. Well done. Next is Mammals."

Judith turns over her answer, Bobcat, 360 points. Judge Haskins claps, "Correct, Judith, you have passed Thomas with 850 points. An aggressive wager may prove to be your salvation."

"Now it's time for Shakespeare. Cassandra, please reveal your answer."

Cassie displays her card, Hamlet, with 100 points.

"That is correct; your total is now 570 points."

Cassie is nervous; her conservative bid has left her vulnerable to Regina. If she guesses correctly and has bid the most points, Cassie will lose everything.

The judge announces, "Regina, please reveal your answer."

Regina displays her card, Hamlet, with 180 points.

A wave of emotion grips Cassie as she realizes the result, standing on the edge of victory and defeat. Regina and Cassie both have 570 points. Tears threaten to fall as she clutches her hands, reminding herself she's come this far and still has a chance to turn the tide in the final two games. Cassie is unsure whether there will be a tie-breaking question.

Judge Haskins turns to the players. "Well, we have a tie between Cassie and Regina. I have decided both will move on. Originally, your next challenge was to be played individually. However, with four players remaining, I believe I'll shake things up and have two teams of two players compete in the next round. Both players will advance to the next game. "

Cassie breathes a sigh of relief. She is still in the game. Cassie shoots a glance at Thomas; he looks confused and angry.

"Wait, so you're saying everyone moves on, and no one is eliminated?" he asks incredulously. Seething anger lingers in his voice; he hopes for a more definitive end for the weaker players.

"I say we settle this now. Eliminate both Cassie and Regina, and let's get on with it. Or are you making the rules up as you go?"

Judge Haskins's expression hardens as he turns to Thomas. Ire flickers within his composed demeanor.

"I am growing tired of your lack of respect, Thomas. You speak of eliminations as if this is some trivial spectacle," he snaps, his voice low but charged with intensity. "You underestimate the gravity of this contest and the resilience of those you deem 'weaker.' Remember that each player's journey is marked by sacrifice and strategy, not just accumulating points on a board. If you cannot respect their struggles, you will find that the game is less forgiving than you expect."

Resuming his stoic demeanor, Judge Haskins gestures for his associates to lead the players back to their rooms. Panic lingers beneath Cassie's calm facade as she ascends the stairs, the possibility of impending danger tightening like a noose around her throat. Her head spins as she considers escape; the stakes are far too high to entertain.

* * *

Back in her room, Cassie realizes she must deliver a message to someone before it's too late. If Haskins detects her intent, she could become his next victim. The mansion's maze-like corridors offer both safety and the risk of getting trapped, and every person could be a threat. With adrenaline surging, she plans her route, watching for moments when chaos erupts, distractions, or mistakes that could give her a chance to escape and send a warning. Her only hope is to avoid the tightening grip of the darkness closing in around her. Time is running out, and failure is not an option.

Cassie is desperate. What kind of man has Judge Haskins become? This once-respected figure, known for his fairness and dedication to justice throughout his lengthy career on the bench, now appears to be a shadow of his former self. What could have driven a man of such esteemed reputation and integrity to abandon his principles and fall into a darkness that defies understanding?

These questions remain unanswered. Cassie is sure that if she loses any round of the game, only one possible judgment will be meted out for her past sins. Death.

Twenty-Nine

As Judge Haskins settles into his study, the afterglow of another riveting game still pulses in the air. His gaze drifts to a framed photo on the desk—himself, a young attorney, captured in crisp black-and-white. The desk in the image is tidy, a testament to his orderly nature. A stack of legal tomes stands proud; papers lie arranged with precision, starkly contrasting the chaotic workspaces of his peers. This snapshot reveals the essence of his meticulousness.

Leaning back, he notices the arc of three gold-framed photos catching the light. Each one tells a story, preserving moments that once shimmered with happiness but now flicker under the oppressive darkness hanging over Eberly Manor.

His heart warms at the first photo: Robert and Constance, both in their teens, stand confidently by the Liberty Bell in Independence Hall. Their bright smiles leap from the frame, pulling him back to that sun-drenched day. He hears their laughter echoing through the crisp Philadelphia air, a joyful soundtrack to a memory that feels both distant and immediate.

* * *

July 1974

As a teenager, Judge Robert Haskins often explored historic sites in Philadelphia with his older sister, Constance. One summer day, the siblings wandered through Independence Mall, their voices echoing off the marble floors and grand columns.

"Robert, look at this!" Constance called out, her voice filled with excitement as she stood before the iconic building. Robert, a lanky teenager with a curious mind, joined her, his eyes widening at the sight of the majestic architecture.

"Imagine the debates and discussions that took place within these walls," Constance said, her voice expressive. "The Founding Fathers shaped the future of our nation."

Robert nodded, his eyes sparkling with mischief. "I wonder if they ever argued about something like parking tickets for their horses," he joked, a playful smile crossing his face.

Constance laughed, her warm smile revealing their close bond. "I doubt it. But who knows? Maybe even the smallest disputes had their place in history."

Their conversation flowed as they strolled, discussing the past and their hopes for the future. Constance, always the more serious of the two, shared her dreams of becoming an educator, inspired by their grandmother's legacy. Ever the adventurous one, Robert talked about his wish to explore the world beyond Philadelphia, his curiosity about people and their stories already engaging his mind.

Constance stopped at a vendor selling historical pamphlets. "Robert, can you hold my bag?" she asked, handing him her tote.

He watched her as she examined the pamphlets. Constance returned with one tucked under her arm. "Did you know Grandpa William helped lay the cornerstone for this mall?"

"I vaguely remember them talking about it," Robert replied, distracted by pigeons pecking at crumbs.

Constance laughed. "You were young then. He loved historical preservation." She looked around. "Come on, let's get ice cream."

At the nearby stand, Constance ordered a strawberry waffle cone, while Robert chose a chocolate. "The pamphlet mentions the Eberly family's contributions," she said, licking her cone.

"Grandfather was remarkable," Robert agreed, wiping chocolate from his chin. "We should visit Eberly Manor more often; it's been far too long."

* * *

Judge Haskins leaned closer to the second photo, his gaze fixed on the date embossed in the corner: May 2nd, 1995. That date shimmered in his memory, a vivid reminder of joy and family triumph. His heart warmed as he recalled the scene: his mother, father, and Constance, each wearing a beaming smile, gathered on the steps of the sixth circuit courtroom. Robert, dressed in his judge's robes for the first time, stood proudly among them. It was a treasured moment, one that seemed to briefly push back the long shadow William Eberly cast over their lives.

He moved to the last photo, and the scene shifted. Robert and Constance sat across from each other in the intimate glow of LeBec Fin, the soft murmur of the five-star restaurant surrounding them. They laughed, glasses raised in celebration of Constance's recent promotion to principal of the Chester Springs Academy for Girls. Constance's eyes sparkled with excitement as she talked about her plans for the upcoming fall semester.

The remnants of their meal cluttered the table, but she

remained focused, and her passion was evident. She spoke enthusiastically about adding law classes to the curriculum, aiming to empower young women by fostering a strong understanding of legal principles. Constance's dreams hovered between them, inspiring critical thinking about justice and rights and preparing her students to become advocates and leaders. Robert listened attentively, feeling a surge of pride for the woman in front of him, who wanted to motivate the next generation to understand and influence a complex legal world.

Tears build in Judge Haskin's eyes as he remembers that this was the last day they were together.

* * *

In 2004, a personal tragedy marred Judge Robert Haskin's distinguished career when Constance was the victim of a brutal carjacking that led to her death. Constance and her two friends had been enjoying a lively evening at the Merben Theater in Mayfair, watching The Notebook. As they left the theater, laughter filled the air, but the joy quickly turned to fear when an armed attacker demanded their car.

Constance quickly handed over the keys, but her friends tried to resist. Sadly, during the chaos, the attacker shot her, and she collapsed to the ground as he ran away, leaving her friends shocked and horrified.

Days later, as her family gathered in the somber hospital room, hope faded. Doctors delivered the heartbreaking news: Constance had been declared brain-dead. In accordance with her living will, Robert struggled with the difficult decision to let her go. With a heavy heart and knowing it was what she would have wanted, he honored her wishes, an ultimate act of love in a moment of profound loss.

The tragedy left the judge reeling, and his world turned upside down. Now he had to navigate the legal system from a different perspective: that of a grieving family member.

The investigation led to the arrest of a suspect, making the case appear straightforward. Thomas DeMarco, an emerging attorney, represented the accused, Jason Carter, in a case that garnered significant media attention.

Robert and his mother, Anne, attended the trial, feeling both anxious and calm. The atmosphere in the courtroom grew tense, especially as the well-known and respected judge appeared angry and emotional during the trial. Judge Richard Sharp presided over the proceedings, a man Judge Haskins knew and respected. Attorney Kevin Rankin, a close friend, believed the case was airtight and justice would be served.

During the initial days of the trial, Rankin built a clear and airtight case, supported by compelling evidence and witness testimony. However, DeMarco continued to exploit subtle missteps to sway the outcome in his client's favor. DeMarco was also well-known for allegations of judicial misconduct that his law firm had hidden on multiple occasions.

During the trial, DeMarco focused on a critical point: documenting the chain of command for the evidence found on Carter's mobile phone.

He had pointed out the missing documentation that verified the chain of custody. They focused on a young officer who was unable to locate a crucial transfer document, which he testified he had signed. Without it, Judge Sharp had to rule the evidence inadmissible.

Judge Haskins shifted in his seat, the air in the courtroom heavy with unspoken tension. As he leaned forward, listening carefully to the witness's testimony, the inconsistencies in the chain of custody gnawed at him, each contradiction fueling a deep unease in his gut. It felt more than procedural errors; it simmered with the unmistakable scent of something more sinister—an orchestrated effort to undermine the case's integrity.

He considered the missing transfer document—a vital piece deliberately removed—a significant gap in the evidence intended to support the prosecution's case. The idea of judicial misconduct haunted him, a betrayal that felt worse than any verdict. Each second felt longer, increasing the pressure of responsibility on his shoulders.

As the jury prepared to announce their decision, Judge Haskins sank back into his chair, eyes sweeping over the courtroom—a space that had always felt familiar but now seemed foreign, laden with unseen burdens. The polished wooden paneling, the rows of seats filled with spectators, and even the jury box all bore a gravitas that heightened his anxiety.

Beside him, Anne squeezed his hand tight, an anchor amidst the tempest of emotions swirling within him. He could feel the knot of anxiety tightening in his stomach, a mix of hope and dread spiraling together. This wasn't just another case; it felt personal in a way he had never experienced before, the stakes higher than ever.

The jury's verdict of not guilty on the most serious charge of second-degree murder devastated Robert. His mother sobbed, "He killed my Constance."

Judge Haskins held his mother close, trying to soothe her trembling shoulders. But as he looked into her tear-streaked face, fury surged within him. The man who had so ruthlessly taken Constance's life was serving a mere five-year sentence for stealing her car. *Five years!* It felt like a slap in the face—a cruel reminder that justice often falls short. The injustice tore at him, igniting a fire that threatened to consume his sense of calm.

As time went on, Judge Haskins withdrew into himself, his once-sharp wit dulled by grief. But as he looked into his mother's tear-filled eyes, he felt a deep sense of helplessness, knowing that justice had slipped away once again. During this period, he turned to the one place he had always found comfort: Eberly Manor.

* * *

Present Day

Amid his study, the judge feels tension creeping back into his bones, as if the air thickens with the memories of those moments. He closes his eyes, wishing he could erase that scene from his mind, yet it remains a stark reminder.

He stares at the photos of Constance again, wishing she were there to share these thoughts and offer her wisdom. Perhaps this is why he orchestrates his games. He's motivated to create a scenario in which the innocent prevail and to deliver the verdict he desires for himself and for those who endure the pain of inadequate justice.

As time passed, Judge Haskins explored the law books that Constance cherished, using them as a refuge from his pain. Each page reminded him of her passion for justice, strengthening his renewed determination to uphold the principles she believed in, even in the face of profound grief. He transformed his sorrow into a relentless pursuit of truth—honoring her memory through his unwavering commitment to justice.

Yesterday morning, Judge Haskins entered the Eberly family mausoleum, the cool air brushing against him as sunlight filtered through the trees. He walked past the weathered markers, each one a silent tribute to a life once vibrant and full.

His thoughts drifted to the fleeting nature of status and wealth. In this sacred space, grandeur felt empty; beneath the surface, everyone shared the same fate. He traced a finger over a chipped headstone, feeling the cold stone—a reminder that in death, all souls rest equally in the earth, leaving only echoes of their lives.

As he walked through the dimly lit tomb, a feeling of reverence filled the surrounding space. Carefully carved plaques decorated the cool stone walls, each one representing his family's legacy.

William Ryan Eberly	Beatrice Elizabeth Eberly
Born: May 1st, 1904	Born May 13th, 1910
Died: January 14th, 1975	Died: June 1st, 1970
Anne Eberly Haskins	John Charles Haskins
Born January 2nd, 1932	Born: June 14th, 1928
Died: January 22nd, 2007	Died: June 1st, 1999
Constance Beth Haskins	Robert William Haskins
Born: November 24th, 1953	Born: March 29th, 1959
Died: April 19th, 2004	Died:

Judge Haskins stood by his sister's marker, holding a single white rose. "Constance," he began, his voice low. "It's Robert. I have something here for you." He placed the rose beside the marker.

"I've come to update you. On the path I've chosen." He paused, adjusting his tie. "The gavel is heavy, Constance. Heavier than it should be. The cases ... they've been challenging. You always said I had a head for details."

"Being a judge, it has its ... disappointments. There were a few times when I obtained information outside official channels. Information that helped shape my decisions. Decisions that some might think ... unbecoming of a judge."

He cleared his throat. "I did what I thought was necessary. For justice, Constance. That's what I tell myself." He looked down at his hands, then back at the marker.

"Eberly Manor ... Grandpa William would be proud. Or maybe he wouldn't. I haven't quite figured out how he would feel about all this. It's been a life of choices, hasn't it, Constance? Some good, some less so. I hope you're not disappointed in me. I hope you can forgive me."

"I will be joining you soon, concluding the Eberly line as it should be. I have a few more tasks to do, justice to serve, in my own way, and then it will be over."

He kissed her marker. "I love you, Constance. I always will."

He stood for a moment longer in silence before turning and walking away, the white rose still resting on the plaque. He did not look back.

Thirty

C assie sits in her dimly lit room, weighed down by guilt and uncertainty. She sees the cameras trained on her every move. Judge Haskins's revelation that the next game will involve teaming up with another player leaves her wrestling with many choices.

She remembers the vow she made long ago in her bedroom when all felt lost: *Never give up on yourself.* She grounds herself and releases her tension. *I need to find an advantage. That's what you do better than anyone else here.*

Cassie surveys the room. She weighs her choices. Each second passes quickly, like sand through her fingers. She understands the stakes—life or death.

She steps closer to the leaded glass windows; the light filtering through their intricate designs casts a mosaic of shadows across her face. If only she could break through, but it's a three-story drop beneath her, the ground beckoning with danger and uncertainty. She glances around for something heavy—furniture, perhaps—but the room holds little that could serve her needs.

Pacing, she bites her lip, the decision weighing on her. Forming a temporary alliance could provide a lifeline, another set of eyes to spot weaknesses in this place—an overlooked door, a hidden passage, or perhaps an inattentive guard. But the risk chills her. What if they turn on her? What if trust leads to betrayal?

Cassie looks back out the window, estimating the distance

below. There's no time to waste, and every choice feels like a gamble. The walls close in, and with each breath, the pressure builds. She could stand alone, but the idea of doing so, vulnerable and exposed, fills her with dread.

Alternatively, if she chooses to go alone, every creak in the floorboards and every shadow on the wall could lead her toward freedom. The manor holds many secrets, and her decision depends on her instincts and the urgency of her situation. Should she risk asking for help or navigate the labyrinth on her own? Time is ticking, and every second counts.

She paces the floor, trying to find a solution, any option besides playing another deadly game.

In the next game, Cassie's partner is crucial. If it's Thomas, she knows any alliance would be risky. He's a ticking time bomb, and his reasons are unclear. His anger during the 'Locks' game still unsettles her. Any other player might be worth the risk. However, both Regina and Judith remain mysteries to her. She can't shake the feeling that a shared burden weighs on their shoulders.

With his knowing eyes, the judge holds the key to that secret. Whatever it is, it's powerful enough to keep Regina and Judith in this state of submission, living under the shadow of their past.

Whatever decision Cassie makes, it needs to be made soon. The game's losers are being executed, and she can't afford any mistakes.

She takes a deep breath to steady herself. *You've come this far; don't give up now.*

Thirty-One

The cramped confines of the eighth precinct's documentation room feel suffocating as Janelle, Detective Coles, and Detective Fenn settle at a small table covered with papers, pens, and a flickering fluorescent light overhead. The dim lighting casts long shadows across their faces, reflecting the weight of the task ahead.

Janelle spreads out the warrant along with the evidence they have meticulously gathered.

"Okay, we need to document everything before we head out," she instructs, her voice firm but steady. She can still feel the adrenaline pulsing through her veins from the earlier rush, but now it is time to focus, to get it right.

Detective Coles nods, his brow furrowed in concentration as he opens his notebook.

"Let's begin with the timeline. We need to connect the dots clearly so that any judge can see the necessity of what we are doing."

He quickly notes key dates and events, his pen gliding across the page. They have both spent weeks collecting leads, weaving together witness testimonies, and piecing together the scattered evidence that has surfaced amid the case's chaos.

Detective Fenn leans closer to the papers, tracing the outline of the warrant. "We should include a list of the evidence we expect to find in Thompson's condo and car," she suggests, her usual brightness dimmed by the seriousness of their task.

Janelle agrees, feeling the weight of responsibility. "If we find nothing, this could backfire. We need to prepare for any objections."

As they work, the room fills with quiet determination, the sound of pens scratching against paper mingling with the rustle of sheets. The minutes pass as they focus intensely on their meticulous work, rechecking each detail. They transfer evidence logs, summarize the cellphone tracking reports, and carefully note the probable locations where relevant evidence might be found—every single detail weighs heavily on them.

Finally, as they finish their last bit of documentation, Janelle leans back in her chair and takes a deep breath.

"Alright, I think we have everything we need. This should be enough to convince the judge that we're justified in this search."

Detective Coles and Detective Fenn exchange tired glances; the exhaustion now settling into their bones.

"Let's hope the judge signs off," Detective Coles murmurs, with a faint trace of anxiety in his voice. "No turning back now."

With a final flick of her pen, Janelle signs off on the last page, feeling a mix of accomplishment and worry.

Janelle states, "Let's move. Judge Miller is expecting us."

Thirty-Two

Game 4: Escape Room

C assie, Thomas, Judith, and Regina stand in the darkened conservatory as the clock ticks towards the hour. The once serene space has transformed; tables mirrored on either side of the room are laden with cryptic items, casting long shadows that dance across the walls.

The faint rustle of leaves outside teases a storm on the horizon, a palpable tension threading through the room. Cassie shifts in her seat, her pulse quickening as her eyes flit from one table to another, scanning the bizarre array of artifacts that might unlock the mystery of their predicament.

Glass jars, their surfaces slick with condensation, stand stoically on one table. Another table sprawls beneath an assortment of small boxes, each one filled with faded memories—yellowed photographs, delicate letters, and trinkets that whisper stories from the past. Nearby, puzzles and games lie strewn about, their complexity an invitation to unravel hidden truths.

Regina stands rigid, her jaw tight, a shadow darkening her brow as if bracing against an unseen force. Judith's fingers tremble slightly as she plucks at a loose thread on her sweater, each tug a silent expression of her anxiety. Thomas leans against the cool surface of his table, his expression blank, a mask of contemplation that betrays nothing.

The door creaks open, slicing through the heavy atmosphere, and a musty draft sweeps across the room. A figure steps in—the judge—commanding their full attention with a decisive stride. He clears his throat, the sound ringing like a bell in the tense silence, signaling that their next challenge was about to begin.

"Welcome, players," he begins, his voice deep and steady. "Tonight, this conservatory becomes an escape room. You'll need more than luck to escape. It will require wit, courage, and maybe even a bit of betrayal."

His gaze sweeps over the group, lingering on each player to gauge their determination. "You must solve puzzles and riddles designed to push you to your limits. The answers will unlock your path to freedom. But I warn you, the clock will be ticking and your time to escape is running out."

The judge's voice cuts through the silence. "Before we get started, we have a little game of chance to decide your partnerships." His smile is mysterious, with a mischievous sparkle in his eyes.

He gestures toward a table in the center of the conservatory, where an array of cards lies face down, each concealing a number. "Select one card and only one. There are two sets of matching cards; your partner will be the person who has the same number as you."

Cassie glances at Thomas, Judith, and Regina. The cards lie before them, but the judge's tone suggests a dark undercurrent to this simple selection.

"The team that escapes my conservatory first will be the winners. If no team has escaped when time runs out, the winners

will be the team with the most puzzles solved. The losing team
—well, we will discuss the sad repercussions once the game is
concluded."

"Now, listen closely. Each of the five puzzles requires a
four-digit number as the correct answer. The lock on the door
will accept your responses. Five correct answers will open the
door. If any number is incorrect, the lock will flash red, and you
must reconsider your choice. Both teams will try to solve the
same puzzles."

As the players shuffled forward, Cassie couldn't help but
notice the judge's grin, which seemed to stretch across his face.
Who will join forces? Who will find themselves trapped with an
enemy? With her instincts on high alert, she knows this game of
chance could either be her best chance at escape or her downfall.

As the players' Cassie glances at the judge, whose eyes gleam,
the atmosphere in the room grows even more charged.

The players select their cards one by one. Thomas picks first,
revealing the number one. Judith picks next and displays a two.

Cassie watches Regina walk up. Tension lingers heavily, an
undeniable weight. She glances at Thomas, leaning against a table,
a smirk curling his lips. The thought of teaming up with him sends
a shiver down her spine. His unpredictable personality could turn
this game into a nightmare.

Regina steps forward, her brow furrowed in concentration
as she reaches for a card, each movement deliberate and cautious.
Please ... not two, Cassie thinks. She watches Regina flip the card;
the only sound is the gentle flutter, as time stood still. The
number glimmers under the dim lighting, and Cassie's breath
catches in her throat as she realizes it's a one. Cassie turns over
her card, revealing the expected two.

"Ah, intriguing pairings!" the judge declares with a grin. "Let's see how these alliances will shape your fate. You may begin."

* * *

9:00 pm.

The clock tolls, and the two teams approach their first table. Cassie reads the clue while Judith checks out the objects on the table, which include four bottles labeled with descriptions of objects and a series of four lit buttons.

This task requires players to identify the correct order of the four objects on the bottles by the date they were invented, from earliest to latest. Once the order is determined, press the buttons in that order. A correct guess will turn the button green. A wrong guess, red. Additionally, an incorrect guess will disable the buttons for two minutes, so please make your guesses wisely.

Judith considers the labels "Ballpoint Pen (1), Phonograph (2), Pasteurized Milk (3), and Incandescent Light Bulb (4)."

Cassie leans forward, nervously tapping her fingers on the table. Glancing at the scattered blueprints, she whispers, "Judith, let's take our time and get it right the first time. We can take advantage of Thomas's approach to the games so far — bulldozing his way through them."

Judith nods her head. "Let's go."

The ticking of the clock fills the silence, intensifying their sense of urgency. She grabs a pencil and examines the first design. "Which invention do you think we should tackle first?"

Judith takes a deep breath, her voice trembling as she responds. "I believe the phonograph is one of the oldest items here. Thomas Edison created it in the late 1870s."

Cassie nods; the logic makes sense so far. "I think you're right. After that, let's go with the incandescent light bulb. I remember in science class we talked about its involvement in some major world fairs before 1900."

"Sounds right," Judith replies, her eyes wide. "Let me think about pasteurization. Louis Pasteur developed it in the mid-1800s, so I guess it might be earlier than the light bulb or the phonograph."

Cassie settles her mind. "So ... if we go with that order: Pasteurization first, Phonograph, followed by the Incandescent Light Bulb, and finally the Ballpoint Pen, I think that was invented after 1900 ... Is that it?"

Judith swallows hard. "What if we choose the wrong order?" she says, fear creeping into her voice.

Cassie steadies her gaze, ready to guide their decision. "We rely on our first instincts and trust each other. Let's try it."

Judith manages a half-smile and pushes the buttons: 3-2-4-1. They turn green. Cassie's excitement bubbles over as she rushes toward Judith, wrapping her arms tightly around her in an exuberant hug. "We can do this! I know we can!" she exclaims, the adrenaline of the moment fueling her sudden hope.

* * *

9:10 pm.

Cassie and Judith tackle the next game on the list: Missing Cards. They study the instructions.

In this game, you must identify the four missing cards from the deck. Once identified, sort the cards by their count in numerical order. Then, create a four-digit code from the ordered cards to unlock this puzzle.

Judith suggests, "Cassie, you can focus on Aces through nines, and I will look for eights through twos."

After three minutes, Judith identifies that the three of diamonds is missing, but Cassie remains unsuccessful.

Cassie slams the deck onto the table, frustration boiling over. "I can't believe I haven't found a single card yet! I can't keep track." Judith looks up and touches Cassie's shoulder. "Let's regroup and focus on the pattern. We'll find it together," Judith says, her voice steady.

Cassie nods, and a sense of renewed purpose appears in her eyes.

Cassie exclaims after the next run through the cards, "The Queen of Spades is not here. I'm pretty sure. I'll check it on the next pass through the deck."

At the other table, Thomas yells, "Got the first missing card; let's keep going." Cassie knows Thomas and Regina currently have the lead.

Judith says, "I think the eight of hearts is missing," she says, her voice steady. "One more to go."

Judith exposes the deck again, and Cassie focuses on it. "The Jack of clubs is missing," she remarks, her voice trailing off. "Let's run through the deck one more time to be sure."

Judith turns the cards over at a quick pace. "I've confirmed the missing cards, but what about the face cards?" Judith's voice rumbles with urgency. "What number should we assign them?"

Cassie looks at their list. "We are missing the three of diamonds, eight of hearts, Jack of clubs, and Queen of spades. Would be …3-8-10-10; but we need a four-digit number."

Judith suggests, "Let's use the first digit for each of the face cards."

They race over to the master lock and enter their guess: '3811'

The lock flashes red, and the judge announces, "That will be a two-minute penalty for an incorrect guess."

Tears run down Judith's face.

Cassie leans in closer to Judith, her fingers anxiously twisting a loose strand of hair. "We've got this." A small smile creeps onto Judith's lips, igniting a flicker of hope amidst the pressure of the ticking clock.

As they wait for their next turn, Thomas and Regina rush over and enter their code. Green. They move to the next table.

Cassie takes a steadying breath to calm herself. She thinks about the face cards and what they could represent. "I have an idea, Judith. If the Ace is one, and two through ten cards are obvious, what if…the Jack is eleven and the Queen is twelve? 3,8,11,12. We tried 3, 8, 1, 1…".

Cassie enters 3, 8, 1, 2 into the lock display and holds her breath … Green.

∗ ∗ ∗

9:30 pm.

Cassie leans over the scattered jigsaw pieces, her brows furrowed in concentration as she locks the last edge into place. Beside her, Judith brings the log cabin to life, connecting colorful sections with a satisfied grin.

"Got it!" Cassie beams, excitement bubbling as Judith adds another piece. Within moments, they triumph, exchanging proud smiles just as Thomas and Regina finish their puzzle nearby, and they are still in the lead.

Cassie sees a four-digit number hidden in the trees. She runs over and punches in the number. Green. Two more challenges to go.

Next, they move to the neighboring table and face the following challenge: a grid of letters twisting and turning like a maze. Judith squints thoughtfully at the layout, while Cassie taps her fingers in anticipation.

Your task is to find five words in the grid below. You must continue to move your pen to find the words. Move in any direction once a word is found, except backward.

Once all five words are found, add a new, additional word to make a new word.

For example, if the words found are 'man', 'wood', and 'place', you can add 'fire' to create 'fireman', 'firewood', and 'fireplace'. Once you guess the word, use the first four letters of the new word to create a 4-digit code to solve the puzzle.

Cassie's heart races as she stares at the jumbled letters, her fingers tapping anxiously against the table. Each letter seems to mock her, refusing to form the words she needs. The ticking clock weighs heavily on her, intensifying the anxiety coiling in her stomach. She takes a deep breath, pushing aside self-doubt and reminding herself that this is a shared challenge—they will find a way through it together.

	C	U	R	R	
E	N	S	O	R	I
S	B	R	Y	Y	C
Y	N	R	V	M	U
L	I	A	A	A	L
I	X	L	S	R	A
R	R	U	C	I	R
A	O	L	A	T	O
	N	I	D	R	

Cassie stares at the word grid, trying to make sense of the directions. She turns to Judith. "Do the directions make sense to you?"

"No. I am not sure how to do this ... yet."

Cassie stares at the puzzle, and her hands sweat. She recognizes patterns and connections, searching for words or phrases that might catch her eye. The noise of the conservatory fades into the background, leaving only the puzzle and her determination to solve it. As she rearranges the letters in her mind, hope grows within her.

Judith appears lost; her eyes give away her concern.

Find a word ... find a word, Cassie...let's go. She starts at the top. CURR ... Y, okay, MARITR is not a word. There must be a connection here somewhere.

This is a word search, Cassie. Find a word ... Back and forth she scans. Judith stares blankly at the puzzle, which adds another layer of stress.

'CURR ... Ignore the top right space. 'CURR ... ICULAR.' "Yes," she yells out loud, for everyone in the room to hear. "Got one!"

She continues across the bottom row, then up, 'ORDINARILY'. *Okay, keep going.*

She swings around to the top, '*SENSORY,*' then down and across '*MARITAL.*' Cassie circles the word giddy with excitement, while Judith looks on in amazement.

Around in a circle, the letters fly '*VASCULAR.*' "Done."

Cassie and Judith look at the words. 'Curricular', 'Ordinarily', 'Sensory', 'Marital', 'Vascular'.

Judith looks at the words and starts murmuring to herself. "Cassie, I think 'extra' completes the words. I'm not sure about 'Extravascular', but the other words fit. How can we make a four-digit number from 'extra'?"

Cassie thinks for a moment. The instructions said to use the first four letters, so *e-x-t-r*. "I have seen something like this before, in a high-end robbery case involving a digital safe. It involved number replacement for letters. A = one, B = two, etc. For letters with two-digit numbers, use the second digit."

Judith mutters, "You can try it, I guess. I have no idea what you are talking about."

Cassie writes numbers on the instruction sheet. "'E' = five, 'X' = twenty-four or four, 'T' = twenty-two or two, 'R' = eighteen or eight. The number is 5-4-2-8 if we use that substitution method," Cassie says.

At that moment, Thomas and Regina race to the lock and enter their guess: Green. "*Yesss,* Thomas screams. One more to go."

Cassie turns to Judith. "Do you want to try my guess?" Judith nods as if in silent prayer, while Cassie runs toward the lock and punches in the numbers, feeling the sweat on her fingertips. Green.

Cassie celebrates in silence and runs to the last table with Judith. *Stay focused. Ten minutes left.*

* * *

9:50 pm.

Cassie and Judith stand at the last table. The novel *War of the Worlds* and a single index card are waiting. There are no instructions, only the following clue:

'course', 'earth', 'falling', 'appeared'.

"Must be words in the novel," muses Judith. She examines the words, and the clock on the wall shows it is 9:51 pm.

Cassie guesses, "It must be either the page number or the number of the word's first appearance in the book. My guess is to find the word number."

Judith says, "So if 'course' is word number 200 in the book, that's the number to use."

Cassie thinks for a moment. *How to get a four-digit number from four numbers...? Fuck, just add the numbers up.*

"Judith, I think the best way to create a four-digit number

from four numbers is to add them together."

"Sounds good. Let's review the words and see what makes sense."

Cassie opens the book, and Judith grabs the pen, ready to jot down the words. Cassie starts with Chapter One. No one would have believed, in the last years of the nineteenth century, that this world was being watched keenly ... She counts the words as quickly as she can.

She reaches word 302, 'course.' Judith jots the number down, and Cassie continues. As Cassie reads down the page, Judith reads behind her, trying to verify Cassie's count. Word 631, 'Earth.' Judith says, "First word count is correct, moving to the second."

Cassie groans, "I think I lost count. Judith. What number did I say was word two?"

Judith looks at her notes. "*631.*"

Cassie continues to count, trying to be steady and accurate. "*1700 - 1764*, 'falling'."

Judith writes it down and continues, "The word count for 'Earth*'* is correct. Counting words for 'falling*'*."

With each word, Cassie's apprehension grew as she read down the page. *Appeared ... Come on.*

Judith glances at the clock. "Third word count is correct ... It's 9:55, Cassie."

Cassie hears the eager voices of Regina and Thomas and knows she is running out of time. She flips to page thirteen ... Got it! She says "1919" to Judith. I'll add up the numbers, and you check my count. Judith nods and reads page thirteen.

Cassie adds the numbers: *4616*.

Judith exclaims, "I think the count for word four is incorrect. I think it's 1918."

Cassie needs to make a quick decision. She decides to trust Judith. "OK, we will go with your count."

The time is now 9:58 pm.

As they rush toward the door, Thomas pushes past Cassie, nearly knocking her over. He dashes to the door and enters his final code. Red. Thomas shouts, "Fuck. That's the right code, dammit." He yells at Judge Haskins and takes a threatening step toward him. The judge's guards block his way.

The judge mocks him, "That will be a two-minute penalty for an incorrect guess. Please move away from the door ... *now!* This is your first and last warning."

Cassie turns back to the lock, takes a deep breath, and enters '4615'.

Green.

As the door opens, a wave of exhilaration washes over Cassie. Adrenaline surges through her as they realize they have unraveled the last puzzle.

Congratulations to both of you," Judge Haskins announces. "You will both play in the last game. My associates will escort you back to your rooms, where food and drinks will await you." He turns to Thomas. "As for you and Regina, we now need to decide who will continue and who will not.

The air in the room shifts, the tension thick enough to cut. All eyes turn to the judge, who stands tall behind the podium, shadows playing across his stern features. A crisp envelope rests in his hand, an emblem of uncertainty and fate.

"Thomas and Regina," he begins, his voice booming, echoing off the walls like the toll of a distant bell. "It has come to this moment. A game of chance awaits you. Only one of you will advance."

Thomas's jaw clenches, his hands curling into fists at his sides. Regina stands beside him, wide-eyed yet resolute. She adjusts her posture, readying herself.

The judge places the envelope on the table, the sound of paper sliding against wood sharp in the thick silence. "Inside this envelope are two cards. One will grant you a place in the last game; the other will eliminate you from the game." He pauses, watching the expressions of both contestants sharpen with fear and determination.

Thomas steps forward, defiance sparking in his dark eyes. "It's all chance then? After everything we've done? After all this bullshit you put me through? Are you out of your fucking mind!"

"Chance is the only friend left to you," Judge Haskins replies, reveling in the tension. "Are you ready to embrace it?"

With a nod from Judge Haskins, they both step to the table, the importance of the moment bearing down on them. The judge's hand hovers over the envelope, the thin paper trembling between his fingers.

"On the count of three," he intones. "You will each draw a card. One of you will escape this game; the other..." he lets the words hang, thick and ominous, "...will not."

"One," Cassie and Judith watch the tension unfold. Cassie knows that if Thomas loses, chaos could erupt. The atmosphere is electric. "Two." Regina closes her eyes. "Three."

In unison, they plunge their hands into the envelope, fingers brushing against each other as they fumble for their fate. The rustle of paper fills the silence, each sound magnified.

"Now," the judge commands, his voice low and authoritative. "Reveal."

With a collective breath, they turn the cards toward the room, revealing their destinies. A moment stretches long, the players' sharp inhalations a shared gasp. Thomas's card shows a green check mark, Regina's a red X. Thomas's eyes widen, the glimmer of triumph flickering on his lips.

A smug smile deepens on the judge's face; "It appears chance has not favored you today, Regina."

Regina stands by the door, her expression unreadable as the guards step toward her.

"Goodbye, Regina," the judge says, his tone carrying chilling finality.

As Regina turns to leave, a flood of emotions—frustration, pain, and relief—overwhelms Cassie. With each step Regina takes away, the room feels smaller, and a single tear traces down her face.

With the judge's voice fading into the background, the moment's reality settles on all of them. The game continues, but the shadow of what has transpired looms large, carving its mark on each.

One more game remaining, one more nightmare to endure.

Thirty-Three

10:00 pm.

T he fluorescent lights in Judge Dorothy Miller's chambers hum a monotonous tune. Fatigue shows in the lines around the judge's eyes. She stretches her arms and hands Janelle a signed copy of the warrant dated Friday, October 11th, at 8:00 pm.

The paper feels fragile and rough. Janelle has spent the last week gathering enough evidence to convince the judge that Cassie Thompson's car and condo are key links to the Cochrane case, despite two unsuccessful warrant requests. Now, the pressure is on to confirm her theory.

"Thank you, Your Honor," Janelle says, her voice low and steady. She doesn't linger, knowing Coles and Fenn were waiting outside.

Janelle steps out of Judge Miller's chambers, the signed warrant heavy in her hand, easing the burden on her shoulders. She knows that if they find evidence of the accident and the cover-up, the next step will be issuing an arrest warrant. She joins Derrick Coles and Carolyn Fenn, informing them on the way to Cassie Thompson's condo.

"We've got the warrant for her condo and her car," she says, her voice tense with urgency. "Let's move. We need to act before Thompson catches wind of this and tries to cover her tracks again."

Coles nods; his eyes fixed on the road as he navigates through the city traffic. "Yes, ma'am," he replies, his tone respectful. Sitting in the back seat, Fenn reviews the warrant, her eyes scanning every detail.

The trio maintains a tense silence as they drive to Cassie's condo, each lost in their thoughts about the case. Janelle replayed the events of the past five weeks that led them here—the evidence that convinced the judge, and the life hanging in the balance.

As the car glides down Route 95, crumbling buildings and graffiti-strewn walls give way to empty lots, where children's laughter mingles with the echoes of city life. But as they near Society Hill, the transformation is striking: manicured lawns replace asphalt, and elegant townhouses rise beside the shimmering Delaware River. Moonlight glints off upscale cafes and boutiques, their polished displays beckoning affluent passersby, marking a stark contrast to the lives left behind just a few miles back.

When they arrive in the lobby of Cassie Thompson's condo building, Detective Robinson approaches the building manager, Mr. Graves. Janelle wastes no time in showing the signed warrant and explaining their authority to search the premises.

Janelle asks Graves, "Does 1505 have a private spot in the garage?"

"Yes, Detective, parking spot C26."

Janelle asks Coles to go to the garage and find Cassie's car, to which he replies, "On it."

Graves escorts Detective Robinson and Coles up the elevator to the fifteenth floor and condo 1505.

Janelle bangs on the door.

"Cassandra Thompson," her voice cuts through the silence, amplified by the street's stillness. "This is Philly PD. We have a search warrant for your residence and vehicle. Please open the door." The only response is the frantic chirp of a nearby cicada, a tiny, insistent noise.

"Ms. Thompson, open the door *now*."

After another minute with no response, Janelle tells Mr. Graves to enter the code and open the door.

∗ ∗ ∗

As Detective Robinson and Fenn step into Cassie's condo, they're both struck by the sheer opulence that envelops them. The spacious layout, accented by high ceilings and floor-to-ceiling windows, allows the moonlight to cascade in, casting an eerie glow.

Fenn raises an eyebrow, taking in the plush scarlet rug that anchors the living area, the sleek lines of the black leather sofa, and the striking art nouveau paintings that adorn the walls.

"This is how the other half lives," she mutters in envy.

"Lily Cochrane deserved to live her life, too." Janelle added. "In her small twin home in Mayfair."

They start in the living room, methodically examining each surface and drawer. Janelle's gaze darts from one spot to the next as she tries to take in the entire scene.

"We're looking for anything that could link her to the accident and the subsequent cover-up," Janelle says as she pulls on a pair of gloves. "Any correspondence, photos, or personal items that appear out of place. Also, any evidence of her fixing the damage on her car?"

"Yes, ma'am," Fenn replies as she continues her systematic search. A laptop on the desk in the corner of the room catches her attention. She examines the surrounding area, checking for any signs of disturbance.

Janelle, meanwhile, searches the bedroom, her eyes remaining sharp and alert. A drawer with a wooden sign features an Amish hex sign. Janelle pulls the drawer open, revealing a collection of documents and mementos. She sifts through the contents; her gloved hands gently hold each item.

Personal items reveal a life that goes beyond wealth. A silver locket glimmers next to a well-worn leather journal, its pages filled with notes and sketches, the ink smudged from frequent use. A hand-painted box opens to show mementos: a smooth seashell, a faded Rush concert ticket from 2008, and a tarnished key. Colorful postcards fan out, each depicting lively travel scenes. One captures a stunning sunset over the Grand Canyon; another exudes Parisian romance with the Eiffel Tower in silhouette. A third features Santorini's iconic white buildings set against the deep blue Aegean Sea. In a busy Tokyo street market postcard, cherry blossoms and paper lanterns burst with vibrant colors, embodying the city's energy.

Janelle steps into the wardrobe closet, its shelves overflowing with neatly arranged clothing. Rows of tailored blouses and crisp blazers showcase Cassie's sophisticated style, while vibrant dresses hint at nights out. Floral fragrances fill the air, along with rich leather from luxury handbags on display.

Janelle's eyes fixate on a striking red dress, intricately embroidered, paired with heels that steal the spotlight. But admiration isn't what she's here for. She rummages through casual sweaters instead, her fingers dancing over the fabric, searching for any clues related to her investigation. Each movement is deliberate amidst the stylish clutter.

As she sifts through the clothing, her fingertips graze a small box nestled in the corner. Curiosity surges as she pulls it out and lifts the lid. Inside, a collection of photographs tied with a delicate ribbon awaits. Each image showcases Cassie in different settings—some candid with friends, others more formal at professional events. One photo captures Janelle's full attention: Cassie stands next to an older gentleman, a radiant smile on her face at a charity gala. A spark of suspicion ignites in Janelle's mind. Could this man be the key to peeling back the layers of the cover-up surrounding the accident?

As Janelle takes in the opulent surroundings, she wonders how Cassie's life had spiraled out of control. The luxurious decor was like a gilded cage, masking the isolation and desperation that had likely consumed her. She imagines a younger Cassie, innocent and hopeful, now transformed into a ruthless persona, both within and outside the courtroom. Janelle's mind flashes back to the Young murder trial, a case that had haunted her with lingering doubts about justice. *She had it all and threw it away.*

Janelle looks closer at the bottom drawer. Inside, she finds a stack of letters, each addressed to Cassie and postmarked from various locations across the country. The return addresses differ, but the handwriting remains the same. She considers these letters a valuable source of information.

* * *

Detective Coles joins the team inside the condo. "Anything?" Janelle asks, her voice thick with excitement. Coles shakes his head, frustration evident on his face. "The car isn't in the garage or anywhere on the premises." Janelle nods and points to the desk. "Let's focus our attention there."

Janelle's attention shifts back to Cassie's laptop. She powers it on, aiming to access Cassie's digital footprint. The password prompt stares back at her, a silent challenge. Unfazed, she tries common password combinations, determined to break through this digital barrier. After several failed attempts, she shuts the laptop and closes the lid.

"Fenn, box up the laptop for the forensics team," Janelle says, "and all her peripherals."

A calendar featuring Lancaster County landscapes hangs on the wall. Janelle's gaze falls on the scribbles and notes that mark specific dates. Each date had a different location written on it, and Fenn's curiosity piqued as she recognized these could be potential travel plans or alibis for Cassie. She makes a mental note to cross-reference these dates with the Cochrane case file.

She looks at what's written for today: *Dougherty Witness statement, noon at EM.*

'EM'. She wonders what it could stand for. A place? Where? Perhaps it was a critical code. She knows that unraveling this mystery could be the key to finding Cassie.

As Janelle shares her discovery, Fenn's interest is evident. "EM could be a person or a location, maybe even where Cassie is right now," Fenn speculates. "Let me think about this. I'll get the forensics team involved as well." With Cassie's car also missing, their window to act was narrowing.

Janelle takes a moment to assess the situation, her instincts guiding her next move. "Coles, let's search the condo again and set up a stakeout in front of the building. Fenn, call in a BOLO on Cassie's car and head back to headquarters and see if Cassie's law firm will give anything up."

Everyone starts work as the clock nears midnight.

Thirty-Four

Game 5: Books

The heavy footsteps of the guards resonate through the hallways of Eberly Manor once again, an ominous herald of the night's events. Judge Haskin's men take Cassie, Thomas, and Judith from their rooms; the hallway looms ahead as the guards usher them into the unknown.

Descending the grand staircase, Cassie can feel her pulse echoing with each step. Flickering candlelight dances, casting grotesque shadows that writhe and twist on the cold stone walls. The manor's breath transforms into a symphony of creaking wood and distant murmurs, deepening her unease. Her fingers brush the cool banister, grounding her and amplifying her dread.

Ahead, the heavy door of the library beckons, inviting yet foreboding. As the guards push it open, an intoxicating chill sweeps through Cassie, thickening the anticipation in the air.

The library is a captivating sanctuary within Eberly Manor, steeped in mystery and intrigue. Towering wooden shelves, intricately carved and cloaked in shadows, rise from floor to ceiling, harboring an extensive collection of books holding centuries of forgotten lore.

Dim light filters through stained glass, casting patterns on the floor. The room hints at the past, centered around a large, ornate table with plush leather chairs, inviting contemplation and debate. However, Cassie senses that a battle of life and death is about to begin.

Distant thunder echoes as the heavy wooden door slowly creaks open in the quiet room. As the judge enters, tension fills the air as he approaches the ornate table—Cassie's heart races as shadows close in around her. Thomas's presence beside her feels overwhelming; she can't shake her unrelenting fear of him.

Judge Haskins announces, "Welcome back, players. I trust you're ready for the ultimate challenge of the evening."

The judge gestures toward the massive shelves of books. "Our last game is called 'Books', which, considering the atmosphere of this room, is hardly surprising. Each of you will receive a book title to find in my library. This won't be simple, since there are over 5,000 books in my collection. Here's a clue to help you: I have displayed the books in a particular order, but it may not be immediately obvious."

"Once you find the book, you will be asked a question about the first chapter. If you answer correctly, you'll earn credit for the book, and I will give you another one to find. If you answer incorrectly, you will not receive credit and will be assigned a different book to locate. You may read the chapter if needed before I ask you the question."

"Whoever answers the most questions correctly in sixty minutes will win the last game. I'm afraid I will eliminate the two losers."

Cassie sharply inhales, stunned by the judge's announcement. She pushes aside her worry and clears her mind. *This challenge is perfect for you. Books have been your salvation, and they will be today. You are the best game player here.*

The judge announces, "We will start shortly."

Cassie gazes at the bookshelves, examining the books to determine their arrangement. She focuses on the information printed on the spines, visible from the shelf. She thinks *Titles and authors are too simple. There must be something more to it. Could it be the publication date?* She scans the titles to give her answers.

11:00 pm.

The clock on the wall chimes eleven times. The three players line up, receive a card from the judge, and race to the bookshelves. Cassie reads the first book on the card, *The Time Machine*.

Cassie sprints through the library of Eberly Manor, her card reading *The Time Machine* clenched in her hand. Her heart pounds as her eyes dart over the towering shelves packed with books. The musty scent of aged paper fills the air, merging with the surrounding tension. Each title hints at adventure, but she has no time to lose.

Cassie leans closer to the towering shelves, her fingers grazing the spines of the books as she tries to decipher their elusive order. She races across the shelves in search of a pattern.

Cassie, you have been to dozens of indie bookstores. How are the books arranged!... Think! The answer comes in a flash. *fiction and non-fiction ... next by genre. Science-fiction novels.*

Cassie identifies the fiction shelves and looks for science fiction titles in the stacks. She finds some toward the bottom of the towering shelf. Cassie starts her search. *'Foundation'...'I Robot'...'The Naked Sun'...Isaac Asimov... Genre, Author, by title... Got it!*

Cassie runs to the end of the row. H. G. Wells.

She spots it; its well-worn cover is a map of its many readers before her. It sits between *The Invisible Man* and *Tono-Bungay*.

Cassie pulls the book from its space with a sense of triumph. Her fingers trace the embossed title, grounding her in purpose. This book isn't only about time travel; it symbolizes the essence of risk and the fear of the unknown.

She walks back to her chair and reads the first chapter. She's unsure of the characters' names, except for the Time Traveler. When she finishes, she quickly goes to Judge Haskins for the answer. Judith is reading her card to find the next book, with a puzzled look on her face.

"Cassandra, what is the name of the Time Traveler's red-haired friend?"

"Filby. George Filby."

"Correct. Well done." The judge announces the next book. "Treasure Island." He hands her the card.

Cassie returns to the shelves: *Treasure Island, Classics*.

As she searches the shelves, Thomas walks by holding *The Great Gatsby*. He glances at Cassie for a moment before heading to the judge with his question. What is he up to? Cassie notices Judith examining the titles of *translated works* on a lower shelf in the library, their gold-embossed spines shining in the dim light.

Cassie walks to the Classics section, her heart pounding as she hunts for *Treasure Island*. Every spine she passes feels like a tease, and doubt grips her; *Who is the author again?* The name was eluding her. Her fingers glide over the titles, but her mind races to remember the author's name.

At that moment, Judith walks by and says, "Stevenson," as she heads toward the non-fiction section. Cassie is stunned, both by the fact that Judith knew exactly what she needed and by the fact that she would offer to help at all.

She scans the 'S' books. "Salinger, Shakespeare, Steinbeck, ... Robert Louis Stevenson. There it is." Frustration wells up inside her. *How could I forget his name?* she scolds, admonishing herself for not recalling the author of a book that had once captivated her.

She shakes her head, determined not to let this lapse in memory bring her down, and grateful for Judith's help. Cassie races back to face Judge Haskins.

"Ms. Thompson, what is the name of the doctor in *Treasure Island?*"

"Dr. Livesey," Cassie pronounces correctly, and heads to find her next challenge, *Great Expectations.*

* * *

11:30 pm.

Cassie races toward the judge, *Wuthering Heights* in hand.

The judge asks Cassie, "What is the old man's name in *Wuthering Heights?*"

"Joseph," Cassie responds confidently.

"Well done, Ms. Thompson. Please select another title to find."

Cassie takes the next card, *All Quiet on the Western Front.* She glances at the table, books stacked by each player's chair. She has six books, Judith has five, and Thomas has four. *So far, so good,'* she thinks as she returns to the shelves.

Cassie has answered questions about *Around the World in 80 Days* and *A Tale of Two Cities*, spending extra time reading the lengthy first chapter of the latter. Judith is right behind her. She also demonstrates that she has mastered The judges' library's organizational system and is now searching for *The Adventures of Sherlock Holmes* next to Cassie.

Cassie races past Thomas, who is fixated on something in the corner by the fireplace. Flickering candlelight casts eerie shadows on his tense features. *What's he doing?* Cassie thinks as she starts in the 'R' author books.

Erich Maria Remarque ... Re...there!

Cassie hurries back to her chair with the book in her hand. *Better read the first chapter. I haven't read this one since Mrs. Joyce's high school English class.*

Next to her, the judge asks Judith, "What is the name of Tom's younger brother?" She responds, "Sid."

"Correct, Mrs. Whitehall."

Cassie glances at the stack of books, frustration bubbling beneath her composed exterior. "*Damn, tied six to six,*" she mutters under her breath, trying to suppress the wave of anxiety that washes over her. She can feel the eyes of her opponents piercing her, each one calculating their next move, anticipating her slip-up. She devours the first chapter and hurriedly leaves her chair.

The judge asks, "Who is the forty-year-old veteran named in the first chapter?"

Cassie replies, "Stan Kaczinski."

"That is correct, Ms. Thompson. Well done. You have taken the lead. Here is your next book to find."

Cassie feels a rush of confidence as she grabs the next card and rushes back to the bookshelves.

* * *

11:45 pm.

Cassie sprints to the mystery section, where her card reads, *And Then There Were None.*

"*Agatha Christie … Christie…there!*" Cassie slips the book off the shelf and heads to Judge Haskins, confident in her knowledge of the classic whodunnit.

The judge asks, "What is the secretary's name?"

Cassie thinks, "*Shit, Claythorne, something Claythorne … Dammit.*" She answers, "Miss Claythorne."

"First and last name, please, Ms. Thompson."

Cassie's mind races as she struggles to recall the judge's names. The urgency churns her stomach, and anger simmers; she regrets not reviewing the chapter. The library feels stifling, her mistake weighing heavily as she glances at the anxious faces around her.

"Miss … Katherine Claythorne," she guesses.

"That is incorrect, Ms. Thompson. The correct name is Vera Claythorne. Here is your next card."

Cassie knows she's in trouble. She's tied with Judith with ten books, and Judith approaches the judge holding the book 2001: A Space Odyssey.

Judith hesitates before replying, "The Watcher?"

Judge Haskins intones, "That is incorrect, Mrs. Whitehall. The correct answer is *Moon-Watcher*."

Yes, Cassie thinks as she heads to the horror section to find *The Haunting of Hill House* by Shirley Jackson.

As Cassie ventures further into the library, her heartbeat quickens, and she feels more tense with each step. She spots Thomas, his eyes sparkling with wild intensity. He appears to move among the bookshelves aimlessly. When he passes the fireplace, he suddenly stops. He lunges forward, grabbing something from the mantel. Fear tightens in her chest as he turns around, now a threatening figure ready to strike, holding the fireplace poker in his hand.

Thomas turns to face Cassie.

"I've been waiting so long for this moment. This farce of a game ends *now*."

Cassie is frozen in her tracks. Before she can respond, he lunges at her. Cassie sidesteps him. "Stay away from me," she cries, adrenaline rushing through her.

He swings the poker at Cassie again, missing her by inches. Thinking quickly, Cassie grabs a heavy book from a nearby shelf, brandishing it as a shield.

"Stay back!" she screams, the weapon hitting the cover of the book with a *thud*, her wrists screaming in pain from the blow.

The judge's men spring into action, their heavy footsteps thudding against the polished wood as they converge on Thomas, blocking his path. They overpower him in a flash, stripping him of his weapon.

"You fucking bitch, I will kill you! " Thomas screams as the men subdue him.

Cassie's breath catches in her throat, and raw panic floods her, her wrists aching. A chill courses down her spine as she realizes how she could have been seriously hurt or worse. Fear ignites her instincts, and she scans the dim library, finding Thomas.

"Why?!" she gasps, betrayal and despair flooding her voice as she locks eyes with him, now a twisted harbinger of chaos, the shadows deepening around him. He stares at Cassie, his eyes bottomless black pits.

$$* * *$$

11:55 pm.

Cassie glances at the clock; five minutes remain. She devotes several minutes trying to find *The Secret Garden*, her heart pounding after Thomas's attack. Cassie races her fingers over the titles. She sees it. *There, thank God.* She grabs it and races to her chair. *Frances Hodgson Burnett, idiot.* She opens with the first chapter. She notes places and characters. As she does, Judith runs from the far shelves, book in hand, headed to the table.

Cassie closes the book and faces the judge. Judith stands behind her.

"Who is Mary Lennox's missing caretaker?"

Cassie takes a deep breath, her heart pounding as she steadies herself. She recalls the characters, settings, and intricate details from the chapter she read. Many possible answers flood her mind, each one a potential lifeline in this moment of uncertainty, but now, this is her time. "Ayah, Your Honor."

"That is correct, Ms. Thompson," the judge says as the clock strikes midnight.

* * *

The atmosphere in the library shifts as the judge's voice rings through the walls, slicing through the thick tension. "Time's up, players," he announces, his tone carrying an air of finality. "You both played valiantly, but only one of you can emerge victorious tonight."

Cassie's pulse quickens, panic surging like a tidal wave, coiling tighter within her chest. The two stacks of books loom around her. Her breath quickens as the moment's gravity hits her, and each heartbeat magnifies the urgency of the situation.

She gazes at Judith, her body marked with complete exhaustion. Judith may have gathered more books than she has, and that uncertainty gnaws at Cassie, amplifying her dread.

The judge's voice echoes through the library, cutting through the tension like a knife. "First, Thomas did not finish the game, so he finished in last place. As I warned earlier, I will address improper behavior, as we discussed, when I explain the game rules upon your arrival. Thomas sealed his fate the moment he broke those rules. You see, there are consequences for those who underestimate the seriousness of this place. Four players have already learned this; one more will follow."

"The final tally is in," he proclaims, his tone a mixture of formality and dire seriousness. "Cassie has answered correctly thirteen times, while Judith supplied twelve correct answers. Unfortunately, Judith, you have been eliminated. "

A heavy silence fills the room. Cassie's heart races with a mix of relief and sorrow. She looks at Judith, whose face shows resignation, the earlier spark now fading. With a firm grip, the guards step forward, guiding Judith away from the library's sanctuary.

"Time can be a cruel arbiter," The judge adds softly, "and the stakes are life and death in this game. The world outside these walls will soon forget the names of those who have failed."

Cassie erupts. "How can you even think about killing Judith?" Cassie exclaims, her voice trembling with anger. "What has she done? Why are you the judge, jury, and executioner?"

Judge Haskins ignores Cassie's outburst and motions for his men to take Judith away.

As Judith walks past Cassie, she turns and whispers, "Don't worry, Cassie, I'm going to be OK." Cassie nods, numb and confused by Judith's certainty in the face of death.

As guards escort Judith from the library, Cassie feels she's on the verge of an emotional breakdown. She experiences a cruel mix of elation and pain—joy for her victory, and sorrow for the players who have lost the game and their lives. People who didn't need to die in this terrible way.

Cassie stares at the judge, relief and simmering anger visible on her face. She is relieved to have survived this nightmare. But she wants out of this trap ... now.

Thirty-Five

Midnight, October 12th

Judge Haskins's men guide Cassie back to the Grand Ballroom, their presence a looming shadow behind her. The space has undergone another breathtaking metamorphosis. It is now a stark, impromptu courtroom, dominated by a raised judicial seat, a witness box, and a sea of expectant, empty gallery chairs.

What the hell is this? Cassie thinks to herself, confusion growing. She suddenly feels alarmed as a guard guides her toward a prominent chair in front of the witness box, and she scans the room for any sign of an exit. The guards show no sign of releasing her, and the judge's eyes seem to follow her every move. The judge takes his seat.

"Well, Cassandra," Judge Haskins says, his voice dripping with disdain as she stands before him, her eyes filled with anger. "I can see you don't like playing my games, but we all do what we must, don't we?" A smug smile plays at the corners of his mouth.

Cassie speaks up defiantly, "Judge Haskins, as an officer of the law, I assume you are also a man of your word and will release me as the winner of your … games."

"If you recall, Ms. Thompson, I never said the winner would be freed, only to have the opportunity to evade justice." Judge Haskins' smile fades, and his eyes harden. "And now … you have that chance."

Cassie knows her carefully maintained facade is at risk. Judge Haskins leans forward as he recalls their first encounter—the Young murder trial.

"Ms. Thompson, I must admit that your performance during our first encounter was impressive. The Young murder case—bribing the key witness, hiding crucial evidence ... all to help your client avoid consequences. But let's not forget the actual victim in that case, shall we? You let the murderer go free, and an innocent life was lost." The judge scowls and then continues.

"But your best performance ... Mr. Richard Sharp."

Judge Haskins's tone turns bitter as he describes how Cassie got him off scot-free despite being a pedophile. "A despicable man, preying on innocent children, and yet you used your skilled legal tactics to free him. Tell me, Ms. Thompson, how do you sleep at night knowing you've put a monster back on the streets as he walks free to decide who his next victim will be?"

As the judge's voice booms, Cassie's mind, a whirlwind of frantic thoughts, spins. *How can he know so many details about this case?* She had been so careful, covering her tracks to hide her illegal activities. The realization dawns on her that this man, this judge, has been watching her, following her career, and waiting for the perfect moment to strike.

Her face pales as a wave of guilt washes over her. Her outward calm breaks down, revealing what she usually conceals. The Richard Sharp case has weighed on her mind since the verdict. The public outcry over the decision remains deafening to her ears, drowning out any sense of peace.

Threats flooded her inbox, each one stabbing at her already guilty heart. She grips the edge of the table; her knuckles turning white as the memory of their words presses down on her. The floorboards creak beneath her, mirroring the fragile state of her career. The scent of old paper lingers in the air as his low rumble cuts through the silence. A chill snakes up her spine, leaving her vulnerable to his critical gaze. In this moment, Cassie struggles with the fear that she will never escape the shadows of that verdict.

Haskins leans forward, his eyes gleaming with excitement and malice. "Despite your legal maneuvers over the past few years, you have escaped my harshest judgment. But Ms. Thompson, today you're here to atone for only one of your victims. Lily Cochrane."

"You see, Ms. Thompson, I have my reasons for seeking justice as I see fit. When I heard about the Cochrane case going cold and the investigation being botched, it didn't sit right with me. So, I started digging, offering my help to the 8th district and the dedicated detectives there. Eventually, they reopened the case and found a name that matched the crime: Cassandra Thompson."

"And after a rather adversarial history with your law firm, the same firm responsible for setting my sister's killer free—an associate of yours, Mr. Weller—provided 'helpful' information to lure you here. At our lunch last week, Mr. Weller talked about his plans to become the next junior partner. He was quite an engaging fellow."

Judge Haskins sits back, a satisfied look on his face. "I knew at that moment you would be the perfect target for my game. A lawyer with a talent for twisting the truth, and a dark secret to hide as well."

Cassie's anger erupts, sharp and hot. She has had enough. "Judge Haskins, I believe we are not so different. You may sit on your bench and pass judgment, but your own hands are dirty." She steps forward toward him.

"You're right, Judge Haskins. I made a terrible mistake that night and relive that moment every day. I struggle with that guilt daily, but I can't turn back the clock."

She pauses, steadying herself. "That doesn't give you the right to play God. You may have revealed my sins, but that doesn't make you any less of a criminal under the law. You've used your judicial power to obtain confidential information and manipulate the law to suit your interests. And to create this elaborate charade and involve, who I suspect are innocent participants in this ... horror show, shows me you are just like me, 'Your Honor'."

The judge pauses. "We will get to the truth of the 'horror show' in a moment, Ms. Thompson. I quite agree with your assessment of my past 'activities', and the questionable use of ex parte to bring you here. Considering my sworn duty as a judge to be impartial, based on the facts at hand, I will allow victim impact statements to help you make the right decision about your plans."

"Victim impact statements—what are you talking about?"

"Ms. Thompson, allow me to introduce you to my special guests for this evening." With a dramatic flourish, he gestures to his associate to open the doors.

The heavy wooden doors of the library creak open, and five figures enter the ballroom. Cassie's blood runs cold as she locks eyes with Thomas, Judith, Emilio, Elizabeth, and Regina.

Cassie gasps. *They're all alive. All red herrings.* These faces aren't opponents. They're part of the judges' deadly contest. His game. Each of them is a harbinger of her doom.

"These individuals," Judge Haskins confirms, his voice cold and steady, "will help you decide the important choices you need to make." He pauses, his eyes flicking to each of the five people.

"Each person has their reason for seeking justice for Lily Cochrane, as you will soon hear. They have been waiting eighteen months for answers. I told them I could provide closure, but in return, they needed to let me choose the venue and format for my plan. After gathering conclusive proof of your crime, we scheduled today's meeting to ensure that justice is served."

Judge Haskins motions for the surprise guests to be seated.

"Despite the predetermined outcome for you and you alone to face judgment tonight, their spirited participation was genuine and their passion undeniable. If you had been eliminated at any point, this phase of the evening would have begun immediately. The players were motivated to make that happen. Of course, I was hoping you would stay in the competition until the end so I could complete all my games. I can tell you it took many weeks to work out all the details. I'm thrilled that you've won, which means my plans have finally come to fruition."

"With that information established, let's begin."

PART 3

Thirty-Six

T he Grand Hall hearth blazes; its fiery heart casts dancing shadows across the walls. The five game players occupy ornate benches flanking the room's perimeter. At the center of the space, Judge Haskins, his judicial robes lending an air of solemnity, addresses them from an imposing lectern. The crackling fire is a silent witness to the unfolding drama, the only sound filling the room.

The judge rises, and his deep, commanding voice breaks the silence. "I am grateful to all of you for gathering here today, bearing witness to this serious matter. I understand the significant hardship this has caused, but seeking a fair resolution requires this difficult meeting."

Cassie stands frozen in the dim light, her eyes wide, a faint tremor passing through her fingertips. Her breath comes in shallow gasps as she stares blankly at the scene unfolding before her. A chill runs up her spine as her thoughts spiral, and she instinctively bites her lower lip, unable to tear her gaze away from the chaos swirling around her.

The judge continues. "Each of you has the opportunity to give a 'Victim Impact Statement'. This is not a formal hearing or a mock trial. The purpose is to allow Ms. Thompson to understand the impact that Lily Cochrane's death has had on you."

Judge Haskins approaches the makeshift bench and takes a

seat. "Mrs. Elizabeth Price, if you would, please step forward." Elizabeth, her eyes downcast, makes her way to the stand at the center of the room. She brings a set of notes to read. Her hands tremble.

"Mrs. Price, could you please tell us a little about yourself?"

She reads: "My name is Elizabeth Price, and I have been a youth librarian at the Northeast Philadelphia branch for the past thirteen years. My role involves curating our selection of books and fostering a love of literature in aspiring readers." Her voice, initially shaky, finds its resonance.

"It brings me great joy to see children's faces light up as they discover the magic of reading. I feel privileged to help inspire the next generation and to be part of their journey as they grow and explore their passions."

But as she continues, a poignant change occurs. Her eyes well up with tears; her composure crumbles. "There was one specific student, a young girl who would visit a few times each week, always looking for her next book. She was getting tutoring to overcome a reading difficulty and dysfluent speech."

Judge Haskins pauses before asking. "And who was that student, Mrs. Price?"

"Lily Cochrane," she replies. Tears now stream down her cheeks.

Hearing her name spoken aloud startles Cassie, causing her to shrink from Elizabeth's unwavering gaze. Burning heat floods Cassie's cheeks as the weight of every accusation bears down on her. As Elizabeth speaks, guilt and memories flood Cassie's mind, each wave crashing over her relentlessly.

Lily was not very different from me, but she didn't have time to overcome her struggles and live her life. The life I took from her.

A vivid image of Lily flashes before her: laughing, carefree, the moonlight catching in her hair. Cassie's stomach twists, a knot of remorse tightening. She presses her palms against her thighs as if her fingers can ground her in the present, but the guilt only multiplies, gnawing at her insides.

Elizabeth's voice steadies as she shares her story. "I had the pleasure of working closely with Lily, and it was incredible to watch her passion for literature come to life. Our time together was special for both of us. She discovered a love for books and would often immerse herself in amazing stories about magic while snuggled up in her favorite cozy spot in the children's section."

"Lily adored fairy tales featuring strong female characters," she continues, her voice affectionate. "These brave girls inspired her to face her own challenges." Elizabeth's eyes glisten with unshed tears as she recalls their discussions on good versus evil, bravery, and compassion, and she closes her notes with a sense of nostalgia.

Judge Haskins's expression softens as he listens to Elizabeth's heartfelt testimony, recognizing the profound impact Lily's death has had on her life.

Elizabeth sobs. "I miss her so much." She wipes her tears, her voice breaking. "I can't believe she's gone. Every day without her feels like a piece of me is missing. I wish I could hear her laughter again."

The air grows thick with tension as Elizabeth's voice quivers, telling a story that ensnares Cassie in an uncomfortable grip. Each word, a thread tightening around her, sparking a storm of broken memories—decisions and hesitations—that haunt her. The walls seem to close in, the weight of her actions presses down, as the truth looms, unavoidable and relentless.

Judge Haskins, his expression unwavering, addresses Elizabeth. "It's clear, Mrs. Price, how dedicated you are to your career and the difference you make in the lives of young people."

"If I may ask, Mrs. Price, can you tell us how this tragedy changed your life?"

Elizabeth's steady gaze, filled with emotion and resolve, settles on the judge.

"Lily's death," she begins, her voice laced with sorrow and strength, "has changed my life in ways I could never have imagined. "

"I struggle through each week, reminded of her, and cry constantly. After talking with my mother, I decided to take a leave of absence to get help. A therapist helped me process my guilt and sadness, guiding me to face the reality of what happened."

"I wanted to do something special to honor Lily, so I helped rename her favorite reading spot in the library to *The Lily Cochrane Reading Nook*. Whenever I am there, it feels like she is still with me. Losing her taught me the importance of books in the healing process. I am dedicated to making a difference for young readers, and she inspires me every single day."

"Mrs. Price, what do you have to say to Ms. Thompson?"

Elizabeth steps down from the podium and approaches Cassie. "I didn't want to see you; I really didn't. I only agreed to Judge Haskins's request to come here so I could watch you take part in this life-or-death charade. To see what kind of person you are."

"I cannot understand the experiences in your life that shaped you into this person. I hope that, however long your punishment may last because of the decisions you made that night, it will ultimately lead to a transformation. A redemption for yourself and for Lily's sake."

"You may step down, Mrs. Price. My colleagues will escort you to your car." Devastated and weeping, Elizabeth exits the makeshift courtroom.

Cassie stands frozen as Elizabeth walks away. The door clicks shut. Shadows from the past flicker in her mind—Lily lies still on the pavement, and the screech of tires echoes like a nightmare. Panic surges as she desperately wipes blood from her dashboard, hands trembling—how can she face the reality of it all?

Judge Haskins and Eberly Manor linger like ghosts, reminders of her deception. In the sterile room, surrounded by legal books, Cassie feels her carefully built façade beginning to crack. She fights tirelessly to survive, but now, staring into the depths of her conscience, the truth is a foe she cannot escape. Cassie Thompson, the lawyer who will do anything to survive, is exposed.

Thirty-Seven

T he judge's voice fills the room once again. "Mr. Emilio Garcia, if you would, please step forward." With a stern expression and a steady gait, Emilio walks toward the stand.

"Mr. Garcia, can you please tell us about yourself?"

Emilio takes a deep breath before addressing the judge, his voice steady and clear.

"My name is Emilio Garcia, Your Honor. I am an emergency medical technician, or EMT. We're based near Nazareth Hospital on Knight's Road. I respond to emergency medical calls and provide care to those in need. It's a job I do proudly."

"Mr. Garcia, how long have you worked as an EMT?"

"Eight years, Your Honor."

"Tell us why you chose this path."

Emilio, standing tall and proud, explains with a steady voice, "I've always wanted to help others, and being an EMT gives me that chance. I get to be there for people in their most vulnerable moments. I feel privileged to make a difference in their lives."

The judge's expression turns somber. "Mr. Garcia, can you tell us about the night of the hit-and-run accident?"

"It was a typical night shift, 8:00 pm to 8:00 am, and I was on call at the station. We received a dispatch for a pedestrian accident with reported injuries on Sheffield Avenue, only a few miles from the hospital. My partner and I responded immediately."

"When we arrived at the scene, I saw a vehicle had hit a young girl, and her injuries were life-threatening. I knew we had only minutes. I provided emergency medical care, doing everything I could to stabilize her."

There were multiple lacerations and bruises, showing the severity of the impact. It left her clothing torn and covered in road rash, suggesting she had been dragged or thrown along the asphalt. As I checked for a pulse, I noticed her skin was cold to the touch, and her breathing was shallow.

Emilio pauses, his voice steady and resolute, commanding attention as he recalls the vivid memory. "She was unconscious, and with the extent of the blunt force trauma I observed, internal bleeding was a major concern."

"We placed her on a spinal board and applied a cervical collar to immobilize her neck and spine. I intubated her to secure her airway and started an IV to administer fluids and medications. Despite our best efforts, her condition continued to worsen. We transported her to Nazareth Hospital, where the trauma team took over."

"The next day, I found out she had died soon after she arrived. It was devastating. She had so much life left to live."

Judge Haskins asks, "Mr. Garcia, if the driver had stopped and called for help, would she have survived?"

Emilio replies, "A quick response is critical. If help had arrived sooner, her chances of survival might have improved." He reflects, "Yet, every situation is unique, and we did our best. Some injuries are too severe."

He adds, "I can't help but wonder who could leave a young girl to die like that, even if the driver didn't intend to hit her."

Emilio's voice trembles as he recounts the frantic efforts to save Lily, each word like a stake in Cassie's heart. The weight of regret presses down on her, closing in like the walls of the room. Memories flicker—moments when she believes she can bury her guilt.

Judge Haskins says, "Mr. Garcia, can you tell us how this event has affected you?"

Emilio shares. "I see the worst things you can imagine in my line of work, but I will never forget that night. Every day, I am reminded of how fragile life is and how important every moment is during emergencies. I see tragedies like this all the time. But her accident will stay with me always. Each life I save is a way to honor Lily and others like her."

"Mr. Garcia, what would you like to say to Ms. Thompson?"

Emilio takes a deep breath. "I've seen too many times what happens when people make poor decisions," he says quietly, looking around the room. "Each one has a ripple effect. It reaches far beyond one person."

He walks over to Cassie, tears in his eyes. "I know what it's like to make a life-changing mistake. I spent two years in juvenile detention because I stole a car—I didn't dare to stand up for myself. When I got out, I turned my life around, and now I have a loving wife with a son on the way. I hope you can do the same for yourself and all of us here."

For Cassie, every word he speaks brings her closer to the reckoning she has dreaded—when she must confront the reality of her actions and the pain they have caused.

Emilio embraces Judith and Regina. He turns as if to say something to Judge Haskins, but hesitates, feeling the weight of the moment holding him back. He stares at him and then looks away, choosing silence over revealing his feelings. Instead, he steps back and leaves the Grand Ballroom.

Thirty-Eight

J udge Haskins summons Regina to the center stand. She walks quietly over to the center stand, composes herself, and faces Cassie.

She begins. "My name is Regina Murphy, and I teach fourth grade at Our Lady of Grace Catholic School in Northeast Philadelphia. I enjoy creating a welcoming environment for my students. In my classroom, we study math, English, science, and social studies. I also help guide them on their spiritual journey through prayer and discussions about our values. My goal is to give each student not only knowledge but also the confidence and compassion they will need as they go through life."

Judge Haskin asks, "How did you know Lily Cochrane?"

"I was Lily's teacher before she died."

Regina pauses, gathering her thoughts. "I watched Lily grow over the school year, not just academically but personally. She had an incredible talent for uniting her classmates, always encouraging them to work together and supporting those who felt excluded. It was touching to see how she could lift others with just a few kind words or a small gesture."

"I'll never forget her approach to learning; her enthusiasm was infectious. She was always the first to raise her hand, eager to share her ideas during discussions. Whether we were diving into math problems or exploring new books during reading time, Lily's passion inspired her entire class and me."

The judge asks, "How has Lily's death affected your fourth-grade class?"

Regina pauses before speaking. "After the news of Lily's passing, I noticed a change in my classroom. It was as if a dark cloud had settled over us. With the help of our school's principal, we arranged counseling sessions so the students could share their feelings. It was important for them to understand that it was okay to grieve."

"We built a memory wall where they could draw pictures and write notes about Lily. Watching them come together to honor her memory gave me hope. It reminded me that even though she may be gone, her spirit lives on in our hearts."

The judge asks, "Please tell us, Regina, how Lily's death has affected you personally."

"Lily's passing has created a deep emptiness in my heart. As her teacher, I felt a special bond with her, and losing her has been painful. I often reflect on our time together, and how much she meant not only to me but to all of her classmates."

"It has also challenged my Catholic faith. I have always believed that God not only gives us crosses to bear but also the grace to endure them. This cross has been incredibly hard to bear."

Judge Haskins says, "Ms. Murphy, I admire your courage in providing this testimony this evening. Could I ask how you have honored Lily's memory?"

Regina wipes a tear from her eye. "It's become my mission to ensure that her legacy lives on through the values I teach and the community we build in our classroom."

Cassie sits in silence, her thoughts a chaotic echo of Regina's words. The weight of her choices presses heavily on her chest, each one a stone pulling her down. She grips the chair, fighting the urge to retreat into ignorance. Yet, a fragile spark flickers inside her—a glimmer of hope.

Two paths lie before her: one shrouded in darkness, the other glowing with the promise of change. Goosebumps race up her arms as she feels the tension of her choice, urging her to step toward the light.

As Regina finishes, the judge clears his throat, drawing everyone's attention. "Ms. Murphy, what would you like to say to Cassandra Thompson?"

Regina pauses to compose herself. "Your Honor, I believe in forgiveness, as my Catholic faith teaches. Until this evening, I couldn't understand what had happened on that tragic night. Holding on to my anger won't bring Lily back."

Regina composes herself and looks skyward, as if seeking guidance.

"I choose to forgive Ms. Thompson, who helped me when I fell in the ballroom, even though she had no reason to do so. I see the good in her and pray she faces the consequences of her actions and turns her life around in honor of Lily's memory and everyone else here tonight."

As she turns to leave, her gaze locks onto Judge Haskins. "I respect all that you have done for our community over the years. Keeping us safe. I still don't understand why you had to put us through this ordeal." Regina's voice trembles as she looks at Judge Haskins, her anger spilling over.

"I can see the pain in your eyes, Judge Haskins, and it breaks my heart to think you had to create these terrible games. Why did it have to come to this? We are all suffering here, and it feels unjust to turn our grief into a spectacle."

Regina gazes around the room. "I feel a darkness in this house. I pray you forgive Cassie and restore light to this grand manor and to yourself."

Regina leaves the library in silence, not looking back. Her footsteps trail off as she steps into the Grand Hallway.

Cassie notices the subtle change in Judge Haskins' expression and recognizes it as an opening. When Regina's words hang in the air, showing a mix of surprise and pain on his face, Cassie senses a chance. The judge's usual stoic demeanor softens briefly, revealing the burden he carries and hinting at a vulnerable moment she might use.

Perhaps she still has a chance of escaping.

Thirty-Nine

J udith stands tall and proud as she addresses The judge. "My name is Judith Whitehall. I have been a resident of the Mayfair neighborhood for most of my life. I am a retired nurse and a widow for the past five years." Her voice is steady and clear, carrying a hint of the authority she once commanded in the ER.

Judge Haskins asks, "Mrs. Whitehall, can you tell us about your nursing career?"

"Your Honor, I chose nursing to support patients through their toughest times and provide them with the care they need. I've learned that nursing is about compassion and support, not just medical care."

She shares her experiences in critical care, where she faced the fragile line between life and death.

"Every ICU shift tested my skills," she says. "I celebrated small victories of those who fought hard and held patients' hands as they took their final breath."

"My final days as a nurse involved taking care of my husband before he died. I retired soon after and got busy living life with my extended family."

The judge asks Mrs. Whitehall, "Can you tell us how you knew Lily Cochrane?"

Judith replies, "Yes, Your Honor. My granddaughter, Holly, and Lily became friends in preschool as they lived across the street from each other and attended the same school. I've known Lily and her family for years."

The judge nods and asks her to tell him more about their friendship.

Judith reflects, "They were inseparable during school. Holly often mentioned Lily's kindness and their shared love of art. Lily was a bright, creative girl who joined us for family gatherings, and I always found her polite and well-mannered."

The Grand Ballroom falls silent as Judge Haskins' deep voice resonates again. "Mrs. Whitehall, I understand you were present on the night of the tragic accident. Can you tell us what happened on that fateful evening?"

Judith, trembling with emotion, begins. "Yes, Your Honor. That evening, I was babysitting; my granddaughter and Lily were playing in our living room. As Lily prepared to leave and walk across the street to her house, I heard them say their goodbyes. I was upstairs doing laundry at the time. A few moments later, I heard a muffled sound from outside." Judith's voice breaks as she fights back tears.

"I went downstairs and looked outside and saw Lily lying on the street. Holly was standing next to me, screaming. I rushed outside and saw that something like a car had hit Lily. I called 911 for help. I ... tried to comfort her... but she was unconscious and barely breathing."

Judith collects herself. "After a few minutes, I saw Emilio arriving in his ambulance. He rushed to Lily's side and tried to help her. My granddaughter was hysterical, and I did my best to comfort her." Judith's voice cracks as she recalls the tragic scene.

She took a moment to compose herself before continuing. "I will never forget the look on Mr. Garcia's face as he worked hard to save Lily. It was as if he knew she was dying."

Judge Haskins asks, "Tell us, Mrs. Whitehall, how did the events of that evening affect you and your granddaughter's life?"

"That night left a lasting impact on my granddaughter and me," she begins, her voice steady yet filled with emotion. "The memory of that horrible crash still haunts me every day. I still see Lily lying on the ground, her young life slipping away. That night changed us, and we're still coming to terms with her death."

Judith's voice trembles. "Holly has tried to cope with what happened. But slowly she became withdrawn, unable to come to terms with the loss of her friend. She has struggled in school since the accident, and is still trying to find joy in the things she once loved. I enrolled Holly in grief counseling for pre-teens, and it has helped her. But she is still so heartbroken."

"As a grandmother, watching her suffer breaks my heart, and I do my best to provide comfort and support during those dark times. Neither of us has been the same since."

Judge Haskins listens, a look of sympathy on his face. "Mrs. Whitehall," he says, his deep voice filling the courtroom, "can you tell us about the community's response to this tragic event?"

Judith collected her thoughts, the heaviness of her words weighing on the silent room. "Our neighborhood changed forever. The block where children played and families gathered became a somber reminder of that tragedy. We organized candlelight vigils and supported Lily's family, but the void left by her absence is still with us."

"Mrs. Whitehall, what would you like to say to Ms. Thompson?"

Judith turns toward Cassie, tears welling up in her eyes.

"I am here today at the request of Judge Haskins. I had no desire to see you in person; I dreaded this moment. However, this elaborate deception allowed me to observe you. Like everyone here, I welcomed that opportunity. However, as the day went on, I felt something different. I wanted to hate you. But ... you helped me in the last game today. I saw compassion in your eyes, a person I wasn't expecting—someone who had lost her way, not a despicable killer."

"Judge Haskins has promised us you will receive justice for your actions and a chance to make up for what you have done to us ... and yourself. It takes everything in me to say this ... I want you to know I will be there for you if you need me. You deserve a second chance. We all do."

Cassie's breath catches as she processes Judith's unexpected forgiveness. Warmth floods her, and the tension in her shoulders eases. Tears well in her eyes as Judith's gentle smile wraps around her like a comforting embrace, illuminating the courtroom with newfound compassion.

Judith faces Judge Haskins, her voice firm but tinged with anger. "Your Honor," she begins, pointing an accusatory finger at Judge Haskins, "Cassie must face the legal repercussions of her actions. Your duty is to deliver justice, not to serve your personal agenda. Please remember the impact your decisions have on our lives." Her words linger in the air, heavy with shared grief and anger.

Judge Haskins' face turns cold, clearly upset with Judith's scolding.

Judith wipes the tears from her eyes and leaves the Grand Ballroom of Eberly Manor, her shoulders shaking with silent sobs.

Forty

Thomas, his angry face etched with pain, steps forward. He grips the railing of the witness stand, his knuckles white. His eyes, red-rimmed and fierce, settle briefly on Judge Haskins's before landing on the defendant, Cassandra Thompson.

Judge Haskins addresses Thomas firmly. "Before you give your statement, remember the rules you already agreed to."

Thomas takes a deep breath, his eyes never leaving Cassandra's. The judge's men walk over and flank him, their eyes alert and attentive to any sign of aggression.

"Please state your name and your relationship to Lily."

He grips the podium with white knuckles. "My name is Thomas Cochrane. I am … *was* Lily's father."

Cassie stifles a gasp, her stomach turning to lead.

Thomas's voice remains steady, but his grief is evident as he continues his testimony. "Lily was a kind and compassionate soul. She had a smile that could light up the room and a heart as big as the sky. She was only ten years old when she was taken from us, but in her short life, she had already touched many people with her warmth and generosity."

Thomas's eyes flick to the defendant, Cassie. "My daughter was wise beyond her years. She loved animals and had a passion for art. She dreamed of becoming a veterinarian and traveling the world to help those in need."

"You have already heard how she loved reading, and she shared that love with other students. That was my daughter, always thinking of others…"

Thomas's voice cracks as he speaks, his eyes glistening with unshed tears. "Lily's death has left a terrible hole in my life. My wife passed away in March, losing her battle with cancer. And now I'm alone, seeking justice for my daughter."

Thomas takes a deep breath and addresses Judge Haskins. "I hold you responsible, Judge Haskins, for creating this bizarre situation. If you hadn't insisted on including Elizabeth, Regina, Emilio, and Judith, I could have resolved this matter as soon as Cassie arrived. None of them wanted to be here in the first place. No one wanted to play your ridiculous games. Your games are obsolete, just as your crumbling manor is. And you."

Judge Haskins responds icily, "Remember this, Thomas. I uncovered the truth in this matter and brought everyone here. It is my judgment that will prevail, not yours."

The judge pauses. "Now, Mr. Cochrane, what do you want to say to Ms. Thompson?"

Thomas takes a threatening step toward Cassie; the guards grab him by the arms. "You took my daughter from me," he says, his voice shaking with rage. Thomas presses his trembling hand to his chest, trying to catch his breath, but the weight inside him only grows heavier.

"Lily was just ten years old and already a shining light of kindness. I want you to understand that I will never forgive you for what you've done. You took my daughter's life, and now my wife has died too. You tore apart my family."

Thomas's eyes burn with fury; his words convey a father's deep anguish. "I hope you understand the magnitude of your crime. I will be waiting for you when you get out of jail."

Judge Haskins stands. "Mr. Cochrane, I am warning you..."

Thomas cuts him off. "Lily was my reason for living, and I will make sure everyone understands the depth of my loss." Thomas shakes his head. "Why did you have to kill her ... my precious Lily?"

The judge motions for his associates to move closer to Thomas. "There were moments I wanted to take justice into my own hands ... but even that wouldn't bring her back. The judge may now provide justice as the law demands, but someday I will give you my own form of justice. You will never hurt anyone else the way you hurt my Lily. I will make sure that you suffer for the rest of your life, and you rot in jail."

Thomas turns and storms out of the Grand Hall and Eberly Manor as the judge's associates follow behind him.

Cassie's hands tremble as she grips the witness stand, her knuckles pale against the wood. She blinks rapidly, fighting back tears as Thomas's anguish echoes in her ears. The room blurs around her, shadows creeping in as panic claws at her throat. Her heart races, each beat a reminder of the life she took, and the guilt settles in a heavy knot in her stomach, twisting with every memory of Lily's innocent smile.

Forty-One

A s the last echoes of Thomas and the guards fade, Judge Haskins and Cassie are finally alone in the Grand Hall.

As Cassie thinks of the raw, aching testimonies, guilt coils around her heart. Each word is a stark reminder of the life she extinguished. She sees Lily's face, framed by the pain she's caused. The magnitude of her actions blocks any path forward. What can she do now? Every instinct in her screams to run, to hide, yet a part of her craves accountability. But uncertainty paralyzes her; how can she seek redemption when she is the architect of Lily's death?

The judge addresses Cassie in a firm but measured tone. "Ms. Thompson," he begins, "the matter before us this evening is of significant consequence. You must understand the choices you have to make."

"First, I will proceed to the presentation of the overwhelming evidence that has been gathered in this case. This is a courtesy to you, Ms. Thompson, to help you make the right decision moving forward."

"The charges against you are grave. You are accused of vehicular homicide in the first degree, stemming from the death of Lily Cochrane on the evening of March 14th of last year."

"We have considerable evidence that you were operating a red Mercedes convertible registered to you at the time of the collision."

"Surveillance footage prompted the 8th Precinct to obtain a warrant for GPS and cell phone tracking of your vehicle, confirming you were at the accident scene shortly after you left the Somerton Bar & Grill. We presume you turned off your lights and took a winding route home to avoid cameras. Fragments of a car found at the scene match your vehicle. This evidence proves your involvement in the tragic death of Lily Cochrane on March 14th, 2023, Ms. Thompson. I recommend you record your full confession for the police. I will read you your Miranda rights and ensure judicial review of your statement."

Cassie's mind races as she considers any possibility to help her counter the judge's demand for a confession. She knows she needs a solid strategy to appeal the request on procedural grounds. Judge Haskins' proposal not only appeals to her conscience but serves as a strategic move, as a confession could impact how the court views her character during sentencing, affecting her punishment.

Cassie, usually the epitome of confidence and self-assurance, experiences a chill running down her spine. The testimony offered by Judge Haskins is, on the surface, damning. She tries to clear her mind and decide what to do.

She analyzes the evidence presented by the judge, looking for any flaws in his case. The evidence at the scene matches her car, even though it has been repaired and repainted to look new. She reviews any other supporting evidence not mentioned by the judge.

They lack conclusive evidence that she was driving at the time of the accident. Surveillance footage shows her drinking but not driving. The car parts found at the scene can be explained, and without a confession, there's no solid proof connecting her to the driver's seat. Her law firm has many ways to spin this. She is heartbroken, but is it time to consider the unthinkable? Ultimately, what is right?

Cassie considers her options. Her life hangs in the balance; The judge's circumstantial evidence could influence the jury. With a solid legal team, she might argue that the judge coerced her confession, potentially harming his career. But confessing might bring closure to Lily Cochrane's family and result in a lighter sentence. Still, it also means facing serious consequences—five to ten years in prison and shame for her mother. The weight of her decision presses on her.

Conflicting emotions storm Cassie, leaving her thoughts in chaos. Despite the heaviness of the charges and evidence against her, she knows her legal skills might offer a way out—but at what cost? The silence in the Grand Ballroom is deafening. She wonders, "What would my mom do?" Memories of that tragic night flood her mind: a scream, a terrible impact, her escape. The guilt is overwhelming, and she understands that facing justice means accepting responsibility for the pain caused to Lily's family and friends. Judith's promise sinks in, a final guidepost for Cassie.

In that moment, Cassie realizes that acknowledging her wrongdoing would be the first step toward healing for herself and toward honoring Lily's memory, even if it means enduring the harsh scrutiny of the law. She knows her mother and her friends will stand by her. She can no longer deal with the grief that weighs on her.

Her mother's words from the other day echo in her mind: Forgiveness is the only path to peace. *Don't let darkness overshadow the light of your future, no matter how hard the road.* Cassie understands that the time is now.

She takes a long, deep breath and faces Judge Haskins.

"Judge Haskins," she declares, her voice rising with an intensity that echoes off the cold, sterile walls of the mansion. "I am prepared to face the consequences of my actions. I demand to be taken to the 8th District station now! I will surrender myself and sign my confession there. No more evasion, no more hiding, and no more games!" The frustration surging within her reaches a boiling point. Her fists clench at her sides.

"I owe it to those I faced today to give them the closure they deserve. I will not admit any guilt in this wretched place to you, nor will I sign any document under your jurisdiction. Please take me upstairs now!" Her resolve is unwavering, and she stares at the judge, every fiber of her being radiating fierce determination that leaves no doubt about her stance.

Judge Haskins approaches Cassie. "Very well, Ms. Thompson. If that is your decision…" Judge Haskins turns to his men. "Please take Ms. Thompson to the library so she may gather her possessions."

Forty-Two

Cassie follows Judge Haskins into the library and finds all her possessions folded neatly in the corner. She notices her phone and car keys are not there. She takes a nervous breath as she turns around and faces him, her heart racing. "Judge Haskins," she begins, her voice steady but low, "I want to leave *now*."

Judge Haskins turns to Cassie, his eyes filled with an evil glint. "I'm sorry, Ms. Thompson, I'm afraid that if you will not face up to your deeds under my terms, in my mansion, in my courtroom, there will be no leaving for you. Regrettably, you and I need to play one more game before the night is out. And I'm afraid this is a game that you cannot win."

Cassie's heart sinks as a chilling realization washes over her: the judge's twisted smile reveals his true intentions, plunging her into a suffocating abyss of despair. Judge Haskins had never intended for her to leave Eberly Manor. The games were only a devious MacGuffin. Shadows of betrayal envelop her, and an icy dread grips her throat as she considers the depths to which he has sunk, leaving her trapped in a nightmare of her own making.

She knows her only opportunity to seize the advantage depends on unveiling Judge Haskins' hidden motives and the glaring inconsistencies in the evidence stacked against her. Her only chance is to go on the offensive. *Use her experience and instincts.*

Cassie stares into Judge Haskin's face. "Now that I know what you're involved in, Judge. I can imagine how the diligent detectives in the 8th District will react when they realize how you betrayed them and twisted justice. You may as well follow me there."

Judge Haskins replies, "You believe you can dictate terms? You have no leverage."

Cassie steps closer, voice low. "I have all the leverage I need. Five witnesses to your cruel games and my unlawful imprisonment. Illegal use of ex parte. Should I keep going?"

She studies his expression, searching for any sign of agreement. This is more than a deal; it's her only chance to protect herself while navigating a treacherous game.

The judge raises a finger and sneers at Cassie. "Oh no, Ms. Thompson. You will not walk away unscathed from this. I will ensure that you face the truth of your choices and how they affect others. My role is to guide you toward redemption, but this won't be a simple path to follow."

Cassie takes a step closer, her eyes locking onto Judge Haskins with defiance and determination.

"I saw the photos in your study—of your family, of your family legacy, of the people who loved and respected you.

"There were many photos of a woman you clearly cared about. How would she feel about your actions?"

Judge Haskins replies coldly, "My sister Constance has felt nothing since Jason Carter murdered her twenty years ago. Ironically, it was your law firm that helped free her killer by tampering with evidence. I can see where you learned your skills,

Ms. Thompson."

"You see, with the actions of your associates, your courtroom antics, and your unforgivable hit-and-run murder of Lily Cochrane, all the pieces are in place for this inevitable conclusion."

Cassie feels the chilling weight of inevitability suffocating her, knowing with gut-wrenching clarity that the specter of death lurks just beyond the shadows, waiting to claim her.

Judge Haskins walks over to the fireplace and picks up a well-worn book. He leans back, a smile on his lips as he watches Cassie. "Have you ever read 'The Cask of Amontillado' by Edgar Allan Poe?" he asks, his tone tinged with a hint of condescension.

Cassie composes herself and furrows her brow, confused by the sudden shift in the conversation. "Yes, I know the story," she replies, unsure of where he's going with this.

The judge's eyes shine with a mixture of amusement and threat. "You see, it's a tale of revenge and betrayal, where the protagonist lures his victim into a trap, sealing him away to face a grim fate. Do you understand the implications of such a story, Ms. Thompson? It's a reminder that even in the guise of the law, danger often lurks barely beneath the surface."

A chill runs down Cassie's spine as she makes an uneasy comparison in her mind. The suffocating atmosphere of the library, once filled with the comforting scent of old books and ink, now feels like a crypt. She can hear echoes of laughter and the distant clinking of wine glasses, replaced by a deafening silence that seems ready to swallow her whole.

"Do you want to spend the rest of your life in prison for killing me?"

The judge chuckles, "No worries there, Ms. Thompson. You see, I will soon join you in your upcoming fate. My doctor says I have at most three months to live. Prostate cancer. Such an ugly way to die. But as you ultimately will, I accept full responsibility for my actions."

With sudden resolve, Cassie turns on her heels, her heart pounding as she runs towards the door. The shadows stretch out toward her, mocking her retreat. *I can't let this happen*, urgency flooding her mind.

Cassie reaches for the door handle, her fingers trembling. The door is locked. She kicks it, trying to make it yield.

She feels a prick in her neck, and everything goes dark.

* * *

Cassie's eyes flutter open, the haze of unconsciousness clearing like fog under morning light. She inhales, the musty air clinging to her throat as if it has its own weight. The smell of damp brick envelops her—a mix of earthiness and stale air—prickling her nostrils and making her skin crawl. Pushing up on her elbows, she squints through the gloom, tracing the damp walls. They threaten like silent sentinels, their rough surfaces jagged and foreboding, a chill seeping into the air.

A small opening allowed a weak beam of light to enter, its glow fading and unsteady, as though it was also afraid to confront the shadows. The light stretches out, casting elongated shapes that twist and writhe in the dark corners, where silence wraps around her like a heavy blanket.

A knot uncoils and twists tightly in her chest, each racing thought tightening its grip. Panic blooms inside her, icy tendrils creeping into her heart, constricting as the harsh reality of her isolation seeps in. Her head spins; the air feels thin and stifling—an echoing reminder of the surrounding solitude—a silence so profound it seems a living thing, suffocating her spirit.

She scrambles to her feet, her heart pounding. "Hello? Is anyone there?" she calls out, her voice echoing off the solid walls. Silence answers her, deepening her fear.

In the dim light, Cassie searches the floor for anything to help her climb. The area is sparse, covered with dust and cobwebs, and it feels claustrophobic and uninviting. She presses her back against the wall, feeling for ledges or cracks that might offer a foothold. The smell of damp floors and decaying wood from old barrels surrounds her. It is a frightening place.

With renewed urgency, she tests her surroundings again, her fingers touching the cold, unyielding bricks. If she can reach that opening …

As she surveys her surroundings, fragments of her last words to Judge Haskins flood her thoughts: the menacing smile, the chilling words about revenge, and the sharp prick she felt before everything went black. A wave of realization hits her: the judge has drugged her. She's trapped.

In a sudden burst of inspiration, she stacks loose debris. Large pieces of barrels lie in one corner, their wooden shards giving her a chance to reach the small gap above.

Breathing heavily, she works quickly, adrenaline fueling her movements. Every sound amplified, making her wonder if anyone nearby was listening. As she steadies her makeshift ladder, she hears a distant noise. Footsteps? Her heart skips a beat, and she freezes, straining to hear more.

She needs to hurry; this might be her only chance. Climbing as fast as she can, she reaches for the opening and peers out, her fingertips brushing the edge. As she grabs the ledge, the footsteps grow louder, and she realizes she might not be alone for long. Desperation builds inside her, and she knows she must escape before it's too late.

She watches the door creak open, and Cassie's heart sinks as Judge Haskins steps into the dim light filtering through the opening. He stands tall, a dark silhouette against the faint glow, and a wicked smile spreads across his face.

"Ah, Ms. Thompson," he begins, his voice calm, echoing off the cold brick walls like a sinister lullaby. "How poetic that you find yourself in this little sanctuary of your own making. You see, you built this tomb brick by brick through your choices and actions. Every decision you made led you here, to this precise moment."

Cassie's grip tightens on the ledge as dread washes over her. She can't let him hear her fear. "What do you want from me?" she demands, trying to sound defiant despite the tremor in her voice. He steps closer, his gaze intense.

"What I want, Cassie, is for you to understand the consequences of your decisions. Each time you choose to bend the law for your advantage, you add another layer to this prison. Only extraordinary circumstances can justify bringing this judgment upon anyone. As much as it pains me, today is such a case."

"What do you want me to do?" she says, terror in her voice. "I'll do whatever you ask. I'll sign your confession."

"It's too late for that. All I want you to do now is embrace your final journey, Cassie. Confront your judgment," he replies, stepping back into the shadows. "Only then can redemption be a possibility. Until then, only this tomb remains your reality."

Cassie looks up and sees the judge's face at the small opening. "Four more bricks to go, and not just any bricks. These are bricks extracted by the police as evidence from the crosswalk where Lily met her death. Many thanks to Chief Vanover from the 8th District for retrieving these from evidence for me."

The judge carefully places each brick, and the dim light fades, plunging Cassie into profound darkness. As her fate becomes clear, a chilling numbness spreads from her fingertips to her core, leaving her paralyzed by fear and regret. Every fleeting thought echoes in her mind, a jumble of what-ifs and wishes, drowning out her instinct to fight as she faces the haunting truth that she may never see the light of day again.

The library door shuts behind her, leaving Cassie alone with the echo of his words. Utter chaos. Total darkness. She takes a trembling breath and starts to scream…

Forty-Three

I t's 9:00 am on Sunday, and everyone at the precinct scrambles to find information on Cassie's location. Janelle stands at her desk, the burden of the hit-and-run case pressing on her shoulders. The flickering fluorescent light above cast a harsh glow on the piles of paperwork surrounding her. She taps her pen against the notepad. What do the initials on Cassie's calendar, 'EM', mean? Cassie Thompson has disappeared without a trace and is most likely on the run. The BOLO has produced no leads so far.

As Janelle leans over the cluttered table, the significance of the evidence presses on her mind. She catches sight of Cassie's laptop, its screen dark and lifeless, a fortress of digital information sealed when they need it most.

The forensics team swarms around the scene, their tech-savvy fingers deftly working to bypass the barriers Cassie has erected. Janelle watches them, a gnawing feeling settling in the pit of her stomach. She can't shake the thought that the answers they seek will be as elusive as the woman herself.

Her thoughts swirl with questions: *What secrets lie locked inside? Is there a hidden message, a cry for help, or perhaps even more evidence of Cassie's guilt amidst the chaos?* The urgency of the situation presses on her; each passing second feels like another heartbeat lost in the relentless race against time. *What twisted choice drives Cassie into this tragedy? At what cost will the truth come to light?*

Janelle must carefully strategize her next steps. The shocking revelation of Chief Vanover's collusion with Judge Haskins casts doubt over the investigation, risking not just the case but the entire district. She knows that to weaken their hold, she must gather evidence cautiously—through surveillance, interviews, and discreet methods—building a strong case without drawing attention. Trust is limited, so she needs to find allies within the precinct who share her commitment to justice while avoiding the watchful eyes of Chief Vanover and Judge Haskins.

Lost in her thoughts, she barely notices the buzz of her phone until it jolts her back to the present. The caller ID displays "WHITEHALL, JUDITH", a name she doesn't recognize. A flicker of curiosity mixes with confusion as she answers.

"Detective Janelle Robinson, 8th District, how can I help you?"

Judith's voice is urgent. "Detective Robinson, I heard on the news this morning that the police are looking for Cassie Thompson. The one responsible for the hit-and-run accident that killed the little girl. Is she at your station?"

Janelle says, "No, we're still looking for her. Do you have any information about her whereabouts?"

"I was with her yesterday at Eberly Manor, and I fear for her safety."

Janelle gestures for Detective Fenn and Coles to come over. "Judith, please hold on a moment. I'm going to transfer you to our conference room."

* * *

Janelle, Detective Coles, and Fenn race across the countryside toward Eberly Manor. The mysterious 'EM' on Cassie's calendar. What Judith told them sounded like something straight out of a twisted Agatha Christie novel. Horrific games orchestrated by Judge Robert Haskins aimed to force a confession from Cassie Thompson about Lily Cochrane's death. Detective Fenn confirmed Judith's story by talking with Emilio Garcia and Regina Murphy, and they agreed to come to the station to give their statements.

As Janelle, Coles, and Fenn race toward Eberly Manor, the tension in the car is thick. Janelle grips the steering wheel, her heart pounding. She knows they don't have probable cause for a warrant, and Judge Haskins won't agree to a search without it.

"What the fuck?" Janelle says, her voice edged with disbelief. "Judge Haskins is such a respected judge. How could he have spiraled into something so twisted? It's insanity!"

Coles shifts in the passenger seat, his brow furrowed. "That instability makes him unpredictable … and dangerous. If he feels cornered, there's no telling how far he might go. All three witnesses described several armed guards." His tone is serious, reflecting their growing concern. "We're dealing with someone who's supposed to uphold the law, yet here he is, crossing every line."

Fenn leans forward, scanning the road ahead. "And from what Judith described, he knows every detail about our investigation."

Janelle remembers the mysterious phone call to an unknown judge in Chief Vanover's office, which makes her sick. "Our commanding officer gave it to him. And who knows who else?" Janelle thinks. *Priority one: get Cassie back to face justice and contact internal review to address the matter with Vanover.*

∗ ∗ ∗

Janelle's car pulls up to the gates of Eberly Manor. They are open, with the statuesque ravens beckoning them inside.

Janelle says, "Stay alert—we know armed guards are inside. I don't care what Judge Haskin's reputation is. Be ready for anything. Check your weapons and body cameras now. Look for any signs of Cassie or her car on the premises so we can claim probable cause for a search of the house."

Janelle, Coles, and Fenn approach the imposing door. The house is dead silent, with only the call of hawks in the distance.

Janelle knocks on the door. After a few seconds, the door opens, and a burly man stands in the doorway.

"Philly PD. We need to speak to Judge Haskins *now*."

The man escorts them inside without a word and directs them to the sitting room.

Judge Haskins lounges in his luxurious chair, holding a brandy and smoking a cigar. The crackling fireplace casts sharp shadows across his face. Wearing traditional trial robes, he exudes authority. The deep black fabric contrasts with his crisp, starched white collar. He greets the detectives with a mischievous smile.

Janelle speaks. "Judge Robert Haskins, we need you to come down to headquarters to discuss the whereabouts of Cassie Thompson and the unlawful imprisonment of several other individuals last evening."

Judge Haskins rises and reaches out his hand to Janelle. "Ah, Detective Robinson, so nice to meet you again. I've been expecting you...."

Forty-Four

Six months later

Sunlight, a river of gold, pours through the soaring Gothic arches of Eberly Manor, illuminating the motes of dust pirouetting in its radiant beam. Amy follows her husband, Andrew, through the ornate oak entrance doors, a paint sample gripped in her hand. They walk into the main hallway, their precocious daughter Rachel in tow. Three months have elapsed since they acquired the 100-year-old mansion, a breathtaking Gothic-style residence.

After years of searching, Amy and Andrew Henderson were astounded to find a serendipitous listing. A property that had been unavailable for many years unexpectedly became available after the owner's passing three months earlier. They bought it sight unseen. And today was their grand tour.

Amy envisions the corridor adorned with a luxurious Persian runner. *A rich burgundy,* she ponders, *would beautifully contrast with the light-hued stone.* Andrew and his enterprising wife assess the area with knowing smiles and chuckles.

Amy, the family's home decorator, built a successful business, and a prominent local magazine listed her among the top ten in the Philadelphia area. She is also an accomplished clarinet player and tours three months a year with various Philadelphia Chamber Orchestral groups. The Hendersons' passion and energy are in the early stages of transforming Eberly

Manor into a vibrant home, filled with love, creativity, and a bright future.

They head up the stairs and stop first at the master bedroom. The suite, with its lofty ceilings and ornate moldings, inspires grand plans. "The master suite needs a new chandelier," Amy decides, pausing at the doorway. "Something dramatic, maybe crystal. It needs to be worthy of this bedroom!" Andrew grins, already picturing the sparkling centerpiece above their bed.

"I've also dreamed of a four-poster bed," Amy confesses, her eyes sparkling. "Something regal, with intricate carvings and luxurious drapes."

Rachel, her six-year-old impatience evident, interrupts with a demanding, "Daddy, can I *pleeeease* see my room now?" "Of course, sweetheart," he replies, "it's the next room on our tour."

As they continue down the hall, Amy cannot help but smile at her daughter's eagerness. She shares Rachel's excitement, knowing that her bedroom will be a space of wonder and magic. Turning her creative eye to the task, Amy envisions a space filled with soft, warm light, much like the hallway's golden glow.

A delicate peach hue would adorn the walls, creating a cozy and inviting atmosphere. Underfoot, a plush rug with a subtle floral pattern would add a whimsical touch, providing a comfortable space for Rachel to play and explore. A well-adorned box sits on the end table ... locked.

The centerpiece of Rachel's room will be a beautiful canopy bed draped with sheer curtains, and Amy believes this will create an enchanting space for her imagination to flourish. A cozy window seat will provide the perfect spot for reading and taking in the manor's view of the grounds. Rachel will spread out her stuffed animals to keep her company as she dreams. Amy knows this transformation will surpass her daughter's expectations, creating a room where she can grow and make lasting memories. She can't wait to see Rachel's joy as she explores her fairy-tale sanctuary.

They move to the guest bedroom, but they find the door locked. "Hmmm ... looks like I need to talk to the agent again," Andrew remarks as they walk down the stairs.

The family moves through the bottom floor, buzzing with ideas. In the spacious kitchen with its worn cabinetry, Amy dreams of a modern makeover, picturing sleek appliances and a marble-topped island for gourmet cooking. Rachel excitedly suggests a baking corner for her favorite hobby, and Andrew promises to build a custom station for her. Inspired, Amy envisions hosting elegant dinner parties that mix old-world charm with modern style.

They move into the conservatory; "The light in here is magical," Amy breathes, as if speaking too loudly might break the spell cast by the golden rays streaming through the windows.

Andrew, ever practical, nods in agreement. "It'll be perfect for your recitals. We should host your wind ensemble as well once we're settled."

Amy's eyes light up at the suggestion; her mind is already planning the event. "Oh, Andrew, can you imagine? A summer soiree with the garden in full bloom and the house glowing. It would be enchanting!" Their laughter and lively conversations echo through the halls, a striking contrast to the mansion's former silence and neglect.

The library is at the end of the hall, featuring high vaulted ceilings and tall, half-empty bookshelves that extend nearly to the ceiling. She imagines cozy reading corners and warm lamps, inviting readers to curl up with books. The idea of filling the shelves with a diverse collection—classic novels, historical books, murder mysteries, and children's books for Rachel—excites her. She pictures family game nights with their favorite board games spread out on a large table.

As they approach the magnificent fireplace, a detail catches Amy's eye. "Andrew," she says softly, pointing to a section of the brickwork. "Look at those bricks. They're a different shade." Andrew examines the fireplace. Several bricks near the top of the hearth were of different colors and textures, a subtle discrepancy in the otherwise uniform stone.

"That's funny," Andrew says, his voice thoughtful. "I wonder if it's a repair job from ages ago. Maybe they used salvaged bricks?" He places a hand on Amy's shoulder, his touch reassuring.

"I think it's cool. It gives the fireplace some personality."

"I agree; it gives it charm." She laughs, and Andrew grins.

"We can keep them if you want, but we can always remodel, or tear out the entire wall ..."

Forty-Five

1 Week Later

Detective Robinson stands back, watching as Barry, the Chester County coroner, extracts a body from a wall in the library of Eberly Manor. The process is delicate, and Janelle's keen eye misses nothing. The team lays the young woman's remains on a black tarp.

Barry grimaces under the library's dim glow and gestures towards the remains. As he steps closer, he can't shake the unease curling in his stomach. The remains lay sprawled on a tarp, surrounded by disarray; the half-closed pages of a tattered manuscript and scattered letters, some of which were stained, perhaps by time or something more sinister.

Janelle's gloved hand hovers over a few scattered artifacts, remnants of a life once lived. The dim light catches the glint of a silver locket, its clasp broken, containing a photograph of an aging face next to a farmhouse. She finds himself lost in the image, at odds with the cruel reality of the scene.

Barry says, "My initial estimate places the woman's age between twenty-five and thirty, and the decay suggests the body has been here for three to six months. The cause of death is hard to determine, considering the state of the body. I'll let the lab figure that out."

Janelle pauses over the body, her delicate features and long blonde hair illuminated by the harsh overhead lights. She gazes at the remains, a terrible weight settling in her chest. The coroner methodically prepares to take the body away, but Janelle knows deep down who this is. Justice, she thinks, cruelly served, yet it's not what she hoped for and never what the victim deserved.

Personal documents lie scattered near the body, serving as chilling evidence of a cruelty that defies understanding. The body, still and lifeless, clutches a fragile locket between her fingers—a silent testament to the secrets it holds. Janelle's heart aches as she remembers Cassie Thompson, the vibrant girl full of dreams, now reduced to this tragic fate. If only Cassie could have had a second chance.

Regret swirls in Janelle's mind, each "what if" echoing louder than the last. What if she had made different choices? What if she hadn't crossed paths with Judge Haskins?

As she prepares for this evening's press briefing, Janelle steels herself. She will share the details of Cassie's disappearance, hoping to provide family and friends, including her team of detectives, with the closure they desperately need.

* * *

After his arrest, Judge Haskins refused to discuss Cassie's whereabouts, insisting on silence until his death three months later while confined in a secure medical facility. Janelle searched tirelessly for Cassie, retracing their steps through the busy streets of Mayfair and making unsuccessful subpoena requests to her law firm for Cassie's location. Judge Hastings's reluctance to share information only added to the mystery surrounding her disappearance. Despite many inquiries from investigators and concerned family members, Judge Haskins remained silent, leaving Cassie's fate unanswered. As time went on, those close to

Cassie grew increasingly desperate for answers, hoping for any clue that might lead them to her.

Janelle feels regret as she reflects on Judge Robert Haskins, once a symbol of justice, whose family legacy is now tainted by corruption. The magnitude of his downfall makes her speculate how a man who was once a pillar of the judiciary could have fallen so far into darkness.

Janelle signals her team to retrieve the cadaver dogs from the police van and bring them into the hall. Buddy, a basset hound, and Sandy, a golden labrador, wait for their work to begin. Their handlers hold their leashes taut, guiding them first to the body, allowing the ancient wood and stone to signal the scent of death. Then, freedom.

Their hurried paws thump against the old oak floors, creating a frantic rhythm. Buddy shuffles toward the first-floor conservatory, his leash stretching tight. Sandy runs up the stairs, Detective Fenn close behind. Janelle knows Sandy catches a scent. The slight change in her posture and the tightening of her jaw speak volumes. Buddy's bark, sharp and commanding, cuts through the heavy silence.

Janelle pats Buddy's head. "Tell me what you found, boy."

Buddy points with his nose toward the in-wall bookcase and barks to be understood. Janelle rushes in. "Everyone, back up. Now. Sergeant, please radio in. We have another body. This looks like a major crime scene."

In its Gothic grandeur, Eberly Manor feels more like a mausoleum than a crime scene, its secrets whispered by the wind as it weaves through the decaying woodwork. It has become a tomb.

In the distance, Janelle hears Sandy barking upstairs, alerting Detective Fenn to another discovery. Janelle's blood runs cold. *How many more bodies will we find here? How many people have lost their lives because of twisted justice?*

Janelle heaves a deep sigh and gets to work.

Acknowledgements

This book wouldn't have been possible without the incredible support and contributions of many individuals. My heartfelt thanks go out to each of you.

To my editors:
Rachele, my editor-in-chief, and Donna, my line editor, whose guidance and commitment helped to bring this book to life.

Alyssa Matesic, developmental editor. Helped the book come together, although I had to kill a few of my darlings in the process. The happy-hour scene will be re-imagined in the next book.

Becca: line and copy editing, for her excellent job in pointing out how many pet words I used. I killed them as well.

Tami Jeffers for her final edits.

To my beta readers:
Amanda, Matt & Lisa, Chris, and David.
Allison, E.K. Earle, Gemma, and Micheala Stahl
Marina Myles, Mina, Sophia A, Stella T

Also:
- To Ruth Ware, Riley Sager, and S.A. Barnes, whose books and support helped inspire me as an author.
- Alan Parsons, after hearing his first album, inspired me to read the works of Edgar Allan Poe, and this gave me the idea for this book.
- The Dunkin' store in Eagle, PA, for providing much-needed coffee.

Thank you for purchasing and reading my book. I truly appreciate it and hope you enjoyed it. Please consider leaving a review online. Your feedback and support mean a lot and help me continue doing what I love.

Here's how you can leave a review:

1) Scan the QR code on this page and go directly to the review page.
2) Or, visit your Amazon orders page and click "Write a Product review."

Your kind words mean a lot. You've been a great help!

Author Bio

Growing up in Northeast Philadelphia, I've been a fan of mystery novels for as long as I can remember, but it must've started with the Hardy Boys and Nancy Drew. I'm also an avid moviegoer, with Alfred Hitchcock among my favorite directors.

(You should watch the Birds if you haven't yet.) As an adult, my enthusiasm for reading grew, and I devour any mystery or thriller book you put in front of me! My favorite authors are Agatha Christie, Riley Sager, Ruth Ware, and Alice Feeney! But after reading so many, I wondered, "Could I do this too?" And so, you've found my secret passion project! Midnight at Eberly Manor is my first novel, and it mixes all my mystery/thriller loves, and I can't wait for you to read it!

www.ingramcontent.com/pod-product-compliance
Lightning Source LLC
Chambersburg PA
CBHW050034120726
47903CB00006B/2041